PEYTON'S PRICE

A SINGULAR OBSESSION NOVEL

LUCY LEROUX

DISCLAIMER

This book is a work of fiction. All of the characters, names, and events portrayed in this novel are products of the author's imagination. Any resemblance to actual events or persons, living or dead, is entirely coincidental.

This eBook is licensed for your personal enjoyment only and may not be re-sold or given away to other people. If you would like to share this book with someone else, please send them to the author's website, where they can find out where to purchase a copy for themselves. Free content can be downloaded at the author's free reads page.

Thank you for respecting the author's work. Enjoy!

TITLES BY LUCY LEROUX

.

***

The Hex, A Free Spellbound Regency Short
Available Now
Cursed, A Spellbound Regency Novel
Available Now
Black Widow, A Spellbound Regency Novel, Book Two
Available Now
Haunted, A Spellbound Regency Novel, Book Three
Coming Soon

***

Writing As L.B. Gilbert
Discordia, A Free Elementals Prequel Short,
Available Now
Fire: The Elementals Book One
Available Now
Air: The Elementals Book Two
Available Now
Water: The Elementals Book Three
Available Now
Earth: The Elementals Book Four
Coming Soon

Kin Selection, Shifter's Claim, Book One
Available now
Eat You Up, A Shifter's Claim, Book Two
Coming Soon

CREDITS

Cover Design: Robin Harper
  http://www.wickedbydesigncovers.com

Editor: Cynthia Shepp
  http://www.cynthiashepp.com/

Thank you to all of my readers!

CHAPTER 1

*P*eyton Carson craned her neck over the crowd, lifting her arms so she could pretend to be stretching.

I am not searching for Liam Tyler, she told herself. He was out of the country for the rest of the week, and he'd sent a card with his regrets. But she looked anyway. Some habits were hard to break.

But you will...any day now. Her childhood crush on him was over. Peyton had been telling herself that for a couple of years now. Someday, she was going to believe it...

"Here!" Maggie, Liam's sister and Peyton's best friend, thrust an ornately garnished cocktail glass into her hand. They were in the Caislean's exclusive Camelot bar, a hidden speakeasy within the hotel. It had been designed by Calen MacLachlan, and it was opened as a special joint venture between him and the Tylers, the owners of the exclusive hotel chain where she'd worked most of her adult life.

Maggie had commandeered the hotspot for a surprise graduation party, inviting everyone they knew—literally. Peyton had even spotted their seventh grade English teacher dancing with one of the hotel's concierge staff.

Her friend took a big sip of her own glass before standing on a chair. She lifted her glass in a toast. "To the hardest-working woman in town and my very best friend in the world—congratulations on your Ph.D.!"

Peyton had delivered her magnum opus to the computer science department yesterday. After sleeping twelve hours, she'd woken to the hotel's masseuse waiting to give her the works. Once he'd finished, he'd said Maggie had organized an intimate dinner for the two of them to celebrate. Instead, she'd found the party of the year.

Feeling loved, Peyton laughed, standing and holding her own glass high. "Thanks. And to all of you, I can't tell you how much it means you're here—I'm done, bitches!"

There was laughter all around. Peyton chugged her drink, then held out her empty glass for a refill. Patrick, Maggie's other brother, laughed and replaced it with an equally artful glass—a gin-based drink this time. Peyton didn't even bother to ask for one with her preferred rum instead.

Forget that Liam's not here. After four long years, she'd finally completed her dissertation in computer science, a Ph.D. she'd earned while working full time in the IT department of the hotel.

Calen and his wife Maia had set up an elaborate private party in the VIP room of the Camelot, one complete with a private bar and a mustachioed hipster mixologist. Some of her other girlfriends were here as well—Elynn and Sophia had flown in from the UK where they both lived with their doting husbands. Both were here at Maggie's behest, with their men in tow, to help Peyton celebrate.

"I can't believe you guys came all this way," she'd cried when she saw them. Sergei Damov was also here, but he made his home in Manhattan, which was just a short helicopter ride away—a viable travel option for a billionaire.

The music was just loud enough, and the alcohol flowed. Peyton felt great as she danced and drank with her best friends.

"I can't believe I'm finished," she shouted from her spot in the middle of the dance floor, holding up her cocktail like a torch. Whoops and cheers came back from all directions. Maggie threw her arms around Peyton, almost sliding to the floor as her stilettos lost purchase on the tiles. Laughing their heads off, Peyton and Elynn caught her, helping her up so they could keep dancing their butts off.

Sometime after Peyton's third cocktail, she took a break from dancing, collapsing in her seat at the head table. A hush fell over the room as someone came inside. When the music was turned down, Peyton twisted her head to see Sabrina, the hotel's pastry chef, holding a cake lit by sparklers.

A chorus of 'For She's a Jolly Good Fellow' broke out as Sabrina set the cake in front of Peyton.

"It's chocolate and sweet cream—your favorite," the chef said, before leaning over to give her a hug.

Peyton almost squealed. "I don't care what flavor it is! Everything you bake is amazing."

The Caislean only hired the crème de la creme. Everyone in the kitchen was the best at what they did, but Sabrina was exceptional. People from all over the East Coast came to the Caislean just to eat her desserts. The Tyler brothers had fended off more than one attempt to poach her.

Peyton had just finished cutting the cake when she felt *his* presence. Peering over Maggie's head, Peyton spotted Liam. He walked up behind his sister, clapping with the rest of the crowd. Peyton's heart stuttered and she flushed, beaming with joy. She should have been more circumspect, but she couldn't help herself. He had come.

Liam spent most of his days out of the country, overseeing the construction of a brand-new hotel in Australia. The local government had been giving him trouble, and she'd resigned herself to the fact he wouldn't be here for this—the most important day of her life.

"Congratulations," he called over his sibling's head as Alex patted him on the back. Calen came up on his left, greeting him as if he hadn't seen him in years instead of days.

"Thank you," Peyton said, a bit too softly for him to hear. Her hungry eyes drank in the sight of him as he leaned over and dropped a small box tied with ribbon in front of her.

She took the box, but she didn't open it. That would happen later, in private.

Every time Liam left town, Peyton ordered herself not to miss him, but her heart still dipped and soared whenever he returned.

The low light obscured the rich mahogany of his hair, which he wore just a bit longer than was fashionable. His broad shoulders filled out his navy Brioni blue suit to perfection, but it was a tad rumpled. Peyton smiled as she realized that meant he'd come straight from the plane instead of stopping to shower and change like he usually did when he arrived home.

Appearances were important to Liam. He always said presentation was everything in the hotel business, so she was pleased he'd been willing to forsake his image to be here sooner.

Peyton's smile turned brittle as Caroline Wentworth, Liam's on-again/off-again girlfriend, appeared at his arm. "Did you tell them?" the woman asked, tipping her perfectly coiffed head at Liam.

Peyton's stomach churned as Liam dipped to murmur something in his girlfriend's ear. *Why did he have to bring her?* No sooner had Peyton had the thought, she regretted it. This was Liam's hotel. He could bring whoever he wanted to the party.

She tried not to envy the socialite's appearance. Caroline's smooth platinum hair was in a perfect French twist, a hairstyle Peyton never had the patience to try. The woman was also dressed in a sharp white suit, a color Peyton couldn't wear without instantly getting it filthy in some freak accident. The suit was trimmed in sparkling yellow thread.

It's probably real gold, she thought waspishly. Gene, Caroline's father, owned a lucrative string of boutique hotels. The Caislean had a reciprocal loyalty program with the smaller chain. It was how Caroline and Liam had met a bit over three years ago. They dated for seven or eight months before breaking up the first time—a record for Liam. Over a year later, they began seeing each other again, resuming an intermittent but distressingly lasting relationship.

Peyton almost missed the days of interchangeable blonde bimbos.

Those were around for a few weeks at the most before Liam dropped them to find a new, nearly identical model.

But even she had to admit Caroline wasn't part of that mold. Yes, she was blonde, but the similarity ended there. Like Liam and the other Tylers, she had grown up in the hotel business. Caroline helped her father manage the boutique chain, and she was partially responsible for its success.

Liam's expression darkened before her eyes. "I already said not now. It's not the time," he growled.

"Oh, come on Liam—it's a celebration! We'll just be doing more of it now."

Caroline turned, waving with an expansive gesture. Peyton blinked as she realized Caroline was deliberately calling attention to a massive diamond ring on her left hand.

"We're engaged," Caroline squealed, poking Liam when he tried to shush her.

The announcement was followed by a long silence. Peyton's lungs began to burn when she felt all eyes on her.

"Congratulations," she said in a loud, overly bright voice, trying desperately to sound jovial while her heart was silently ripped to shreds.

"Thank you," Caroline said, smiling up at Liam. He shook his head at her as if she were an incorrigible child.

"You should have waited," he scolded. "Sorry. She should have waited," he repeated apologetically, this time addressing Peyton. "This is supposed to be your day."

"No problem," she said in a hoarse voice, grateful for the dim light. "More to celebrate."

"That's exactly what I've been saying," Caroline chided, reaching up to touch the nape of Liam's neck.

Peyton nearly gave herself whiplash when she jerked her attention away. She turned to the other girls. Next to her, Maggie was bone white. Peyton pivoted on her heel, unable to see her own shattered expression reflected in her best friend's eyes.

Elynn gave Maia a hard nudge. The other woman hurriedly stood, then crossed the room to turn the music back up.

Everyone started talking at once. Peyton pushed her plate of cake away, then staggered to her feet. She couldn't make anything out through the haze of tears. Biting the inside of her cheek she inhaled deeply through her nose, refusing to let a single one fall as she made a beeline for the restroom.

Someone called her name, but she didn't stop. The party would have to go on without her.

CHAPTER 2

*P*eyton clung to the toilet, violently retching. It felt like her lungs were being compressed by steel bands—a cage around her chest, one that only let her get one shallow breath at a time. It wasn't enough. She needed more air.

Tears coursed down her cheeks. *You knew this was coming.* Lately, Liam had been spending so much time with Caroline. And he wanted the hotel chain Caroline's father owned. But Gene Wentworth wanted to keep his business in the family. He'd made that clear on several occasions.

Despite his ambition, Peyton never thought he'd go this far. It was Liam after all. He'd built an empire from nothing through sheer grit and determination. Nobody could force his hand this way. Not if he didn't want them to. Which could only mean one thing. He loved Caroline.

Peyton wanted to laugh. At long last, Liam Tyler had fallen in love. It just wasn't with her.

All those people out there… Despite trying to hide her feelings for Liam, they had all known. Not to mention all the lies she'd told herself. She was the only one she'd fooled. Only Liam and Caroline had been oblivious to the pain they'd so casually inflicted. The pity on everyone else's faces had been humiliating.

I need to get out of here. Dying wasn't an option. Caislean employees were not allowed to expose themselves or be unprofessional in any way. She'd been employee of the month all those times because she knew the rules backward and forward.

Grabbing some toilet paper, she scrubbed at her cheeks, giving silent thanks to the makers of waterproof mascara.

"Peyton, are you okay?" Expensive shoes appeared under the stall door.

She had expected Maggie, but the voice wasn't hers.

"I'm fine," she called out. The quiver in her voice called her a liar.

The woman huffed. "Yeah, see...I've been that kind of fine. Sergei's lucky I didn't kneecap him back then for what he did to me."

"*Eva?*"

She pushed open the stall door to reveal the curly blonde perfection of Sergei Damov's wife, Eva Damov, formerly Stone.

"Hi," Peyton said weakly.

She knew the other woman a little. They had run into each other a few times when the Tylers entertained, but they hadn't spent much time together—mainly because Eva was a big-time executive at her husband's company. She traveled almost as much as the Tyler siblings. Sergei constantly bragged about his brilliant wife and how much money she made him. Peyton admired her enormously, but the other woman's busy schedule meant they were almost strangers.

Eva handed her a washcloth with a soft and sympathetic expression. "I arrived in time for Caroline's announcement. I'm sorry your party was hijacked. Maggie is out there running interference."

"Thanks." Peyton hobbled to the sink in her ridiculous shoes.

If she knew Liam, he'd be busting down the door soon enough to make sure she got back out there to enjoy the rest of her party. Desperate to avoid seeing him, she needed to clean herself up to avoid comment when she snuck out of here.

She wiped her face, critically assessing the damage. It wasn't that bad, considering. But it was bad enough.

"I, uh..." Her usually agile mind failed to come up with a sufficiently plausible excuse for leaving.

Smiling brightly, Eva clapped her small hands together. "I'm so glad I caught you since I wanted to tell you in person. I was extremely impressed with your dissertation."

Peyton stared. "You read it?"

The blonde curls bounced as Eva shrugged. "It's sort of in my wheelhouse."

"It is?" Peyton knew Eva had some interests in computers, but not enough to read a boring thesis on the state of quantum computing.

Eva leaned toward her. "You know about Adstringo, right?"

Catching up, Peyton nodded. "Sergei owns it."

The Silicon Valley company had made a big splash a few years ago with some groundbreaking software. She'd heard rumblings that more revolutionary projects were in the works, but there had been unspecified delays.

Eva waved her hand, dismissing her words. "Sergei paid for it, but Adstringo is *my* baby at Damov Industries, one of a handful I take a personal interest in."

Peyton nodded again, wondering why Eva was telling her this.

Eva's heels clicked on the marble floor as she reached for one of the thick paper towels in special holders on the sink. After she ran one of them under the tap, she turned.

Peyton kept still when Eva gently wiped her mouth.

"The guys at Adstringo are brilliant, but they tend to go off on tangents," Eva said casually, pretending she wasn't wiping another grown woman's face like a mother with her child.

"They're an immature pack of geeks, to be honest," she continued. "I've tried bringing in experienced managers to wrangle them. They respond well to authority, but only up to a point. It doesn't last because the managers can't follow the work they're doing at a deeper level. They need someone who understands them—someone who can even pitch in and code sometimes."

Peyton's lips parted as the dots began to connect. "Are—are you offering me a job?"

"I am." Eva grinned, tossing the towel into the bin. "If you can stomach the thought of management instead of a pure engineering position."

Peyton was flabbergasted. "I've never managed anyone."

Eva raised a brow. "Really? Because as I understood it, you've been the de facto head of IT at the hotel for years, all while going to school and getting your degree."

"Well, the work here isn't..." Peyton had been about to protest her work at the hotel didn't involve management at all, but that wasn't true. She'd just never realized it because she'd been doing it for so long.

"It would pay well," Eva said in an enticing voice, elaborating on the details.

Peyton's hands shook as she adjusted her dress, but she listened with avid interest.

I could do this job. The position Eva described could have been tailor-made to fit her skill set. Yes, she'd have to leave her friends behind, but she'd been offered a once-in-a-lifetime opportunity. If she took it, she would have to live on the other side of the country.

I wouldn't have to watch Liam get married.

"Do I need to interview?"

"Yes, but if I'm right, it's just going to be a formality. I can smell talent. It's one of my gifts. I know you'll do well at Adstringo."

Eva reached into her purse, then handed her a card. "I want you to call my assistant tomorrow to make the appointment. He'll handle your travel plans. We'll take care of everything."

Eva broke off, giving her an apologetic glance. "I should add this position is going to be demanding, and we need someone yesterday. You might have to relocate very soon."

Peyton didn't believe that for a second. Tears stung at her eyes. This time, she didn't let them fall.

She dabbed at her face, willing the redness to fade. "Eva, you're fucking amazing."

Eva grinned. The swearing didn't put her off. "So Sergei keeps telling me, but he's too biased to count as—"

The door swung open. Peyton flinched, half-expecting Liam.

"Damn it, Ethan. This is the ladies' room." Eva pointed imperiously at the door.

Ethan Thomas, Jason's partner at the FBI, snickered. "Just pretend I got lost."

Peyton's brow creased, wondering at the familiarity of the pair.

Oh, that's right! Ethan had been part of Eva's rescue mission a few years ago. He had delivered Eva's son on the yacht where she'd been held captive. She even named her son after him. Of course, it stood to reason they would be friends now. Too wrapped up in her grief, she'd almost forgotten their history.

Ethan gave Eva another lopsided grin. "It's turned into a schmooze-fest out there. Caroline's father just showed up. I'm gonna cut out early. Anybody in here in need of a ride?"

He raised his head, his expression matter of fact when he focused on Peyton.

He was good. It was as if he were completely unaware her heart had just been ripped out in front of her nearest and dearest friends.

Eva answered for her. "What good timing. Peyton's come down with a touch of food poisoning. She could use a lift home."

He held out his hand. "Great. C'mon. It's on my way," he lied. His apartment was across town from hers.

Eva gave Peyton a quick hug. "I'll tell everyone you were sick. We can celebrate your thesis later—and maybe more. Call that number."

Her head still spinning, Peyton nodded. "I will."

CHAPTER 3

*I*t had started to rain. The bus ride home would have been a disaster in this weather, but at least the world was keeping pace with her emotions for a change.

What emotions? Blessedly numb, she stared out the window. After a few blocks, she registered that Ethan was carrying on a conversation with himself. It was a steady stream of small talk.

She shifted to gaze at him blankly, trying to piece together what that hell he was talking about just as he lapsed into silence.

"It's going to be all right," he said after a long pause. "That Caroline woman could have kept her mouth shut another day. She and Liam didn't need to ruin your party."

Peyton shrugged. "Doesn't matter."

She was so tired now. She could get in bed now and sleep all weekend.

"Of course it matters. You worked like a dog for that degree. Doing something like that on top of your job at the hotel was insane. Having your thunder stolen like that sucked."

He reached over to squeeze her hand before returning it to the gearshift of the manual car. "Hey…if I tell you something, you won't hold it against me, will you?

"It's okay. Don't bother."

"What?" He laughed, not expecting that.

"I already know what you're going to say."

"And what's that?" Ethan asked.

The wet city streets crawled past the rain-streaked window. They had hit downtown traffic. "You're going to say I'm better off," she supplied in a flat voice.

Ethan and Liam didn't get on. To say the two rubbed each other the wrong way was a vast understatement. They hated each other, for reasons neither had disclosed.

"And then you're going to say I've wasted my time pining for someone who will only ever see me as a sister," Peyton continued. "You're going to say I'm a fucking idiot—that I've been one for years."

"Err…"

It wouldn't have been the first time. Maggie had said the same things —only she had put them more diplomatically. Trick had also hedged and nudged her in other directions, leaving the blunter you-don't-have-a-prayer-with-Liam speech for his sister. Even Calen had dropped a less-than subtle hint last Christmas. That had hurt because she'd always believed only the Tyler siblings had been aware of her secret.

Some secret. It seemed everyone had been aware of how Peyton felt about Liam. Their pity would be unbearable now.

"That's a bit harsher than I would have put it," Ethan muttered, stopping for a red light.

Peyton reached up to trace a falling raindrop on the other side of the window. "Did I ever tell you how long I've known the Tylers?"

"No…a while, right?"

"I was seven when I met Maggie. It was my first day at Eastwood Prep. It's a private school. She was in my class. I sat next to her, but we didn't speak until recess, in the sandbox. These rich girls were picking on me for being new. Somehow, they knew I was a poor scholarship kid. I guess my second-hand uniform gave me away. One pushed me down. I was crying, and Maggie came to my rescue."

"I've never heard this story. What did she do?"

Peyton's mouth twitched. "She barreled into our little cluster like a cannonball, then pushed them right back. She yelled at them to go away…and for some reason, they did. She told me later they'd tried to bully her, too, but her brothers had prepared her for that sort of thing. They taught her to fight back, dirtier and harder."

He laughed. "That sounds like Maggie." Ethan was fond of his partner's wife, but not too fond. He liked Maggie, but he spent most of his time flirting with Peyton when he was around them.

"I met Liam that day, too," Peyton continued. "He picked Maggie up from school. Back then, their parents were still alive. Picking her up was a chore for him, but he didn't complain when Maggie insisted on waiting until my dad came and picked me up. Dad was an hour late. That was around the time he started drinking heavily—he was starting to lose track of time."

Ethan murmured noncommittally. Peyton hadn't mentioned her dad to Ethan before, but Dad's alcoholism was an open secret. Donald Carson had been gone over a year. In some ways, though, she was still dealing with his problems.

"It wasn't long until Liam started driving me home instead of waiting around for my dad to remember what time school let out. It was over twenty minutes out of his way—an eternity for a teenage boy."

"It's an eternity for him now," Ethan sniped.

"True." Liam was the most driven individual she knew. He was also the most impatient. When he wanted something, he wanted it done yesterday. "But he stopped driving me home after he had to help me carry my second-grade science project inside the house. Once he got a good look inside, he took me to his parent's B&B. I practically moved in with their family then."

She could still remember how Liam's face had hardened when he'd walked inside that first time. He'd put down her project—an ancient computer, dissected and laid out with each internal piece carefully labeled. Ever so slowly, he'd done a circuit around the dingy living room, no doubt counting the number of empty liquor bottles.

After he'd peeked into the refrigerator and almost-bare kitchen cupboards, he'd made her pack a bag. That had been the first of many sleepovers with Maggie. Patrick had moved one of the B&B's trundle beds into Maggie's room for Peyton to use. Eventually, they got so tired of moving it they'd left it there permanently.

Liam had become her hero that day, but not yet the love of her life. That status had been cemented later.

"Hey, I get you're grateful to Liam, but—" Ethan began.

"I'd be dead without him," Peyton said flatly. "Or worse..."

He shifted gears. "Don't you think that's a bit of an exaggeration?"

"No. It's not." She flicked a glance at him. "I don't think Jason knows so you wouldn't have heard it from him. Liam doesn't share much. He's rather good at keeping secrets. Patrick has never mentioned it to me, but Calen knows because he was there."

She'd piqued Ethan's interest now. His hands tightened around the steering wheel. "What happened?"

"You've heard about my dad's gambling problem, right?"

He shrugged noncommittally. "What did Donny do?"

Peyton sighed. Ethan was too good an FBI agent to be unaware of her history. That and he seemed to like her. That made him extra nosy.

"In addition to being a lifelong drunk, he also liked to play cards, usually after a few beers. Of course, the more he drank, the worse he played. After a while, it was hard to tell which he liked more—booze or cards. He would have the odd lucky streak, but they never lasted."

"Let me guess? He got in over his head, borrowed money from bad people he couldn't pay back, and..."

"Yeah." She glanced at him. "It's not exactly an original story, is it?"

"And you were there when they came to collect." It wasn't a question. Ethan's voice was clipped and hard.

She nodded. "I was nine. Maggie's parents had just passed away a few months earlier, but Liam was somehow still managing to keep the B&B going with the help of their loyal staff—Constanza and Maria-Elena."

Peyton sank deeper in the seat, lost in her memories. It was amazing to reminiscence on where they started. "For a moment, right after the car accident, it felt like the Tylers were going to lose it all, but Liam pulled everyone together. Even Maggie and Trick pitched in. They cleaned the kitchen together, then took over the gardening. I felt bad hanging around, giving them another mouth to feed, so I told Maggie my dad needed me at home and started catching the bus home from school. And one day, Dad's creditors came. They were inside when I arrived."

Ethan kept his eyes on the road. "How many men?"

"Three big guys. I knew a few of their faces from the bar my dad liked to drink at. Sometimes, when the power or water went out, I'd have to go down there to remind him to pay the bill, so they'd turn it back on."

She ran her fingers over the fine leather interior of Ethan's car. It was just the type of vehicle Donny would have gone crazy over. But his habit ensured he'd never been able to hang onto his driver's license for long.

"What did they do to you?" Ethan braced himself.

"Nothing." Her laughter was harsh. "I was terrified, but I knew enough not to show it. They asked where my father was. I told them he'd be home any minute. Then…I don't know. I guess being at the B&B had rubbed off on me. I pretended I was Maggie when she was greeting guests. I offered them coffee, but I didn't wait for an answer. I just headed to the kitchen like everything was normal."

Peyton picked at the sleeve of her wool coat. "I could hear them whispering in the living room. I wasn't able to make out most of what they were saying, but one had a higher pitched and nasally voice. I could hear him fine."

Ethan hung on her every word. "What was he saying?"

She took a deep breath. "He was bitching about our place being a dump, and how Dad would never be able to pay up. He said they'd get more for me than any amount Dad could scrounge up. He knew a guy who would pay top dollar if I hadn't gotten my period yet."

Ethan swore aloud. "Son of a bitch."

Peyton shrugged. It was a long time ago. And she never had night-mares about it. She only ever dreamed about what happened after.

"I didn't know what to do, so I took the cordless and hid in one of the kitchen cabinets."

He nodded sagely, piecing it together. "And you called Liam."

"Yes."

She replayed the whispered conversation in her mind. All she'd told him was there were men in her house waiting for her father, and she was hiding in the kitchen.

"Liam didn't give me a chance to tell him about the money—not that it would have made a difference. The surviving Tylers operated on a shoestring back then. Things are pretty different for them now."

"What did Liam do against three men?" Ethan appeared confused. "He was still in high school, and they would have been armed."

A corner of Peyton's mouth turned up. "He came in with his base-ball bat. He was on the team at the time—and he didn't come alone."

"Who did he bring with him?"

Peyton's smile was wide now. "Calen. He brought his bat, too."

Liam had swaggered in like he owned the place. The men had risen to their feet at the sight of the bat, but they hadn't been scared. They had been ready to fight. They hadn't known fear until Calen walked in whistling, his bat braced against the nape of his neck, hands hanging over it like boys did when they didn't have a care in the world.

The men hadn't recognized Calen right away. Not until Liam had introduced him. "Liam told them Calen's name and that, yes, he was one of *those* MacLauchlans."

Ethan whistled. Though it had waned in recent years, Calen's father, Colman MacLachlan, was still a name in the city's underworld. For all intents and purposes, Colman was retired, but back then, just the mention of his name would have been enough to give men nightmares.

"I thought Liam had always been against Calen trading on his father's reputation."

"He was...*is*. As far as I know, it's the only time he ever asked Calen to use it that way." She huffed. "And it worked. The minute those three knew who they were dealing with, they almost wet themselves. They were small-time thugs. Colman ran almost a third of Boston at the time."

The men had left in a hurry shortly after, but not before Calen assured them he would be in touch regarding her father's debt. To this day, she wasn't sure if Calen had paid it off in cash or threats. It was equally possible he'd traded a favor from his father. Neither Liam nor Calen would discuss it with her afterward.

After the intruders had left, Liam had found her shivering in one of the kitchen cabinets. Calen had patted her hair awkwardly while Liam packed her things for her. They had taken her to the B&B. Afterward, they left again. Only that time, it had been to find her father.

Donny had been scared of Liam and Calen enough to check into rehab. *Too bad it hadn't lasted.* He would always fall off the wagon after a few months.

There was a long silence as Ethan digested everything. "Well, it's nice to know Liam wasn't always an asshole."

She took a deep breath, hiding the small shudder that racked her body. He had that wrong. Liam wasn't an asshole. He was what she, Maggie, and Patrick had made him.

Liam had been a few weeks shy of his eighteenth birthday when his parents died. He'd stalled the powers-that-be long enough for him to come of legal age. The minute he did, he took custody of his younger brother and sister, making sure they stayed together despite the kind, but ultimately misguided, intentions of distant relatives and the state.

Every flashy magazine profile written about Liam had mentioned how he'd taken charge of his two siblings, but the reality was he'd assumed responsibility for Peyton, too.

Burdened with three underage kids, Liam had slaved away at the B&B, not settling for keeping the place afloat. Instead, he'd insisted on expanding, using Calen's legitimate contacts—the friends Calen made at university—for seed funding on what had become one of the world's most exclusive hotel chains.

"Liam also paid my tuition in high school," she said after a long silence. "My scholarship had dried up halfway through. Liam arranged to take over the payments without telling me—right around the time he opened the first Caislean hotel here in town. I only found out about the arrangement because one of the school counselors let it slip. I also wouldn't have been able to pay for college without the hotel. The Caislean paid for it as part of a work-study program."

The words came out without heat. Back then, she had been furious when she discovered the truth. It wasn't that she hadn't wanted to work in the hotel anymore, but she'd been determined not to rely on Liam and the Tylers anymore. College would have been her fresh start, at least until she discovered she couldn't pay for it. Not until she'd been offered that work-study program.

"Don't bother getting all worked up over it," Liam had told her when she'd confronted him about it. "We need you, and you need us. Besides, it should be a moot point. We're practically family."

Family. The word soothed and stung at the same time. Belatedly, she realized Ethan was still talking.

"If he wants to ruin his life with that cold fish, it's his business," he said. "But you deserve someone who can focus on you and not the empire they're trying to build."

Peyton remained quiet. This evening had been a disaster. She felt eviscerated, but there was almost a strange sense of comfort in a pain so overwhelming it wiped her numb.

"Eva offered me a job."

Ethan's head snapped quickly to her. "She did?"

"Yes. An amazing one, if I can land it."

"That sounds great. Your talents are wasted working at a hotel. I mean, it's challenging in its own right, I'm sure, but I couldn't even pronounce half the words in the title of your thesis. I'm sure it would be a nice change, too."

And there would be the added bonus of not having to see Liam every day. Ethan didn't say it aloud, but he didn't have to.

"It's in Silicon Valley," she said.

"As in California?" He sounded disappointed. "Well, that's quite a big change of scenery," he said after a long minute.

"I'm going to take it."

"*Ah.*"

With the salary Eva quoted, Peyton could pay off every cent she'd ever taken from Liam...and she could pay off the others he didn't know about, the ones her father had left her with a few bookies in Southie.

Ethan didn't say anything until he had pulled up in front of her office building. "So, how would you feel about a visit in a couple of months?"

Peyton blinked. "I'm not sure," she whispered.

Ethan leaned over, getting close enough to unclip her seat belt. "Why don't you think about it and get back to me?"

"Uh..."

He shrugged, the winsome smile still on his face.

"I'll think about it." Peyton didn't know what made her say it, but she didn't feel like taking it back.

This time, Ethan reached all the way across her, brushing against her long enough for her to feel his heat. He unlocked the door. "You do that. I'll be waiting for your call."

CHAPTER 4

*P*eyton reared back, dropping the box cutter as her index finger began to bleed. She pulled off the mangled piece of packing tape she'd been trying to remove with a hard yank.

"Frak," she swore, putting her injured finger in her mouth to suck on the tiny wound.

"It's an omen," Maggie said, setting a half-filled box on her bed. "It means you shouldn't move to California."

Peyton plastered a bracing smile at her best friend. "You love San Francisco. You'll visit me, and I'll visit you."

She snaked out an arm, wrapping it around Maggie's neck. "And I shouldn't have to tell you this—but it's likely we'll see each other just as often. You've been so busy lately with the new hotels, traveling all the time anyway. It'll be almost as easy to meet there as here," she added, stretching the truth.

She didn't add that Maggie's time was also limited due to a happy marriage. Her husband Jason was Ethan's partner at the FBI. Although they had been together for a couple of years, the pair still acted like newlyweds.

"It won't be the same," Maggie said, a hairsbreadth away from whining.

"I know. But we'll both get used to it. This is too good of a job opportunity to pass up."

Maggie pouted. "I know you want to work in your field now that you have your degree, but there are tech firms here in Boston."

"Not like this one." Peyton held up another sweater. "What do you think? Should I bother taking these?"

Maggie reached over morosely to finger the thick wool. "Samuel Clemens said it best. 'The coldest winter I ever spent was summer in San Francisco'. So yes, take all the sweaters and the down vests."

Peyton snorted softly, then started putting the sweater in the box. She loved Maggie like a sister, but this was for the best. Peyton couldn't stand being here, working at the same hotel with Liam day in and day out.

Putting on appearances was exhausting. She felt as if someone had dug out her insides. Peyton was little more than a walking shell now, one capable of walking and talking and even smiling, but a shell, nonetheless. Leaving town, avoiding the man she'd loved her whole life, was her only hope for recovery.

How she was going to do it was still something of a mystery. She'd built her whole life around the Tylers and the hotel chain they'd founded. She'd given up holidays, worked on her birthday, had come in when she was blind sick and had to be sent home, all because Liam had, too. And she had wanted to be near him.

Now he was going to marry someone else. Peyton had to leave for her own sanity. Besides, it was long past time for her to strike out and try to build a life of her own. She should have done it years ago.

Plus, it was only a matter of time before Maggie announced her first pregnancy. It might be a few months or years, but it would happen soon enough. Once it did, Peyton would see even less of her friend. Yes, she felt guilty she wouldn't be there when it happened, but Maggie had the support of an awesome husband and two involved older brothers. There was also a large number of hotel staff who loved the youngest Tyler like a daughter or a granddaughter. Maggie was going to have all the help she could possibly need.

"Are you sure it's a good idea to move in with Dylan?" Maggie asked, naming a mutual school friend who had offered Peyton a room a twenty-minute drive from her new office.

"I think it's a great idea," she said with a little more enthusiasm. "He's got a three-bedroom house all to himself almost next door to Adstringo. He's also in the start-up world, so he knows what kind of waters I'm going to be navigating. I'll get to pick his brain nightly. Plus, judging from his last couple of calls, he's still the same Dylan. Living with him is going to be fun."

Dylan Nguyen had been one of the few other scholarship kids at Eastwood Prep, but he hadn't finished. He was expelled a few months shy of their senior year for selling a dime bag of marijuana to one of their fellow students.

"Liam has hated his guts ever since he found out he got kicked out," Maggie reminded her.

"Then it's a good thing Liam's not the boss of me," Peyton quipped. *Not anymore.*

Maggie wasn't letting it go. "Even Trick thinks he's shady."

"That was high school stuff. Dylan wasn't charged with any crimes."

That would have been too public for their fancy private school. Instead, Dylan had been quietly expelled. A few weeks later, he'd gone to live with his maiden aunt in Novato, California. Like Peyton, Dylan had been into computers. They'd stayed in touch despite the Tylers' general disapproval of him.

Peyton's continued contact with Dylan was something Maggie hadn't understood. But she'd been taught to view life as black and white. Peyton had been raised in the grey. And she was never going to hold that kind of past indiscretion against Dylan. Like her, he'd clawed his way into the light. She admired him.

Her best friend's lower lip wobbled, but she nodded. "I could kill

Caroline for announcing the engagement at your party. You wouldn't be moving now."

Peyton stopped packing. She hurried over to embrace Maggie, squeezing her tight. "You can't blame her. She was excited, the way any newly engaged person would be."

In fact, it was the most amount of emotion she'd ever seen Caroline display. It made Peyton realize she didn't know the other woman at all. She hadn't wanted to. Caroline Wentworth was reserved, but perhaps if Peyton had made an effort to get to know the other woman, Peyton would have been able to accept Liam was never going to be hers long before this. Instead, she'd buried her head in the sand and had subsequently been surprised when she'd been run over by a truck.

"It wasn't her fault or his," Peyton murmured, backing away to study her empty shelves. There was a small jewelry box left on the bureau. She opened it, studying the only item left inside—a silver charm bracelet.

As jewelry went, it wasn't valuable. Nevertheless, the charm bracelet was one of her most precious possessions. It had been a gift from Liam. He'd given it to her on her seventeenth birthday, back when he still did all his own shopping.

His secretary chose his gifts these days. Last year, she'd been given a thousand-dollar watch. She'd tossed it in a drawer unused, well aware he hadn't selected it personally.

Peyton reached into the box, running her index finger over the string of charms. There was a book, which she had later learned was passport, as well as world-famous monuments like the Eiffel Tower and a tiny Taj Mahal.

She always wondered if Liam had bought it because he knew she wanted to see the world or if it were a random purchase. "Promise me something."

Maggie wiped her eye surreptitiously, trying to hide the fact she was near tears. "Anything."

"Don't hold any of this against your brother. None of this is his fault. And you should give Caroline a chance, too. She's going to be your sister-in-law."

Peyton knew she didn't have to ask her best friend not to mention her hurt feelings to the man. Maggie still honored the blood oath never to mention Peyton's unrequited love to another living soul, which she'd taken at fourteen. The fact everyone knew was her own fault. She simply couldn't hide the way she felt when she was near him.

"Do I have to?" Maggie asked, perilously close to whining. Peyton's best friend had never liked the cool ice blonde. She enjoyed trashing the other woman with Peyton when they were alone, but now she wondered how much of that was simply her friend being loyal to her.

Maggie grumbled something under her breath.

Peyton turned. "What was that?"

Her friend sighed dramatically. "I'll try if she tries being human for a change—and if she stops being so damn condescending. She actually lectured me on the best way to flip rooms last week, as if we didn't have that down. Our hotel is five times bigger than any of theirs."

Peyton laughed. "How dare she!"

Well, an effort was all Peyton asked. Caroline had never gone out of her way to cozy up to Maggie. Her singular focus had been Liam. Ultimately, it would be up to him to facilitate a relationship between his sister and his future wife. His comfort and well-being was no longer her concern.

She put the jewelry box back on the shelf, the bracelet still inside.

"Aren't you going to pack that?"

"Later," Peyton lied.

She couldn't take any mementos of Liam with her. It was going to be brutal, but a clean break was what she needed.

CHAPTER 5

"What did you just say?" Liam had just spent eleven hours on a plane, and all he wanted to do was shower and go to bed, but his brother Patrick's report about the hotel wasn't making sense.

Trick sat behind his desk, his feet propped up on the edge. His brother's usual elegance was a bit frayed at the corners. He should have been in bed hours ago, too. Ever since he'd met his wife, Thalia, Patrick had been getting up bright and early every Sunday morning to attend Catholic services with her. At first, Liam had thought it was Thalia's influence, but he'd been surprised to learn Trick was the one behind the regular church attendance.

Liam wasn't sure he was comfortable with his brother's newfound faith. The sudden resurgence of customs abandoned after their parents died struck him as odd. The trappings of the Church felt alien and stifling to Liam now, but he wasn't going to make a big deal about it to Trick. His brother was a grown man. He was expecting his first child for fuck's sake. And Liam would rather chew his own leg off than talk about his feelings.

Trick rubbed his face. Sundays were now his longest day. "I said the hotel is at ninety-four percent capacity. The new schedule has improved room-turnover efficiency by an average of two minutes, and I've started interviewing candidates to replace Peyton."

Liam pulled off his tie. Confused, he threw it on his desk. "I don't understand. Why do you need to replace her?"

Patrick's mouth was turned down. He tapped the leather blotter with the tip of a ballpoint pen.

"*We* need to replace her. She took another job. She told me and HR last week—the day after you left for Singapore."

Liam's stared at his brother incredulously. "What the hell are you talking about? What job?"

Trick leaned back in his chair, meeting Liam's eyes with a flat expression. "You didn't seriously think she was still going to work here after getting her degree, did you?"

Of course he had. Peyton was an institution here. He'd built this hotel with her and his siblings. She'd been with them since the very beginning, doing whatever was needed.

When they'd been struggling to keep his parents B&B open, he'd complained their website was buggy. Their archaic online reservation needed an overhaul, but they couldn't afford to pay a programmer. A ten-year-old Peyton had taught herself to program in HTML on his old laptop to code a new one. She'd later learned Java, Python, and C++—all before finishing high school. Peyton was irreplaceable.

Liam leaned over to put a hand on the front of his desk. Inexplicably, he suddenly felt a little lightheaded and his skin felt clammy. "Peyton can't leave the Caislean. This is her home. We're her family."

His brother snorted. "Technically, we're not...and I don't think we can top the offer she received."

Liam scoffed. "If it's a question of money, we can up her pay. That's not an issue. We'll offer her stock if we have to," he said, suddenly wondering why he hadn't thought about it before.

Trick was strangely quiet, just watching him. "I don't think that's going to be enough. Eva headhunted her personally."

Incredulous, Liam said, "Sergei's Eva? *She* poached Peyton?"

Trick avoided his eyes. "I don't think it counts as poaching if the person is ready to leave. This job is at Adstringo—the tech company that's in the news all the time. It's kind of a big deal, a once-in-a-lifetime opportunity, yadda, yadda…"

So what? Peyton wouldn't leave for a flashy start-up. She was too smart to put her eggs in a basket that might declare bankruptcy in a year or two.

Except Sergei was behind the company, which meant it wouldn't be floundering any time soon—if ever.

"This is insane," Liam groused, waving a hand as if he could ward off more things he didn't want to hear. "I'm going down to her office to talk to her in person."

"It's too late. She's gone."

"*What*? She didn't even give two weeks' notice?"

"Nope. Not that she could have. You know how the start-up world is. When they want something, they want it yesterday. Maggie and Jason helped her pack up and ship her place over the weekend. She's *gone*. Moved to California late last week…and she's not coming back."

Liam had an overwhelming urge to get up and deck his brother, but that would have been shooting the messenger. "Is she still mad about Caroline usurping her party? I know it was bad timing, but Peyton can't be holding a grudge. If she is, I'll make it up to her."

Shaking his head, Trick stood. He put his hands on his hips with an air of frustrated exhaustion. "Don't bother, Liam. We were on borrowed time with her. She's determined to make a new life in California, one that won't include us. Just…just let her go."

Stunned, Liam clenched his fist. Peyton was one of Trick's best friends. "I don't get how you can be so—so blasé about this? Why aren't you willing to fight for her?"

His brother's laugh was sharp and short. "Liam, I love you, but you're a fucking idiot. About this matter, you always have been."

Trick went to the door, opened it, then pivoted to scrutinize him hard. "Can I ask you something? Did you really think Peyton was going to stick around to watch you marry someone else?"

His brother didn't wait for an answer. A moment later, the door swung shut behind him, leaving Liam alone, gut-punched. He staggered to his feet, pressing a fist against his belly until the urge to be sick all over his desk passed.

CHAPTER 6

ONE MONTH LATER

*L*iam gripped the steering wheel, scanning the street for approaching cars. *What the fuck am I doing?*

He sat in a parked car, stalking his little sister's best friend. He'd been here for four hours, and he didn't even know why. It wasn't as if he could talk Peyton into moving back.

It had been a hellish month since she had moved. Maggie was miserable, and both Trick and Jason were short-tempered. It felt as if the entire staff of the Boston Caislean was downcast. No one smiled in Liam's presence anymore.

Except for Caroline. The woman had been looking at an endless stream of linens, table settings, and flowers. She was probably buried in pattern books at this moment. Needless to say, she hadn't noticed that anything was off.

It was going to be all right, he thought, uncomfortably aware his words felt like a lie. Trick had been right when he'd said they couldn't keep someone of Peyton's caliber stuck working in their IT department.

He fingered the check his accountant had sent over a few days ago. It was from Peyton. She'd addressed it to the Caislean instead of to him personally. However, the memo portion of the check made what it was supposed to be for clear.

50% tuition + 50% DC debt.

The reference to tuition had been self-explanatory, but the accountant had wanted to know what bill Peyton had run up in Washington D.C. that hadn't been comped by the hotel. Liam ordered the check to be sent to him directly, without explaining that D.C. stood for Donald Carson, Peyton's father.

The money must have come from her Adstringo signing bonus. In the last month, Liam had done a lot of reading about the company. Even he had to concede the hotel must seem incredibly dull compared to the work being done there.

I should have given her more to do. Perhaps if he'd given Peyton more responsibilities, she wouldn't have gotten bored. He could have easily matched whatever this Silicon Valley outfit was paying her.

Except you know it's not about the money. Peyton had been determined to pay off that old debt for years, but he wouldn't hear of it. Now she was closing the book on it...and him. It was now obvious why.

He gritted his teeth. *Do not go there.*

Liam was spectacularly good at compartmentalizing. It was how he'd managed to keep the family business going when his parents died. How he'd gone on to establish an incredibly successful hotel chain. He focused on what needed to be done, and he never let anyone or anything get in his way. For example, he hadn't asked himself why Peyton spent so much of their time together watching him when she thought he wasn't looking. And he hadn't asked himself why he'd always pretended not to notice. Had it really been because he hadn't wanted to embarrass her?

Reaching over, he fingered the small velvet bag next to him. He'd found the charm bracelet in Peyton's old apartment. She'd been so excited when he'd given it to her. Leaving it behind had to have been an oversight. He'd brought it with him so he could return it to her.

A car turned the corner. He sat up straighter, waiting for it to stop in front of the two-story McMansion Peyton was supposed to be sharing with a roommate. He'd filched the direction from his sister's address book when Maggie had hedged and made excuses not to give it to him.

Liam held his breath as the sedan passed the house, then continued down the street.

Damn it. This was insane. He needed to get out of here. Liam reached for the ignition. He was about to press the button that would start the ignition when a black SUV turned the corner. This one stopped in front of the house.

Peyton stepped out of the backseat. Her brown hair was in a messy ponytail, and she carried a leather messenger bag that appeared to be heavy. She waved half-heartedly to the driver before dragging herself up the walk, the exhaustion of a long day transmitting with every step.

Liam got out of the car. He didn't stop to think. If he had, he might have stopped to consider what a woman alone would do if she heard heavy footsteps running up behind her.

Yelping, Liam ducked just in time to avoid a small terra-cotta planter being hurled at his head.

"Stop right there, whoever you are!"

He straightened. "Peyton, it's me."

She drew herself up to her full height, shaking her head. "What the hell, Liam? You scared the crap out of me. What are you doing here?"

"I was on my way home from Sydney, but I added a layover at SFO. I'm...I'm here to see you," he said, voice faltering.

Peyton's face was drawn and pale. She was exhausted, but that was nothing new. They'd worked a lot of late nights together, but the way she watched him now was different. Then it hit him. This was the first time in his memory she hadn't seemed happy to see him.

"It's been a month, and you haven't called," he said when she continued to stare at him.

"I've been busy," she muttered. "My new job is demanding. I called Maggie. Told her to say hi to everyone for me."

"Did you?" For some reason, his sister hadn't mentioned that to him. But it wouldn't have made a difference. Liam had been used to talking to Peyton almost every day. Even when he'd been out of town or he'd sent her to another hotel to troubleshoot technical issues, he'd called her constantly for status updates.

"Can I buy you dinner?" He twisted his head to the moving curtain next to the door. Someone was there, but they didn't want to be seen.

Peyton shook her head. "I ate at the office. There's a big project due later this week."

Liam frowned, wondering why her roommate was spying and hiding. "Then how about a drink?"

"I'm sorry, Liam, but you should have called. It's not a good night— not even a good week."

He ran his hands over the front of his coat because he didn't know what else to do with them. "I did call. Twice. You didn't answer."

Smile tight and fleeting, she shrugged. "I've been working long and irregular hours. Sorry. I haven't been doing great at keeping in touch."

Liam took a deep breath. He'd bet she wouldn't have said the same to his younger siblings. In fact, he was certain he'd seen Trick laugh at a text message from her just last week.

"Are you coming home for Christmas?" he asked, his voice sharpening.

Peyton winced. "I don't think I can get away."

Liam shuffled his feet, frustration filling him. There were a million things he wanted to say, but there wasn't a single one he could think of that could breach the invisible wall between them. "Can I come in for coffee at least? It's a long drive."

"Uh…"

Liam couldn't believe it. "Are you serious? Can you not even pretend to be friends anymore?"

Peyton sighed. "I apologize, but I don't want to make my room-mate uncomfortable."

He hadn't expected to hear that. "*What?* Who do you live with?"

"His name is Dylan Nguyen. Maggie and I went to high school with him."

It took him a moment to connect the dots. His lips parted, mouth dropping. "Your roommate is that drug dealer who got expelled?"

Was she serious? What the hell was she thinking?

Peyton's expression shuttered. "That's all in the past. Dylan is in tech now, just like me. But he remembers how people judged him for that one mistake. You were particularly vocal. And I don't want him to be uncomfortable in his own home, so, no, I'm sorry—I can't ask you in."

She retreated another step, moving closer to the door. "Thanks for stopping by to check on me, but you should call next time. That way, you won't waste a trip."

Liam couldn't move. Peyton moving away from him was something so unfamiliar, so unexpected, it felt as if he were in shock.

She smiled again. It was almost sad. Wistful. The glow from her porch light shadowed her face, but there was a distinct shimmer in her eyes. "Goodbye," she breathed before hitching her bag higher on her shoulder.

He watched her, rooted to the spot, as Peyton opened the door and disappeared inside.

PEYTON TOOK the drink Dylan handed her without asking what it was. After she took a sip, she coughed as the liquid fire burned her throat all the way down.

"Is that battery acid?" she choked out, her eyes watering.

"Almost. It's Wall Street Whiskey." Dylan held up a matching glass of his own before sitting across from her. "It's extremely popular in Vietnam. My dad used to blow his whole paycheck on the stuff."

Cocking his head, he studied her face. "Have you recovered yet?"

Peyton shook her head. "I'm not sure you can recover from finding Liam Tyler on your doorstep after a twelve-hour day."

34

Dylan shuddered sympathetically. "I don't blame you at all. One glimpse of him from behind the curtain, and I was right back in high school. I would say he hasn't changed, but that would be a big fat lie. He's even more built than he was back then—how the hell does he run a hotel chain if he spends all that time in the gym?"

Peyton huffed out an unwilling laugh. "He likes to work out his frustrations."

"What frustrations does he have? According to Forbes, he's kicking ass and taking names." Dylan took a sip, then reached over to pat her hand. "I'm sorry he came here."

She ducked her head. Since moving, Dylan had become her confidante. Brokenhearted and unable to hide it, she'd spilled her guts about Liam, his engagement, and why she'd felt the need to move across the country out of the blue.

"Maybe it's a sign," he said. "You need to start dating. Try Tinder or something."

Peyton winced. "I don't think I can handle that. I need to start small."

Dylan took another swig of his drink. "Why? I say jump in the deep end. What is that old saying? The best way to get over someone is to get *under* someone else?"

"I've never...I've never been one for casual sex," she corrected.

Her friend watched her with a frown. "You were going to say something else." His eyes widened. "*Oh, my God.*"

Peyton held up a finger. "Stop right there. Don't say it."

"*You've never ever?* Not with anyone?"

Groaning, she collapsed deeper in her chair. For years, she'd treated her virginity like a prize to be claimed by the right man. Only it was a prize no one wanted.

"I was saving myself for true love." Peyton laughed, only so she wouldn't cry.

Incredulously, he waved with his glass. "You need to get out there to make up for lost time. With your looks, you can have your pick of men. Hell, you can have several, one for each day of the week."

"As if I have the time." Her schedule at work wasn't conducive to a love life.

"Well, don't make the same mistake I did and date someone from work." Dylan smirked. "Avoid that at all costs."

She snorted. "Words to live by."

Being in love with a coworker was a recipe for disaster, even when there was no relationship to speak of. Peyton took a second sip of the throat-scorching brew, swallowing it quickly. "I've been an asshole. Love is fiction—the stuff they use to sell tickets to movies and romance novels."

Swirling her glass, she lifted it, watching the way the light filtered through the golden-brown liquid. "You're right. It's time to start dating."

Dylan raised his glass in turn. "Cheers. Here's to moving on."

CHAPTER 7

*P*eyton collapsed against the door, her eyes closed. That was hands-down the worst date of her life. In the last few weeks, she'd been on enough to last her a lifetime.

The minute she'd put her profile up on the dating website, she'd been inundated by chat requests. Most had been unappealing— straight out requests to meet and have sex. She'd ignored those, cherry-picking a few of the more promising leads with disappointing results.

Tonight was supposed to be different. She'd been impressed enough by Dan Collier's profile to go out of her way to meet him at a bar in Oakland. According to Google maps, the location was in a busy strip mall with several shops and restaurants. When she arrived, she found the area deserted. The various business that had made it seem like a safe and lively block shut down after dark. The only people out and about were drinking in the sparsely populated bar.

To add insult to injury, Dan Collier looked nothing like his picture. Peyton had been willing to overlook that detail if Collier proved half as charming as his profile. But the hopeful anticipation she'd felt died in the first few minutes of conversation. That was all her date had waited before launching into a hard sell to try to get her to have sex with him on the first date. The bar Collier had chosen was downstairs from his apartment. When she had turned him down, the creep had told her he felt sorry for her.

"Yeah, I'm okay with that," she'd told him as she hurried to leave. She'd been kicking herself for her misplaced optimism the whole way home.

"Dylan," she called, kicking off her shoes as she closed the front door behind her. "I'm home early. It went terrible—as usual. Have you eaten yet?"

Her roommate was almost always home before her. Rehashing her terrible dates over a few drinks had become something of a ritual. Not to mention she was starving. The bar hadn't offered anything beyond pretzels to accompany their watered-down drinks.

Dylan sat in his usual armchair, but he didn't have his tablet or laptop out. He looked up, a sheen covering his skin.

"I was hoping you would be in later, or not at all."

Peyton checked her progress toward him mid-step. "What's going on?"

A tingle of misapprehension ran up her spine. Something was wrong. Dylan was sweating, and he wasn't looking at her. He was looking behind her.

Feeling a sudden movement, she spun around. There were two men behind her, one thin and covered in tattoos. She didn't get a good look at the other larger one, but she felt his hands as he grabbed her by the shoulders.

"Is this her?" the smaller man said, walking around to Dylan's side. The stranger ran his eyes over her as the big man forced her down into the seat across from them.

"What's going on?" She twisted away from the restraining hold.

The tattooed man smiled. "Our mutual friend has struck a deal to cancel out his debt."

"Debt? What debt?" Peyton's head spun. Dylan was a successful programmer. He made plenty of money. Aside from his house and car, he didn't have big expenses. He still wore the same brand of hoodies and jeans he'd favored in high school.

Dylan shuddered. "I'm so sorry, but I've run out of time."

"Time for what?"

"To pay us back for the drugs he stole, of course," the tattooed man said.

"Drugs?" Peyton's stomach twisted. "You're dealing again? What about your job?"

The one he never seemed to go to, her brain supplied at the eleventh hour, far too late for it to make a difference. Dylan left after she did in the morning. And he was always back before she got home, but she'd foolishly assumed it was because he had seniority at work.

"The company went belly up last year," Dylan said. "I got another coding job, but they cut me loose. After that, I couldn't get another job."

"But good programmers are in demand," she protested with an anxious glance at the man behind her. He didn't have a gun in hand, but instinct told her that he was armed.

"He made more money selling our drugs. The hours were better. He had it made," the man said with a thin smile. "At least until he decided it was easier to rob them."

"I told you I didn't steal anything. The bag was stolen." Dylan's tone was petulant.

She still didn't understand. "Marijuana is legal now. How lucrative can it be getting into the illegal drug trade when dispensaries are opening up all over the state?"

"You'd be surprised," the stranger said. "People still want variety and the newest greatest high."

Peyton measured the distance to the door longingly. "You make designer drugs," she guessed.

"And your friend lost a backpack full of our best merchandise," the man said, making air quotes around lost. "It was worth two hundred Gs. Luckily, he's found a way to make amends."

"I can make the cash back some other way. You don't need her."

The man laughed. It was harsh and ugly. "This was your idea. Don't tell me you're getting cold feet now."

The neurons in her brain were firing too slow. Eventually, though, enough dots connected to realize they meant her.

"*What?*" Peyton tried to stand, only to be forced down by the goon behind her.

Pain flared in her neck. At first, she thought his hold had pinched a nerve. But the cold feeling seeping into her skin wasn't horror. She'd been jabbed with a needle.

The liquid in the syringe flooded her system, sapping her energy. Struggling against the restraining hand, she tried to open her mouth to scream, but the big man clapped his meaty hand over her mouth.

The suited man's expression grew calculated. "She's a bit too old for the auction block, but if she is as you said, we might make our money back fast. If she's not, then it's going to take some time. Either way, consider this a down payment only—if I were you, I'd hit the bricks and start making back our money now."

Her vision was darkening quickly. Dylan stared at her, his eyes narrowed and tight as he blinked rapidly. She wanted to tell him to go fuck himself, but something quite different came out.

"Liam is going to k-kill you," she slurred before passing out.

CHAPTER 8

*L*iam sat at his desk, fingering the charm bracelet in his pocket as his mind wandered, replaying the night he saw Peyton in front of her home. He couldn't forget the way she stared at him, as if he were a stranger.

Or like someone she used to know but wanted nothing to do with now.

She was only tired, he told himself. He'd surprised her after a long day at work when she was exhausted and hungry. The next time, he'd call in advance and make reservations at a five-star restaurant, something near her work so she could meet him easily.

He'd find one where they could both walk over. There was less chance she'd back out that way.

"Liam, are you listening to me?"

He frowned at Caroline. "No," he said curtly.

His beautiful fiancée scowled. "Honestly, I don't know why I bother."

Snapping the folder on her lap shut, she stood. "It's as if you don't care what our wedding is going to look like."

This was an old argument. Stifling a sigh, he picked up the book displaying vases. He'd been told they were to hold the centerpieces at each table. "I don't see why you aren't going over this with the Caislean's wedding planning team. They're exceptionally good at what they do. God knows that's why I pay them so much."

"I know they're good, but I want our wedding to have a certain *je ne sais quoi.*" She reached over to brush lint off his shoulder. "It may be the merger of two hotel dynasties, but it also needs to include a few personal touches—things that are both meaningful and sophisticated. People will be expecting more from us. Our wedding has to be new and surprising."

Liam groaned. He knew this was what he'd signed up for when he'd agreed to marry Caroline, but now that he was facing the minutiae of stationary and beribboned flower choices, he wanted to crawl out of his skin. "Well, if you want surprising, let's shock them and elope."

Caroline rolled her eyes. "You know perfectly well that my father would have a heart attack if we did that. Our wedding has to be the event of the century."

"I can't think of anything I'd rather do less than have a big wedding," he groused.

Used to his usual taciturn disposition, she ignored his grouchiness. "And that's why I will soldier on with the wedding planners on my own."

"You can?" Liam sat up, hope lightening his mood.

Her smile was tinged with amused condescension. "Yes, darling. That way you can focus on the details of the hotel merger. Father is understandably eager to have everything settled."

He got to his feet with a smile. This was what Trick didn't understand about his relationship with Caroline. As a hostess, she was unsurpassed. She always knew what to say and do in the rarified circles they moved in. Plus, she was self-contained. Caroline didn't need him. Her most appealing trait was that she would never make demands or set standards that would be difficult to meet.

Caroline understood their hotels came first. He leaned down to kiss her cheek, but she shied away, patting him on the arm.

"Don't mess up my makeup dear. I'm meeting the Grove sisters for lunch in a few minutes."

He nodded, putting his hands in his pockets. "Thanks for taking over the wedding prep," he said, feeling particularly grateful.

He'd have to ask his secretary to pick up something special for Caroline, maybe a necklace or some earrings. Tina always knew what Caroline liked.

His fiancée's laugh was light and frothy, like chilled champagne. "Don't thank me yet. If you find anything objectionable in the proceedings or the reception, I don't want to hear any complaints. In fact, I expect you to be very vocal in your compliments."

He grinned, but it didn't reach his eyes. "Even if I end up hating the flowers?"

"Especially if you end up hating the flowers." On that note, she departed with an airy wave.

Liam watched the door, wondering if he should have mentioned he was heading back out to the West Coast.

His stomach felt a bit unsettled over the omission, but Liam dismissed the idea the feeling might be guilt.

He was only going to check on a friend. He'd go tonight, and he'd use the charm bracelet as an excuse. Liam knew Peyton would want it back.

CHAPTER 9

*P*eyton's head lolled as she fought the effects of the drug.

The atmosphere was making it difficult. If only there was some sort of breeze or something to shift this stale air, but there were no windows in this damn dungeon. Metallic and heavy, the air in the cell settled over her like a dirty blanket.

She had no idea what day it was. It felt like she'd been in this hole for a week, but she knew it hadn't been that long—it had been two days at the most.

Maybe it's more. Her memories were hazy. She remembered voices and movement. Someone had tried to question her, but she wasn't able to recall any of the conversation. And despite her isolation, it wasn't quiet. It seemed like there was always someone talking or crying in the background.

Hands had touched her.

Peyton didn't think she had been raped, but she still felt violated.

I could be wrong about that, too.

She had been given something to make her weak, but her aware-ness seemed intact. An ultra-light sleep was either a side effect of the crap they'd injected her with, or her stress had kept her on edge enough to keep her in this zombified, but mostly conscious, state.

A few hours later, she had worked herself up to a seated position. Her vision was clearer, enabling her to make out details of her location. Then she wished she couldn't.

It was a cell. The walls were painted metal. A bare toilet was positioned in the corner, but it appeared rough, the bolts shiny and half stripped as if someone had forced it into position—an afterthought in a makeshift prison.

Forcing her feeble muscles to obey her, Peyton dragged herself to that toilet to make use of it, but judging by the state and smell of her clothing, it was too late. She did her best to clean up with the water she found in a bucket, but she cut her ablutions short. This might be all they were going to give her to drink. There was no sink in the room.

Drinking from a tap would have been safer. Did she even dare drink the bucket water? What if that was how they'd been administering the drug? She only remembered that first shot. Surely that single injection hadn't lasted till now?

She glanced at the remaining water. How long could a person go without? A few days at most. People could survive much longer without food.

They won't starve you. That wasn't the point. She had to stay attractive. Dylan had traded her to pay off his debt, which meant she was worth something to these people. Letting her die of starvation would be counterproductive.

Peyton knew her future was bleak. She had no skills that criminals would value. Yes, she was a fair hacker, but they didn't know anything about that moonlighting stint of hers in college. She hadn't had enough time to make a reputation for herself in Silicon Valley, so clearly Dylan hadn't sold her for her way with computers.

That left two options. Either she was going to be forced to be a drug mule, or she was going to be sold for sex. Of the two, the latter was more likely. If they had wanted a drug mule, taking her from her home seemed an unnecessary step. They could have forced her to agree to terms back at Dylan's house.

So sex it is. It was almost funny. She was going to be a prostitute instead of a programmer. After all these years, Peyton was going to find out what she'd been missing—in the most appalling circumstances she could possibly think of.

It was worse than a nightmare. Despite the near miss she had told Ethan about, she hadn't dwelled on the incident after it happened, except perhaps to canonize the man who had rescued her. Peyton had channeled all that fear and angst into something else...love. Sure, it hadn't been wanted or even recognized, but at least she had loved once in her life. Just once.

It would have to be enough. After what was waiting for her, she was fairly sure she'd never love anyone or anything again. Which meant she had little choice about what she had to do next.

The first chance she got, Peyton was going to escape...or die trying.

A VICIOUS SLAP WOKE HER. Rearing back, Peyton pulled away, wincing. She blinked up at the man and woman who stood over her, struggling to focus on their faces. *Shit.* The fact her captors weren't wearing masks was a bad sign. It meant they didn't care if she could identify them. They were either confident in their ability to stay out of the reach of the authorities, or...

There were a million questions going through her mind, but she knew better than to waste her time asking them. There would be no answers, not when the odds were two against one and the muscle at the door was armed.

"What happens next?" Peyton's voice was hoarse from disuse.

The woman, an attractive brunette in her early fifties, smiled hatefully. "I heard you were smart. Thank you for not wasting my time," she said in a thickly accented voice. Peyton couldn't pinpoint the accent. It sounded vaguely Baltic in origin.

The woman checked her clipboard. "Well, well. It seems you're top tier. I hadn't expected that at your age."

"Top tier?" Peyton asked, a sinking feeling in her belly.

"A verified virgin," the woman supplied, sniffing and running her finger along the paper. "It means you'll go on the auction block after the others. We always save your kind for last."

"How was I verified?"

"A medical test when you arrived," the woman answered without looking at her. "Of course, between you and me, those results don't mean much. However, men set such a store by them. At best, we can confirm a lack of recent sexual activity. With your seller's assurance you are pure, it's enough for us to sell you that way."

The woman's head drew back as she studied Peyton up and down. "Personally, I don't think an oddity such as yourself will fetch very much, but my employers seem to think a virgin of your age can make as much as the preteens."

Never in her life had Peyton ever wanted to be a man more. If she were as big and as strong as Liam, she could wrestle the gun out of that asshole's hand and shoot this evil bitch.

"If I'm so worthless, why bother selling me at all?"

The woman smirked. "Be grateful you're going to auction. If you hadn't, we would have put you to work the minute you arrived, awake or asleep. It wouldn't have mattered. The men who pay us don't care."

The woman retreated, waving forward a small bent woman carrying several buckets of water.

"Wash. Once you are done, we will bring you fresh clothes, then you'll be transported. You will reach the auction site in a few days."

"And if I don't what? A bullet in the head now?"

"Of course not. We simply market you to different buyers. The unwilling ones make some profit. Some clients enjoy the fight, although the poor dears don't last as long. My advice—if you want to survive, keep your head down. Be subservient and docile. You might get lucky. With your college grades and advanced degree, you might well be chosen as a breeder. It helps that you are white. Other races aren't chosen for that honor nearly as often."

The woman gestured at the buckets. "So now you wash."

"I guess it would be too much to ask for privacy, huh?" Peyton kept one eye on the armed man watching her with slumberous eyes.

The woman's face tightened. "*No.* We don't take chances with our merchandise. But have no fear. This one has seen it all, and he knows better than to depreciate your value."

Lips compressed, Peyton reached for the hem of her shirt, pulling it off before standing to strip off the rest of her soiled clothes.

CHAPTER 10

*L*iam pounded on the door of Peyton and Dylan's house. He'd flown in yesterday, sending half a dozen texts and voicemails to her phone, requesting dinner.

When she hadn't replied, he'd gone to her work, announcing himself as a family friend only to learn Peyton hadn't been at work for days. She had emailed to let them know she'd contracted the flu. Simultaneously relieved and concerned, he'd driven out to the house without warning her that he was coming.

The 'For Sale' sign on the lawn of the McMansion caught him off guard, but the lights were on. The television was playing loud enough to be heard on the sidewalk.

Maybe she couldn't hear her phone. Now that he was here, Liam had texted and rang the doorbell, but he was being steadily ignored by the occupants inside.

"Fuck this." He went down the concrete path leading to the driveway, slipping along the side of the house, searching for windows out of the line of sight of the neighbors.

The rear window just beyond the driveway was open a tiny crack. The room behind it was dark. He pulled out his phone.

. . .

ARE you too sick to come to the door? Or are you so mad at me that you can't stand the sight of me?

THE MINUTES STRETCHED WITHOUT A RESPONSE. Jaw clenched, he fished out his keys. He wedged the thinnest one under the frame of the mesh screen, then worked it up and out. Then he opened the window wide enough for him to squeeze through.

Breaking and entering Peyton's home was a bit high-handed— even for him—but Liam was at his wit's end. He needed to talk to her. They had to get back to normal somehow. Even if she did decide to stay out here in California, they could still talk on the phone or something…

A flash of shame coursed through him, but he ignored it, hefting one leg over the sill and climbing inside. He certainly hoped Peyton would be in a more receptive mood than her silence suggested. Otherwise, the headlines were going to be very colorful. *'Hotel magnate arrested breaking into San Mateo home'.*

I can't believe I'm doing this. Only Peyton could reduce him to breaking and entering, but there wasn't anyone else in his life who would ignore him like this. Why was she so damn stubborn?

This is humiliating, he thought, brushing himself off as he took stock of the empty bedroom he found himself in.

This is Peyton's. Enough light filtered in from the window for him to be able to tell.

He recognized her things. Maggie had helped her pick out the dark bedspread embroidered with star constellations. The Tiffany lamp on the desk was from his brother, and Jason had bought the silly cartoon mousepad at a street fair as a joke.

What was wrong with this picture? Liam couldn't put his finger on it. He flipped the light switch, scanning everything that was visible and out in the open. It took him a long moment, but then it hit him.

None of the objects were from him. True, he wasn't a big gift giver, but he'd known Peyton forever. Over the years, he'd bought her enough knickknacks to fill several shelves at least. But there was nothing of that here. Not even one of the picture frames she'd claimed to love.

She left the charm bracelet. Peyton had treasured that thing. It was as if…

His skin broke out into a cold sweat. Peyton hadn't just left Boston —she had left him.

Liam dropped onto the bed, sitting on the edge with a thump. This wasn't about the job or because she wanted to make enough money to pay off that old debt. Peyton had moved across the country to get away from him. She'd intentionally left everything that reminded her of him behind. He was being cut out.

Bile rose up his throat. Swallowing hard, he sat there, willing Peyton to come into the room so they could talk. When he took a breath, he was surprised at how difficult it was to draw one deep enough.

Fuck. Liam rubbed his face, but he put his hand down when he noticed it trembling. He hadn't felt pain like this since his parents died.

You have to get ahold of yourself. For a moment, he weighed leaving, crawling out the window and returning when he had a plan. Maybe all she needed was time…

No. He was here, now. He could fix this—fix them. He didn't know how he was going to do it, but he'd think of something once he saw her.

When it came right down to it, Peyton had never said no to him. Not about anything important. Taking a deep breath, he headed for the bedroom door.

PEYTON WASN'T SITTING with Dylan. The young man was alone, hunched forward and holding a phone in each hand. One of them was familiar. Peyton had chosen that model as standard issue for the hotel IT staff for its extensive bags of tricks and flexibility—that and she'd drooled over the distinctive metallic blue casing. She'd cajoled him into approving the expensive devices because they matched the Caislean's hotel uniform.

Liam frowned. The last time he'd seen that phone, it had been surgically attached to Peyton's hand. If it wasn't there, it lived in her pocket. She never went anywhere without it.

A creeping disquiet began to climb up his spine. Scowling, he froze where he was, deciding not to announce his presence. Something was wrong here.

Dylan was drunk. A half-a-dozen empty beer bottles were scattered on the coffee table in front of him. More were lying haphazardly on the floor.

If Peyton were here, she'd have already picked them up. She was a very neat person. After growing up with an alcoholic father, she didn't approve of excessive drinking. Peyton never had more than two cocktails a night unless they were very spaced out. She never stopped anyone from having fun, but she watched out for her friends when they went out partying. Liam found her attitude about alcohol to be healthier than a lot of others with similar backgrounds.

On a hunch, Liam fished his phone out and texted Peyton's number, asking her to call him back. His hand fisted as Dylan picked up the blue phone, checked the screen, then dismissed the message.

Liam's self-control vanished in a blink. Growling aloud, he stalked up behind Dylan, grabbing the smaller man by the scruff of the neck, knocking over the armchair in the process.

"Wha—how did you get in here?" Dylan sputtered, reaching up to try to break his iron hold.

Tightening his grip, Liam shook the man. "Where is Peyton?"

"I don't know! She's probably still at work."

Liam narrowed his eyes on Dylan's face. The guy was sweating. Despite the amount of alcohol in him, he was stone-cold sober.

"No, she's not there. They said she was at home sick. I've checked her room. Her bed is made. It hasn't been slept in today. So, tell me again...*where is she?*"

"I don't know! She must have gone out. Maybe she had another date. The house was empty when I got home after work."

Liam shifted his arm, glancing at his Bvlgari watch. "It's not even seven. I'm supposed to believe you drank all those beers in that amount of time?"

He threw Dylan on the couch, shifting the heavy piece of furniture back an inch or two. Liam put his hands on his hips and scowled down at him, counting the number of bottles again. "Did you even go to work today?"

"Of course I did." He didn't stutter this time, but Liam knew he was lying. It was in the evasiveness of his eyes, and the slight tremor in his hands.

Liam had brokered hundreds, maybe thousands, of deals. He'd trained himself to read his adversaries in the boardroom. It was a science to him—he studied them, broke down and dissected their every reaction to give him the advantage. Becoming adept at spotting liars was a natural consequence. He saw something else in Dylan's expression, too—guilt.

The crawling feeling in the pit of his stomach redoubled until it felt as if he were going to burst.

Peyton wasn't here, and she wasn't out on some date. Dylan's behavior combined with his damning possession of her phone screamed of something nefarious.

She was in trouble, and Dylan had something to do with it.

Liam bent until his face was inches from the younger man's. "*What did you do?*"

BREAKING Dylan down was harder than Liam would have guessed.

His opponent was weak, but he was also recalcitrant and stubborn. Combined with Dylan's intense dislike of him—a grudge he'd been holding on to for years no doubt—made the bastard clam up tighter than his own asshole. But Liam wouldn't be deterred, not now that he knew Peyton was in danger.

The nightmare threats of the world rose up as Dylan covered his face with his hands. Whatever he was hiding, it was fucking big.

Liam yanked Dylan's hand away from his face. "You tell me what the hell is going on, and you do it now, or I swear I will *ruin* you."

Cowering, Dylan leaned as far away from him as he could, pressing against the couch cushions.

"I can't tell you. They'll kill me."

Red filled Liam's vision, and he stiffened until his muscles screamed with tension. Liam flexed his fists. "Who are you talking about?"

But Dylan just shook his head. *Don't kill him. Whatever you do, don't kill him.* If Liam gave in to the rage coursing through him, he might never see Peyton alive again.

He was going to make him talk if it was the last thing he did. Liam snaked out a hand. Dylan reared back, trying to curl up in a ball, so Liam ended up just grabbing a leg, but that was fine. He used his superior strength to yank the man off the couch, dragging him along the floor.

"What are you doing, you psycho?" Dylan flailed as Liam dragged across the carpet of the spacious living room.

I hope he gets rug burn, Liam thought as he headed for the stairs. "I came in through the back, so I noticed your lovely McMansion has a nice little balcony. Unless you tell me what you know, I'm going to hurl you off it. It's only the second story, so you probably won't die. However, if I aim right, I'm fairly sure I can fracture your skull." Every other word was punctuated with a thump as Dylan's head banged against each step.

"You can't do this. I have neighbors." Dylan twisted, trying to pull away. At the top of the stairs, he reached out to grab the banister, but

Liam hauled on his leg hard enough to dislocate it at the joint. Dylan let go, then Liam hustled him through the bedroom door and across to the balcony doors.

"I'll scream," Dylan gasped as Liam pushed them open. "My neighbors will call the police."

"I doubt they are all that fond of you, given how loud you play your television. In fact, I doubt they'll hear this over that crap you're playing downstairs."

Liam reached down, yanking Dylan to his feet. "But if the police do come…well, I guess my lawyers will be earning their exorbitant retainers."

With that, he threw open the double doors leading to the balcony. In only a few steps, he was holding Dylan against the balcony railing.

"Wait—"

Liam grabbed the man's legs. Hefting Dylan's entire body over the edge was easy after the years of weightlifting and martial arts with Liam's brother, but telling his adversary that would be counterproductive.

"Damn, you're heavier than you look," he said, shaking him before shifting to hold him by a single leg.

"You crazy *fuck*. You're going to kill me."

Liam scoffed. "Like I said, you won't die. Not at this height. I will be going for permanent brain damage, though. If I can smash your head against the concrete hard enough, you'll be drinking your dinner out of a straw for the next few years."

"I can't tell you anything," Dylan cried, flailing his arms and free leg.

"Then get ready to kiss the pavement," Liam hissed. He loosened his grip, so the shithead slid down a few inches.

"Wait, *please*."

He let Dylan slip down another inch until Liam was holding on by a single ankle.

"I traded her!"

Shocked, Liam almost dropped the shit. "You did *what?*"

55

Dylan began to sob. Liam decided to haul him in, tossing the smaller man against the corner of the balcony. He didn't have a choice. Liam had to stop touching the scumbag or he might actually kill him.

Liam knelt in front of him. "What are you talking about?"

"I owed these people money. Two hundred grand. They were going to take the house, but I don't own it anymore. The bank does. The dealership even repossessed my car."

The entire story came pouring out—Dylan's unemployment and his decision to make ends meet by selling drugs, then losing his latest shipment a mere hour after picking it up.

The fucking moron thinks the mugging was a coincidence.

Snarling, Liam yanked Dylan's collar, bringing their faces inches apart. "I want names, phone numbers, locations, and every other detail you know, and I want them *now*."

CHAPTER 11

*L*iam paced up and down, ignoring the shouts and occasional screams that came from the trunk of his car.

"This is insane. This can't be happening," Trick said for the tenth time.

"Well, it is," Liam rasped, banging on the top of the trunk. "Shut up in there!"

"I'm claustrophobic," Dylan screamed.

"I don't care."

"Are you seriously adding kidnapping to this whole mess?" his brother asked.

"I'm not letting the asshole off the hook. He stays where we can get at him until we get Peyton back."

"Jason and Ethan might take exception to that. If they were here, that is—they're staking out an operation in upstate New York."

"I don't care if they arrest me as long as they do it after we get Peyton back." And as long as she was missing, Ethan wouldn't touch him—the FBI agent would probably help him beat a confession out of Dylan once he learned what the little shit had done.

"I can have Maggie try to call Jason. They've got some sort of system in place for when he is away on a stakeout."

"They won't be able to help anyway," Liam muttered, his mind a million miles away.

It was true the agents had broken the rules for his friends before, but this was different. The FBI couldn't infiltrate a ring of human traffickers without reams of paperwork and months, maybe years, of surveillance.

Liam had known people in danger...women he cared for, the wives of his friends and his brother. Even his brother and sister had come under a sniper's crosshairs, though they hadn't been the actual target.

This was a different corner of hell entirely. There wasn't a single fixated psycho behind this, or a family as had been the case with Tahlia, his brother's wife. A group that would take a woman had to be sure they could keep her hidden, make her disappear. Most preyed on the defenseless, girls and women who had no one to help them and wouldn't be missed.

Peyton didn't fall in that category. Even if Dylan hadn't told his drug supplier about her connections in Boston, he would have shared the fact she had a job at a prominent Silicon Valley company. They had to know someone would search for her.

And they took her anyway...

His chest compressed as he racked his brain, trying to recall everything he knew about human trafficking. Thanks to a series of whiskey-fueled conversations, it was a bit more than the average man.

The people who took Peyton were either complete amateurs or an established-enough outfit that didn't care if the disappearance came under police scrutiny. Liam started to pray it was the latter because he knew what to do then—the one thing he swore he'd never do again.

He had to call Matthias.

CHAPTER 12

*S*omeone was going to buy her today.

There were no voices here. The man who'd escorted her to this bare but well-lit room had dragged her by the arm with a grip so tight he left fingerprint marks. Peyton briefly considered trying to kick off one of her heels to use as a weapon, but she'd been dissuaded by the second and third man trailing behind them carrying machine guns. All were long gone now. She was alone…waiting yet again.

Peyton hadn't expected to see her again, but roughly a week after the heinous woman with the clipboard visiting her the first time, she'd come back to inform Peyton auction day had arrived.

Peyton had been scrubbed clean, then given a pristine gown the color of driven snow. Again, she was warned to be subservient, not to speak—at all. Not that they would ask her to.

"Your only job is to stand there and look pretty," Mega-Bitch told her.

Peyton was tempted to claw her own face open, anything to stop this atrocity, but she was too afraid. The machine guns had smelled of spent gunpowder, an odor she had learned to recognize after her best friend had married an FBI agent. She'd noted the distinctive tang on both Jason and Ethan, usually after they went to the range to practice with their service weapons.

The scent of these guns had been so much stronger…as if they had just been used. Peyton didn't want to imagine on who. Instead, she did as she was told and went into the room to wait.

Will they bring the other girls in soon? Or would they be dragged onto the stage individually?

Peyton hadn't seen many other prisoners in the complex where she was being held, but her instincts told her there were quite a few. The amount of infrastructure and security told her this was a big operation. Big, but secretive. She'd only caught a glimpse of one of her fellow prisoners during mealtime. A guard had unlocked her door to leave a tray. A young girl, no more than seventeen, was being escorted down the hallway.

For one brief moment, they locked eyes. The pale blonde beauty had been terrified. Peyton didn't blame her. The girl hesitated, but the guard had given her a shove, moving her along. The next second, she'd been gone.

Peyton had spent the rest of the day brainstorming how to rescue that girl when she succeeded in breaking out.

She knew that was a foolish fantasy now. There hadn't been any missed opportunities where she could have snuck away. The only time she was ever alone was in her cell or in this waiting room.

Her eyes watered under the bright overhead lights. She wobbled in the sky-high stiletto heels she'd been forced to wear with the long white dress that denoted her status—*virgin.*

Peyton's neck was so stiff she thought it might snap, but she couldn't will her muscles to relax, even for a moment. But she waited and waited, trying in vain to calm her racing heart.

And still, nothing happened.

When were they going to transfer her to the auction room? She kept picturing a stage with a small and select crowd of men hidden in the shadows. They wouldn't want her to see their faces. Even the man who bought her might have her blindfolded so she couldn't identify him. Unless… *They wouldn't pluck out my eyes, would they?*

Stop that. Peyton was letting her imagination run away with her. She would probably be beaten in addition to being sexually assaulted, but she would survive that. She had to…

I just have to wait for my chance. Sooner or later, there would be an opportunity to escape. She had to be ready for it.

It was the faint whirl that alerted her to the camera. Squinting, she looked up, directly into the bright lights against the wall, quickly turning away when her vision swamped out.

I'm an idiot, she realized. She wasn't going to be carted off and forced on a stage before an audience. She was already on the auction block.

IT WAS OVER QUICKLY. Peyton had just come to the sickening realization the auction had started when she was informed it was over.

The mood of her captors was jubilant.

"Well, well, I guess I was wrong," Mega-Bitch said, her arms sweeping out in a gesture that encompassed Peyton. She entered the room, flanked by her ever-present set of guards.

"You set a record for the year. Most of the others went for average sums, but you went for close to quadruple. Our new buyer must be very keen. He snatched you up, despite having bought three other girls from one of our competitors a few years ago." Pausing, she sniffed. "Of course, those were bottom-of-the-barrel offerings—girls without your kind of looks to recommend them. In fact, one was quite ugly. But your new owner has a reputation. He's what people in our business call an eclectic collector."

Peyton didn't know how to respond, so she said nothing.

The woman didn't care whether she received a reply. She was too busy gloating. "We've been trying to get in bed with this particular buyer for years. Who could have foreseen that *you* would be what he was looking for?"

She finished with a shrug as if her clients' tastes in sex slaves were none of her business.

Peyton's stomach did back-flips. "What had happened to the other women he bought? Are they still alive?"

Mega-bitch shrugged. "I suppose. Unless they annoyed him too much. If that's the case, they're fish food." She glanced at the guards, annoyance flitting across her features. "Well, get on with it."

The smaller man reached into his pocket. He pulled out a syringe.

Peyton's scrambled back, almost losing her balance on those high stilettos. "Wait, that's not necessary! I'll come quietly. Haven't I cooperated?"

The woman didn't answer. Her gaze was fixed on her phone, reading a message—no doubt her mind had moved to her next set of victims. She didn't bat an eyelash when the guard grabbed Peyton, twisting her arm so hard she screamed as the syringe was jammed into her neck.

Peyton slid down to the floor, her voice dying to a hoarse whisper. The last thing she registered was the woman's heels clicking on the concrete as she walked out the door.

MOVEMENT AND NOISE penetrated the thick fog. Peyton struggled to clear her vision. Bleary-eyed, she sat up as her seat swayed, her hands numb from the cold.

She was on a helicopter. A grey blanket had been tossed on top of her, but it had slid off, leaving her in that thin white dress in the icy air. She squinted out the window, trying to make out any landmarks, but it was pitch black.

There were four seats in the cabin, but the one next to her was empty. She was alone in the backseat. Two men were in the front, the pilot and another man, presumably a guard. Both wore earphones with little microphones attached to them.

Her first muddled thought was she should try to escape now. She could hit the guards with something, but when she raised her aching arms a few inches, she realized her hands were bound together with a twist tie. Another had been looped through it, securing it to the chair's metal arm.

Peyton swore aloud, but the men didn't react. They couldn't hear over the noise of the motor. She closed her eyes, trying to get her bearings, but it was damned hard to focus on anything except the frigid cold. Unable to use her hands, she shifted her legs experimentally, lifting then until she could grab the blanket. She drew it over herself as best she could.

A few minutes later, the man next to the pilot noticed she was awake. He got out of his seat and fitted her with a helmet, jamming it roughly on her head.

"You're lucky," he said, his voice tinny and digitized in her ear. "The buyer has generously decided to meet us halfway. We'll be landing shortly."

He turned and nudged the pilot, pressing a button on the console. "The depraved fuck must be eager for fresh meat. God knows he doesn't have to pay for it, but he still gets girl after girl every year—or at least, he used to. It's been a while. The boss is pretty happy he started up again."

Peyton grimaced, pressing her hands hard against her abdomen to keep from being ill. "Um, I think you pressed the wrong button."

He hadn't cut the audio to her helmet, as he'd intended.

The man laughed. "Whoops."

Shrugging, he turned back to the dark in front of the windshield. Neither man said another word for a long time. After she'd had enough time to calm down—and grow slightly bored—the pilot pointed.

She craned her neck to glimpse over their shoulders. Gasping aloud, she gawked at a massive yacht, its light bright enough to illuminate the sea around it.

It was the biggest non-military vessel she'd ever seen, a floating island in the middle of nowhere.

"I had no idea we were over the ocean," she muttered as they circled the boat. No one answered her.

The boat grew larger the closer they got. There was a raised platform with a giant H at one end. Blinking, she shuddered as the pilot brought them closer, touching down with a soft clang of metal on metal.

A uniformed man and woman appeared at the end of the platform. The man was tall and blond, almost Nordic in appearance, but his female counterpart was smaller—and Indian. They were wearing the dress whites she'd always associated with fancy yacht staff. She snorted softly. *I guess the movies have some of the details right.*

But not all of them. In a movie, she'd be able to fight her way past the staff, then commandeer a speedboat to get off the yacht. The reality was depressingly different.

The uniformed staff waited until the rotors slowed enough to let them approach. The man opened the door as the guard next to the pilot climbed out. He came around to the opening, opening a small pocketknife. He cut her restraints and retreated, letting the uniformed man help her out.

She rubbed her wrists, massaging the deep indentation and small abrasions on her wrists.

The woman approached, examining the marks on her wrist. She whirled to scowl at the guard. "You were told to deliver her without a mark. My employer paid a premium to make this so," she said in a crisp British accent.

The man shrugged. "It's standard for all our deliveries, Ms. Priya."

He shifted to the pilot, giving him a let's-get-out-of-here signal, but the woman blocked his path. Her expression was glacial.

"Priya is my first name. And next time, we expect our orders to be followed to the letter."

"Of course. The customer is always right." The words were respectful, but the smirk that accompanied them was not.

Priya certainly didn't think so. She put her head close to the man's ear. Peyton couldn't hear what she told him, but the man's face got very red. He backpedaled with a jerk, then climbed into the helicopter as if he couldn't wait to leave.

Priya inclined her head in Peyton's direction, indicating she should follow her. Trying not to betray her discomfort, she trailed the woman down a flight of metal stairs to the deck with the male guard behind her. More uniformed staff moved around in the background, doing boat upkeep.

Damn it, when was she going to get a break? Not only was she trapped on a floating island, but there was also a never-ending supply of guards here, too.

But they didn't appear to have weapons. That was something. Her opportunity to escape would be much harder, but escaping from a yacht wasn't impossible. In fact, she knew someone who had done it all on her own once.

But Eva ended up in the hospital after almost dying in her bid for freedom. And she lived only because her captor had been in love with her, enough to give her up to save her life.

Peyton doubted her new owner would care if she were bleeding to death. Why would he? He could just buy another girl to replace her. No muss, no fuss.

Priya recaptured Peyton's attention by opening a door and leading them down a level. They were below the main deck, but the many windows showed they were still well above the waterline.

The hallway was lined with a thick carpet. Every few dozen feet, there was something—a painting or a table topped with a priceless vase. Peyton had never had money, but she'd worked in five-star hotels for most of her adult life. She knew how to spot a real antique when she saw one. Even the door handles gleamed like polished silver.

The boat beat every Caislean hotel she'd ever visited in the luxury stakes. The opulence surrounded her was staggering. Which meant the man who now owned her body and soul was rich beyond measure.

How the hell am I going to get out of here?

CHAPTER 13

*P*eyton lost track of how many turns they'd made getting to this hallway. Priya opened a set of double doors, then led them inside a sumptuous cabin. It was spacious, with deep red Oriental carpet in front of a massive four-poster bed with bedding made of a shimmery champagne fabric.

It was a beautiful room, but the surroundings only strengthened the sick feeling nearly overwhelming her.

Priya cleared her throat. "My employer has been notified of your arrival. He'll be here momentarily. You may want to freshen up before he arrives. The bathroom is through there," she added, pointing at a door. Then she left.

"That's it?" Peyton said to the empty room. No threats or warnings not to try to escape?

It's a boat, smart ass. What would be the point?

With a pounding heart, Peyton went to the door. She tried the knob. The door swung open on soundless hinges. She poked her head into the hallway, but quickly pulled back when she heard footsteps approaching.

Hurriedly, she closed the door. She stood frozen with her hands bracing it shut, but whoever it was passed it without pausing.

Peyton let out a shaky sigh. *Stop being a jackass.* She had to think. She needed a plan.

Any minute, her new owner was going to walk through that door. She pictured a fat Middle Eastern man like in that Liam Neeson movie, but it could be anyone.

Her options were limited. She could make a desperate last stand... or she could let the man who walked in that door use her body. She'd cooperate long enough to lull him into a false sense of security. Once he was confident in her complacency, she'd slip away somehow. There had to be speedboats on a craft this size. It was too big for most ports. A speedboat would be necessary to ferry its passengers to land.

The fact she couldn't drive a speedboat was a problem for another day. She had to pretend to be docile. But acting weak and frightened went against her nature.

You are frightened. Being honest about that might be the best tactic. But after spending years trying to hide her emotions, letting that fear show felt like defeat.

Voices in the hall interrupted her pity party. Suddenly, none of her reasoning was worth a damn. She wasn't going to let anyone touch her without a fight.

Peyton grabbed the nearest object—a vase—but the damn thing didn't budge. It was glued to the surface. Abandoning it, she spun, searching for anything else she could use as a weapon. Nothing came to mind. She ran to the bureau and tugged it open, swearing when she found it empty.

Everything is a weapon. Liam had told her that when she was sixteen. He'd been showing her and Maggie some self-defense moves in the then-new Caislean gym.

The drawer came out easily. She raced to the door, standing just behind it. The voices faded. For a second, Peyton thought she had overreacted once again, but then there was a knock. When she didn't answer, the door cracked open and began to swing toward her.

All Peyton saw was a bright golden-white shock of hair. She swung the drawer up high with all her might, trying to hit the newcomer on the head, but she lost her balance in the process.

The man must have heard the movement, but he didn't have enough time to get out of the way, not completely. He managed to get his hand up, partially shielding him from the blow. However, she came crashing down on him next. They hit to the floor together.

Peyton landed on his long body. It was like throwing herself against a brick wall—a wall covered in a fine suit.

Her new owner had arrived.

~

THE STRANGER LIFTED a hand to his temple. His fingers came away stained red with blood. Peyton scrambled away as three uniformed goons ran into the room. One hurried to help his boss up while the other two ran toward Peyton.

"It's okay," the man said, waving them away. He stood, brushing himself off with his non-bloody hand, then he did the most shocking thing she could have imagined. He laughed.

"Well, Peyton, I must say you don't disappoint. You're exactly as advertised."

Her first blurry impression had been that he was old, with white hair, but he was, in fact, incredibly young. Mid-thirties at the most. His hair was a light white-blonde, very Scandinavian in appearance, with an accent to match.

Standing, he was an intimidating figure—tall and broad-shouldered with a muscular frame that was lean and long. His face was disturbingly handsome with sculpted cheekbones and ice-blue eyes.

Why couldn't his outsides match his insides? Shouldn't villains be ugly?

After a moment of staring at each other, he signaled his men with a little motion of his hand. They disappeared out the door without a murmur.

"What does that mean?" she asked, hoping to stall whatever was coming.

Keep them talking. That was what the television said to do when confronted by someone who wanted to hurt her. Except he hadn't taken a step toward her. He also hadn't asked his people to tie her up.

She continued backing away, putting an armchair between them. Peyton eyed the matching drawer on the bureau, but she stopped herself from reaching for it. It wouldn't be an effective weapon if he saw it coming.

"I cooperated with the slavers. I did everything they told me to," she elaborated. "I won't be any more trouble—I swear." Peyton shifted to stand just in front of the remaining drawer. She put her hands behind her back, hoping he didn't notice.

His lips quirked. "I know well enough to know you'll never stop trying to get away. I would expect no less after the way you grew up. I, too, had a challenging childhood."

Peyton narrowed her eyes. "You don't know me," she said in a low voice.

What the hell was this guy playing at? Unless the slavers had pulled her bio from the Caislean website...but the information there had been very brief. She'd wrote it herself, and she made sure it included little personal data.

"I know quite a bit about you actually," he said, immediately contradicting her. He put his hands in his pockets. "Why don't you try opening the drawer instead of hurling it at my head this time?"

When she didn't move, he sighed. "They're clothes. I thought you'd like to change into something more comfortable before dinner."

He started for the door, but twisted around to face her at the threshold. "I originally planned to have our talk now, but I think I'll go wash up and find a bandage. Why don't you have a hot shower and join me in the dining room in half an hour? Stop any staff member you see. They'll show you the way."

He was gone before she could think of a decent reply.

"What the hell was that?" she said aloud to the empty room.

Unable to stop herself, she slid the drawer open.

Peyton expected to find a dress, perhaps lingerie. With a frown, he pulled out a pair of navy-blue sweatpants.

Okay, now this was getting weird.

THERE WAS a matching hoodie and a long-sleeved t-shirt to go with the sweatpants. She found a set of brand-new sneakers next to the bed. In the closet, she found an identical set of sweats and under-clothes. There was nothing remotely sexy.

He doesn't care what you wear because he expects you to be naked around him. Not that she'd do it willingly, even if he did look a bit like a Nordic god. *Thor-lite.* She smirked before realizing there was nothing to smile about.

Frustrated and confused, Peyton decided to do as Thor asked. She showered, making sure the bathroom door locked first. Then she put on the sweats and went to go find him.

Despite the luxury of the yacht she'd glimpsed, Peyton gaped when she found the dining room.

The walls were a delicate creme with dark cherry wood molding. There were at least a dozen chandeliers, with a larger central one over the single table in the room. Instead of chairs, it had two matching leather booths encircling it. It was almost as if a cozy diner's booth had been set in the middle of the room, except it was far more elegant.

Thor-lite was sitting alone, nibbling on canapés. She crossed the room, freezing halfway when a uniformed man came in. But all he did was bring an open bottle of wine to the table, which was set for two.

She approached cautiously. "You'd never guess we were on a yacht by the look of this place. I can't even feel it moving."

"Trust me, we are." He waved her over with a welcoming gesture. "Rather quickly, too."

"Why only one table?"

He shrugged. "I don't entertain a lot."

"No, I guess you wouldn't." This was a man who bought people. Even in the most corrupt circles of the uber-rich, there would be people who weren't okay with human trafficking.

She slid into the leather seat opposite him, wondering why this place reminded her of the Caislean's main dining room. Thor poured a glass of wine before offering it to her. She shook her head.

"It's just wine—completely unadulterated," he assured her. "I think you'll like the vintage."

He pushed the bottle toward her. She frowned. It was a brand she was familiar with.

"An Italian red. It's one of your favorites, isn't it?"

"How the hell did you know that?" She hadn't had the wine in months—she hadn't been able to find it on the West Coast after her move.

"I was telling the truth when I said I knew a lot about you."

All right, this was starting to creep her out. "*How?*"

He sat back, pursing his lips. "Let's just say I was once very close to someone who is close to you."

He leaned forward, elbows on the table. "Allow me to formally introduce myself. My name is Matthias Fredrik Leif Raske the third. But I just go by Matthias."

When she only stared, he blinked, steepling his fingers. "I guess you're not familiar with the name. I shouldn't be surprised. Liam does like to keep his secrets, doesn't he?"

Her eyes widened. "*Wait, what?*" The story came back to her in a rush.

"I—I do know you," she said. "You lent the guys your boat so they could rescue Eva Stone when her stepbrother took her. Am I on *that* yacht?"

"No," he said with a little slashing motion. "The *Sha* is quite a bit smaller than this. It's currently in the Azores, so my great-aunt Bente can escape the cold of Norway. This is the *Ormen Lange*, my primary vessel, the one I call home."

"Oh." Peyton reached out for the wineglass, but she hesitated. "But you are *that* Matthias, right?"

His eyes twinkled disconcertingly. "Yes, I'm that Matthias. Or you can call me the cavalry if you like."

Peyton searched his face. Matthias seemed to be enjoying himself. Suddenly in need of a drink, she grabbed the glass, downing half the contents in one gulp.

"How did you find me? And why did you rescue me? Or rather, how?"

He lifted his glass. "Well, it wasn't with a superpower or anything exciting like that. I just used cash. I happen to have a lot of it."

"I can see that," she muttered, finishing the rest of her glass. "But you *bought* me. And from what I've seen and heard, it's not the first time. The people holding me said so—you'd bought from their competitor before. You're a consumer in the human-trafficking trade. Aren't you supposed to be one of the good guys?"

Matthias poured himself more wine. "Now Peyton, there you go making assumptions. Whoever said I was a good guy?"

CHAPTER 14

*P*eyton stared at Matthias, aghast. "But you helped before. How can you just *buy* people?"

His smile was devilish. "I mentioned the buckets of money, right? As it turns out, when you have enough, people start offering to sell you...just about anything. Even other people."

"But you're Liam's *friend*." At least she'd thought he was before realization struck. Liam avoided talking about Matthias. Whenever he'd been asked about the elusive billionaire who'd pitched in to help Eva, he'd quickly changed the subject or answered evasively. He must have been aware of Matthias proclivities, and that was why he'd cut him off.

A little corner of her heart shriveled inside her. Liam wouldn't have just let something like that go, right?

Perhaps Matthias had threatened him. This cut-rate Norse god had more money than anyone she'd ever met—and that was saying something. As a Caislean insider, Peyton had rubbed elbows with some of the richest people in the world. But that was how she knew there was a dark side to all that shiny money. Wealth of that kind made people think they were above the law.

Thor-lite was looking less and less like the hero and more like a villain.

But would Liam have turned to him for help if that were the case? And not just once. Her rescue made two times.

No, no! Liam wouldn't do that. He was a principled man. Or at least, she'd always believed he was…

More waiters entered as her thoughts churned. She stared at the plate they set in front of her like it was radioactive. The conversation hadn't done anything to dampen Matthias' appetite. He picked up his fork and knife, cutting up a large medallion of filet mignon as he spoke.

"I definitely wouldn't go as far as to call what Liam and I shared friendship, but, yes, we do have a history. And because of that history, he knew I might be able to help you."

The idea the man she'd loved for so long kept close ties with a slaveowner didn't sit well with her, but she knew better than to say so.

Live to fight another day. A new motto to live by. "Are you going to let me go home?"

Matthias stopped eating, pausing to study her. "Do you really want to go back to Boston?"

Peyton shook her head. "Boston isn't my home anymore. I live in California now…although I suppose I'll have to find a new roommate after this. The last one didn't work out."

"That may be the understatement of the year."

She stilled, her hand halfway to her water glass. "You know what Dylan did? Does Liam?"

"That's how he learned what happened to you." He leaned back in his chair. Again, she cursed the fact he was so handsome. "Tell me honestly, did you believe he'd let you go off to the other side of the country without interference?"

"I assumed he would," she said with a shrug. "I was never a very big part of his life."

Matthias laughed aloud. One look at her confused expression made him subside. "Oh. You were serious."

She didn't understand his reaction. "I am close to the Tyler family —well, Maggie and Patrick, anyway. I watched them build their business together."

"As I understand it, you were a key part of their success," he said. "You were there at the very start with that charming little B&B their parents founded. You changed beds, booked reservations, cleaned…"

This conversation had veered off into the surreal. Hearing him speak about her and the Tylers as if he knew them was unnerving.

She eyed him up and down. "Liam wouldn't have told you that."

Had Matthias hired private investigators? She knew from experience that kind of thing was second nature to certain members of the elite. Was he obsessed with the Tylers or something?

Matthias seemed lost in thought for a long time. She thought he wasn't going to answer when he finally spoke.

"Except he did. Admittedly, getting that much out of him wasn't easy. Liam is what my mother liked to call a tough nut to crack—as you're well aware, I'm sure. But don't downplay your role in the Caislean's success. Liam was quite upset to lose you to Silicon Valley…"

He waited for a reaction that didn't come, which made her wonder. Why did it seem like he was trying to tell her something without actually saying it?

She shrugged defensively. "I helped a little. But my role wasn't that significant."

A tide of self-pity rose up as she pictured Liam's face in her mind. Even now, he was riding to her rescue, fixing all her problems and leaving her more broken than ever because of it.

"I wasn't a big part of Liam's life," she repeated tonelessly.

Those icy-blue eyes gleamed in the dim light. "Well, for someone so insignificant, he certainly spent a lot of time talking about you."

Peyton sucked in a steadying breath. "Are you still in touch?"

"On and off. Mostly off. I thought I'd heard the last of him after our last conversation. But then he called me about you." He leaned forward with something like a smirk on his face. "I bet Caroline loved that."

"You know her, too?" Peyton was unsurprised when he inclined his head. Caroline Wentworth being friendly with a slaveowner made a lot more sense than Liam knowing him.

"Caroline is the one who introduced us. She'd been courting me as an investor in her father's hotel chain, and she brought Liam along to an event in the hopes of impressing me with her connections. I'm sure she regretted that later. I never did invest in the Wentworth chain."

She'd been listening without expression, but a sudden thought made her eyes almost bug out of her head. "You didn't invest in the Caislean, did you?"

Oh, God. Please don't let it be true. Don't let the hotel I've poured my sweat and tears into have been helped by this man's blood money. It would destroy Maggie, and even Patrick, if they ever found out.

"No. Liam never asked, and I never offered."

She hung her head, too emotionally wrung out to hide her relief. When she recovered enough to look at him, he was obviously trying not to laugh.

"Peyton, I'm starting to think you don't like me."

She bit her lip to keep from speaking the cutting remark she was dying to make.

Wiping all traces of mirth off his face, he set down his knife. "All right, it's time for the serious conversation. Integrating into society after this kind of trauma won't be easy. In cases like yours, when you've been in a high-price auction, it's even harder. Sometimes, the slaver keeps track of the merchandise with the buyer, particularly when they think they can make another sale to him or her down the line. Staying out of sight when you're back in Boston will be critical."

The sudden no-nonsense twist in the conversation gave her confused mind whiplash.

"I'm sure Liam will have a plan in place," he continued after a pause. "You may not like hearing this, but it'll be simpler to let him have his way. At least then, I don't have to worry about you getting snatched up a second time. Liam would burn down the hotel before he let that happen. Just make sure he doesn't do anything stupid like marry you too soon. That would be sure to make the papers. You don't need that kind of attention."

"What?" Was Matthias having a stroke? She wasn't following him at all now. Why would he think Liam would want to marry her?

His fork tapped the table. "I know there's quite a bit I'm leaving out. You'll have to excuse me. I've never met one of my acquisitions before. Priya usually took care of them, explaining how everything works. Between you and me, she enjoys it. It gave her a purpose...a sort of higher calling."

Matthias frowned. "No doubt Priya has a checklist of recommendations and guidelines. I should have asked her," he said, trailing off as if he were thinking about calling for the woman.

"You don't meet the people you buy?" Peyton seized that detail like a lifeline.

"Bought. Past tense. I don't do it anymore. And no, it wasn't necessary to meet them. You're an exception. However, you didn't come to my attention in the usual way."

"What's the usual way?"

"Priya," he answered. "When I still indulged in the practice, she took care of all the details. She chose who would be bought, took care of their purchase, and facilitated their eventual departure or secured them a position somewhere. There's never been a reason for me to meet them."

Peyton tried not to gape. She shook her head to clear the muddied thoughts. "Never? But then you...then you didn't have sex with the women you bought?"

"It would be pretty hard to have sex with someone you never met," he pointed out.

Peyton forced her hand flat against the pristine white tablecloth. "Then what did you do with them? Are they a part of your staff?"

She scanned the room for the servants, seeing their presence in a new light.

"Some of them are, I think. I prefer not to know. A few were able to go home, but that wasn't always possible. But anyone who works for me does it by choice. And they would have to be skilled. I'm very selective. I can afford to pay anything I want, and I only hire the best."

"Through Priya?" she asked, her chin lowering as she searched his face.

He inclined his head. "She is terrifying in her efficiency. I like to let her handle all staff issues for that reason. Anyway, if she'd chosen you, she would have explained why it's not always possible to go home. It would be better to start a new life somewhere else, but, in your case, you have powerful friends. It gives you options the others never had."

Once Peyton was sure she wasn't going to hit him, she raised her hands and rubbed her face. "You rescue women and secure their freedom. Why did you let me think you were some sort of monster who *bought and raped them?*"

By the time she finished her question, she was screaming at him with tears in her eyes.

Matthias winced. "I'm sorry, Peyton. It wasn't a joke at your expense. More like Liam's in a perverse way. I didn't mean to mess with you. I shouldn't have done that."

He scratched his head, inadvertently calling attention to the mark she'd left by hitting him with the drawer.

"You should have explained who you are and what you do from the start," she said, trying to get a hold of her emotions. Her voice still shook.

"I know." His face was drawn and tight. She waited for him to say she hadn't given him a chance before she'd hit him with a drawer. But he didn't make any excuses or try to justify drawing out his explanation. Instead, he poured her more wine.

Drained, she settled deeper into the low booth and clutched the wine in her hand.

She was so exhausted she could barely hold the glass up, but nothing could have made her give up alcohol at this moment. "What did you mean it was a joke at Liam's expense?"

"I...I suppose I enjoyed the thought of him being knocked down in your eyes. For what it's worth, I don't think Liam was ever okay with my former hobby. He said rescuing a few people here and there did no good when all the money I spent propped up the system. I told him I had a plan to make a bigger impact, but he didn't care. He was convinced it would blow up in my face. Turns out he was right..."

His icy eyes went flat. Darkness crept into his expression, but it wasn't frightening or threatening. More like desolate...

"What happened?" she whispered.

He didn't answer.

"Well, for what it's worth, thank you," she murmured. The words were inadequate, but they were all she could offer.

Matthias inclined his head, but then laughed. "It's ironic. Liam was dead set against me trying to take down the traffickers, but it didn't stop him from using my contacts when it benefited him. Although looking at you now, I can't blame him," he said with another appraising glance.

An unwelcome flush crept up her chest, but she ignored the sensation.

"You could tell the authorities about the traffickers," she suggested. "I'm sure they could take out the organization with everything you know."

"*No.*" His tone was cold, implacable.

"Why not? They have the resources and expertise. It might take a while, but it would be worth it."

He looked as if he were sorry he'd started the conversation. She waited, and he finally sighed. "You would think so. But you would be wrong."

Oh. "You already tried that, didn't you?"

"Yes." Matthias averted his gaze, his face set.

"And?"

He downed the rest of his wine, then put down the glass with a thump. "And everyone died."

CHAPTER 15

*P*eyton grasped the rail tightly, trying to recall the details of her dream last night. She had woken up in the morning afraid and ready to run, but she couldn't remember what it was she was supposed to be running from.

Well, I can guess, and maybe some things are better left forgotten.

Below her, the black ocean churned as the massive yacht cut through the water. It was a mistake that made her head swim. Hastily, she turned away, focusing on the horizon instead.

That's better.

It was a vast understatement. The night sky was full of stars. Entranced by the view, Peyton lingered outside after sunset to see them. However, now that night had settled, the temperature had dropped too much for the evening gown she was wearing.

Peyton had protested the extravagance when Matthias presented her with several gowns over breakfast, but the deed had been done. Besides, the only other clothing she had were those the jogging suits, which she later learned Matthias provided for the staff to wear in their downtime. So it was either wear the gown or grab one of the yacht uniforms. She'd go naked before she wore the white dress from the auction ever again.

Of course, Matthias might enjoy it if she did.

Peyton wasn't a stranger to masculine appreciation. Although her job had been in the background at the Caislean, she'd had enough run-ins with male guests and men at clubs to know she was reasonably attractive. But since the man she wanted most had never looked at her as a woman, she'd always felt inadequate in that respect.

Matthias looked at her as if he wanted to eat her. Or at least strip her naked.

Flushing, Peyton focused on the ship's movement. It felt as if they were flying across the ocean, but her host had explained the trip to Boston would take several days, almost a week. The *Ormen Lange* was one of the most luxurious mega-yachts in the ocean, but it could only go so fast. A boat would never beat a plane in a race.

Truthfully, she didn't mind the delay. She would have never admitted it to Matthias, but she was in no hurry to see Liam and the others.

And that must make me the most ungrateful person in the world, she thought, pulling away from the railing. Liam had arranged for her rescue from a terrible fate. The least she could do was thank him. If only she could do that without seeing him again.

"It's cold out here."

She spun around to find Matthias. Eyes warm, he watched her. He was wearing a black suit that set off his blond hair and blue eyes. In his hand was a length of dark material. He shook it out to reveal a cape.

"Hi," she said, jerking her head toward him.

After their rocky start, Matthias had gone out of his way to be a wonderful host. He'd eaten every meal with her and had taken her on a personal tour of the ship, including the engine room and the bridge. Matthias had even taught her how to steer the massive craft, much to the surprise of the crew.

The only thing he hadn't done was elaborate on the slavers' sting that had gone wrong. All he'd said was that Interpol had carried it out and almost a dozen girls had died. That had been enough to get her to stop asking questions.

"Is that for me?" She moved to him, then caressed the rich fabric of the cape before he slipped it over her shoulders

"It goes with the dress," he said, tightening the ties at the neck. The cape was lined with more velvet the same color as her gown. It was also deliciously warm as if someone had been holding it over a heater.

"This is wonderful," she said, stroking the cape, unable to help herself. "But it's too fancy for me. I'm a jeans-and-a-sweater kind of girl."

He laughed. "Peyton, you look lovely in sweatpants. You could be wearing sackcloth, and you'd still shine like a pearl."

She blushed furiously despite her best intention not to. "You better be careful. With compliments like that, I'll get a big head and become insufferable."

"Sure you would," he said in a wryly skeptical tone. He stepped closer, his large hands gripping the railing as he faced the horizon.

"The stars are so much brighter here," she said, turning her face up to the sky.

"I know. They never look as bright from land. Even in the desert, far from any city lights, it's not the same." Matthias pointed to a cluster of stars. "That is the constellation Cassiopeia. When I was little, my father taught me how to navigate by the stars on a small sail-boat—a dinghy really. There was no motor, no amenities of any kind."

"And no GPS?" she guessed.

He shook his head with a grin. "Just some charts and a sextant. He wanted to make sure I never grew dependent on technology, or even on other people. Which was why he sent me off in that boat for a week-long trip along the coast of Norway near Arendal when I was fourteen."

"Alone?"

"Yes, alone. No video games, no music players, and no comics. Just me and an old copy of *Hunger* by Hamsun. It's a Norwegian classic. It wasn't the first time he sent me off either. The year before, I had to spend a week alone in the wilderness in Hardangervidda National Park in the dead of winter. However, I was allowed a few essentials that time—a tinder box, waterproof shoes, and a coat."

"Wow," she murmured, impressed despite herself. Peyton had been working at the hotel at fourteen, but she had been surrounded by her friends among the staff. Going off for a week on a small boat or into the woods alone would have been beyond her at that age.

He shifted and took her hand, placing it on the crook of his arm. "I hope you're hungry," he said. "My chef is doing a Cantonese duck tonight."

"Not even a little." She laughed as they walked toward the dining room. "After that lunch, I'm surprised you can even think about food."

The meal had been a light mix of Mediterranean goodies, but they had spent so much time talking, nearly two hours had passed before she knew it.

"I worked up an appetite in the pool," he said, continuing on with an easy gait.

"I may have to try that." Otherwise, she'd gain twenty pounds before the *Ormen Lange* docked.

Ahead of them, a uniformed man came toward them in the hallway. He lit up at the sight of his employer, but he grew a little stiff when he spotted her. Red-faced, he nodded quickly and ducked his head.

It wasn't the first time something like that had happened.

She waited until they were sitting at the dining booth again before she said anything. "Matthias, have you noticed how awkward the staff seems to be around me?"

"Have they not been helping you?" He frowned. "If they haven't been doing their duty…"

"Oh, no. It's nothing like that. They're very attentive." In fact, they bent over backward to help her whenever they could. "It's just that they're not very talkative. Except for Priya, I seem to make them anxious."

The Indian woman was the sole exception. But even she never dropped the conservative professionalism she'd displayed since Peyton arrived. Her conversations with the woman had been stilted at best. Only Matthias seemed comfortable around her.

Her host wrinkled his nose. "I apologize. I'll speak to them."

"No, don't do that," Peyton said hastily. The last thing she wanted was for their boss to shame them into being friendlier. "I simply wondered what was wrong."

"Nothing. At least, nothing to do with you," he assured her. "I should have realized earlier. Given the circumstances, it's not a big mystery. I think the staff is afraid I'm going to resume my underground railroad."

"Oh." Peyton felt foolish. "Of course. They were all with you the last time when things went bad."

His voice grew clipped. "It wasn't *bad*. It was a bloody disaster— one I don't intend to discuss in any detail, so don't ask."

He reached for the fork with an abrupt gesture, then proceeded to eat in silence.

Peyton felt ridiculously small. She could only imagine how difficult it must have been, trying to help people and having everything go wrong. The guilt he must have felt...

"I'm sorry," she whispered. "You don't have to talk about it. I understand."

He huffed lightly, and his expression softened. "Let's just have a nice meal and talk about nothing at all."

With everything that was hanging over her head when she got back to Boston, that was an appealing offer. "Sounds good to me."

The meal was superb. There were four courses, a mixture of Asian and French cuisine, followed by dessert. Each course had its own wine pairing. She begged off dessert, pleading for mercy. "Anymore and I may explode. Tell me, do you always eat like that? Because if you do, then why aren't you a thousand pounds?"

"Most of the time, my staff has to remind me to eat," he confessed. "My business interests are...extensive. I spend most of my day locked in my office. I have to set reminders to do things like bathe and eat. I hate being sedentary, so I periodically stop working long enough to throw myself in the pool. I also like lifting weights."

"Yeah, that's kind of obvious," she said, trying not to stare at him. The breadth of his shoulders and arm definition alone spoke to hours spent in the gym. It put her new sloth-like existence to shame.

Peyton was going to have to ask him about the weight room. She hadn't been aware the boat had one. But she should have. The *Ormen Lange* was bigger than any cruise ship she'd ever seen.

"But you're right I don't usually eat this richly," he said, shaking her out of her reverie. "I asked my chef to treat us to something special while you're a guest here. When you're back with Liam and the others, I wouldn't want you to forget us."

His words sent a wave of emotion crashing through her. It was hard to pinpoint which was the strongest. Relief mingled with anxiety, along with something else she didn't want to name.

Seemingly unaware of her introspection, Matthias got up and offered his hand. "There's another way to work off these excess calories. Dance with me."

Peyton huffed, but she took his hand with a grin. "We'd have to dance all night to work off that meal."

"Which we could do," he said, pulling her close and turning her into a spin.

As if on cue, music began to play, piped in from God knew where. Peyton stopped, twisting to glance around. It sounded like a full-blown orchestra was in the room with them.

"How the hell did you do that?" she asked, wide-eyed.

Matthias fished out his cell phone, then pressed a few buttons. "Bluetooth."

The volume of the music lowered, and she laughed. "I should have guessed that."

Peyton walked back into his arms, letting him twirl her into a fast waltz. "That's a hell of a sound system."

"It's the best money can buy, or so I've been told." As they spun in a circle, she fell against him. He grinned. "You're incredibly good at this. I wouldn't have thought someone in IT would be so good at ballroom dancing."

Peyton laughed. "You forget Maggie Tyler is my best friend. She's been in charge of events at the Caislean since before they were a chain. That's hundreds, or even thousands, of weddings, quinceañeras, sweet sixteens, and charity balls. For years, she was stuck attending them as a party planner, which meant I was, too."

Matthias steered them into a tight turn. "The last time I checked, party planners didn't waltz."

"Yours might not have, but you'd be surprised at how often a bridesmaid or attendant would drop out at the last minute. Rather than ruin the elaborate choreography those parties had planned, either Maggie or I had to squeeze into dozens of horrible bridesmaid's gowns so we could fill in. Well, it was sometimes a squeeze. There were a few occasions when the dresses were so big we had to use safety pins to make them fit. I still have a scar on my back when one opened mid-promenade."

He wrinkled his nose. "Ouch."

He drifted his hand up her back, then stopped. When he looked into her eyes for a long moment, Peyton held her breath, half-hoping, but half-dreading, that he would kiss her.

As soon as she realized what she was thinking, she pulled away. And then she wanted to throw herself off the boat for being so stupid.

Every time she began to enjoy a man's company, she'd be overcome by guilt. Which was crazy. The man she loved had never looked at her twice, not in the way she'd wanted him to.

Matthias put his hands on her shoulders. "It's all right, Peyton. I haven't been thinking too clearly since you got here. I know you can't…"

She spun around, her eyes filled with unbidden tears. "Of course I *can*. I'm being such an ass. I don't know what's wrong with me."

His smile was tinged with sadness. "There's nothing wrong with you. I haven't been playing fair. My only excuse is I didn't do it on purpose. I know you have to go back to him."

Peyton frowned. There it was again, the suggestion she was going back to Liam.

"I don't know where you got this idea I'm going back to anyone. I'm single. Depressingly so."

Matthias gave her an indulgent glance. "After all that has happened, you won't be staying that way, not with the way Liam was carrying on. He may be hardheaded and obstinate, but he's no fool."

She crossed her arms over her chest. "He's marrying Caroline Wentworth."

Staring at her in disbelief, Matthias gave himself a little shake. "All right, I take it back. He's an idiot."

CHAPTER 16

*P*eyton didn't expect Matthias' reaction to the news. For a moment, his lips twisted as if he tasted something sour. Then his face cleared and he laughed, grabbing the bottle of wine at the table.

"I think this calls for a celebration," he said. "Let's toast to the happy couple!"

Pursing her lips, she blinked. "I'll pass, thanks."

Matthias winced. "Sorry. I doubt the wedding will happen. I know those two well, much better than they realize. Neither will be satisfied with half a life. Granted, Liam does love self-flagellation so he might go through with it, but I doubt it. Not once you go home."

Peyton passed a hand over her face. "I don't know what makes you so confident he cares about me."

He raised one blond brow. Peyton waved dismissively. "Well, he obviously cares enough to save me from sex traffickers. He's not a monster. But his feelings aren't romantic. He sees me as a sister."

Matthias put the bottle down, then spun her into his arms. "I'm willing to bet you're wrong. You see, once upon a time, I spent quite a bit of time with Liam. Long enough to see how he interacts with people in his sphere—his siblings, his staff, and, yes, even how he acts with the women in his life. Granted, it was mostly when he was on the phone, but that's one of the few times he lets his guard down."

He paused to stare down into her eyes. "With you, he was always different. It was subtle, but whenever he talked to you or about you, there was something…distinctive. As if he were frustrated."

She snorted. "No doubt he was. For an underling, I gave him a pretty hard time."

They had often butted heads at work, sometimes for no reason at all. Maggie and Trick had given up trying to intervene long ago. Whenever she and Liam got into an argument, they would just sigh and find something else to do for half an hour.

Matthias gave her a gently chiding glance. "And I think it was because he was fighting his instincts, burying his natural impulses around you."

"Are you sure you're not reading too much into a few arguments?" How much time could Matthias and Liam have spent together if neither she nor the other Tylers had ever met him?

Well, Liam does spend most of his life traveling on business for the hotel. It was possible some fraction of that time had been spent here, with his mysterious friend.

Matthias leaned down. This time, she could smell the wine on his breath. "Like I said before, Peyton, you're a good bet. And not to brag, but my instincts have always served me well."

"I would say I have to take your word on that, but you do live on a mega-yacht, so I guess they can't be half bad," she said, surreptitiously checking her own breath on the next turn.

Well, at least if he does kiss me, we'll match, she thought wryly, although it was obvious his desire to kiss her had dwindled away.

"Caroline understands Liam in her way, too," Matthias continued as he slowed them to a stop, making the wine in Peyton's stomach swirl unpleasantly.

"Caroline knows better than to demand more than he's willing to give. She probably doesn't think him capable of more. But she's underestimating him. The fact she is willing to marry him now, after what she vowed...well, that tells me she doesn't realize that." He stopped abruptly. "Unless she changed her mind—but no. She wouldn't do that."

Fascinated, Peyton raised an eyebrow. It was almost as if he was having a conversation with himself.

"About what?" she prodded.

"Sex," he said with a shrug.

"*What?*"

He blinked as if he'd forgotten she was there. "I didn't mean to say that. Discretion being the better part of valor, etcetera et cetera."

Matthias' warm hand came up to cup her cheek. "But...if anyone deserves to know where the bodies are buried, it's you."

Her heart skipped a beat, but it wasn't because of his touch. Or at least, not completely because of it.

"Tell me," she whispered.

He hesitated. Gripping his hand, she willed him to speak. "The reason I don't have much faith in the future success of Liam and Caroline's marriage is because she once vowed never to let him touch her again. And if I know Caroline, she will stick to that. For all her faults, she's a woman of her word."

Peyton didn't understand. "But she's crazy about him. I've seen them together." All over each other in fact. Granted, those public displays of affection had tapered off since the early days of their relationship.

Just thinking of it made her stomach hurt. She lurched away. "I think I drank too much. And none of what you are saying makes any sense. Caroline loves Liam."

"Caroline *needs* Liam. That's something else entirely. You see, he's the perfect foil for her. She looks great on his arm, and he's a tour de force in the hotel world. Liam can satisfy her father's sexist desire to turn his hotel chain over to a man. Caroline likes to pretend it doesn't bother her, but the fact her father is passing her over to head the family business hurts. The old man is holding out for this marriage, but if Caroline marries Liam, then the sting of the insult lessens. She'd be half the hotel industry's foremost power couple. But trusting Liam with her body after what happened is another matter entirely."

Belatedly, light dawned. "He *cheated* on her?" Shock nearly knocked Peyton over.

Never in a million years would she have guessed Liam would do such a thing. He was a man of integrity. He prided himself on keeping his word, which was why he never made promises to the women he dated. Until Caroline, that is.

Matthias pursed his lips. "Cheating is a strong word. They weren't actually together at the time, but when you're off and on like that, I suppose it's a technicality. Regardless, she wasn't able to look the other way, like she might have if she had found him with anyone else."

Pivoting on his heel, Matthias put his hands on her shoulders. "Peyton, you've been trying to convince me that Liam doesn't have any feelings for you, but you never asked how I knew how *you* felt. You see, I happen to know the signs. Only one man can inflict the kind of damage I see in your eyes. And I know because I've been there."

Holy shit. It felt as if the floor under her feet was disintegrating. Or maybe it was her heart.

"*You* and Liam?" she breathed.

He nodded. "Caroline swore she'd never let Liam touch her again after she found him in bed with me."

CHAPTER 17

*P*eyton sat on the floor, clutching her middle. She was in danger of losing all four courses. Matthias sat next to her, pressing against her side.

"It's going to be okay, Peyton."

It was difficult to make out what he was saying. Her eardrums were vibrating as if her head were going to explode. "I had no idea he was gay. Or that you were…"

Had she been imagining that Matthias wanted to kiss her? What kind of an idiot was she?

Peyton had known for years there was something wrong with her. Only a glutton for punishment would pine for a man like Liam Tyler. But this revelation was it—the proof she was simply wired all wrong and always had been. Not only had she spent most of her life in love with a man who would never love her back, but also the only other man who'd managed to turn her head even a little bit was *his lover*.

Except—except Liam was marrying Caroline. What the hell was that all about?

Matthias nudged her. "That's because he's not gay. And neither am I."

Peyton's head drew back, and she stared at him as if he were insane. He took her hand, then brought it to his lips. "Peyton, for some people, life is never that simple."

Suddenly, he groaned and let her go. "And the fact I want to pick you up and carry you to my stateroom is only making it more complicated."

"Now I'm really confused," she said hoarsely.

He moved, settling cross-legged opposite her. His knees almost touched hers, but he was careful to leave a little distance between them. He reached for her hand, but then checked himself as if thinking better of it.

"Peyton, I know what I am. I had the benefit of learning it the hard way. Those painful lessons taught me to never compromise on what I need." He shrugged. "I want what I want, and it's to enjoy the pleasure of a man—or a woman—in my bed. Preferably both."

"Oh." So he was bisexual. "Err...would that be at the same time?"

The corner of his mouth kicked up. "On occasion."

Peyton slammed the door on the mental image that popped into her head, but she couldn't hide the heat across her cheeks. "Isn't that a bit greedy?" she asked, her voice barely more than a squeak.

"Is that what you sincerely believe?" He risked touching her cheek with his index finger. "Or does this blush mean you find it a bit exciting?"

Tongue-tied, Peyton bit her lip, stalling until she could think. "Just because you are...omnivorous doesn't mean Liam is."

Laughing, he swiped his hand down his face. "Omnivorous. I like that. It's not accurate, but I like it. In reality, there's a whole spectrum of sexuality, each little wavelength with its own nuance their name or label can't capture, but I digress."

He leaned forward. "My point is I'd bet everything I owned on Liam's true nature being omnivorous, too. Whether he will ever admit it is another story. The man does like to get in his own way sometimes. For your sake, I hope this isn't one of them, because after meeting you, I sincerely hope you get your happy ending. One of us should."

She snorted even though it wasn't funny. "Wishful thinking won't make it so."

"Never underestimate the power of positive thought." He tapped his temple. "I think that's enough revelations for one night. Tomorrow morning, we dock in Boston Harbor. You're almost home."

Peyton's breath caught, her belly churning once more.

Matthias took her hand, putting it in the crook of his arm. "Let me walk you to your stateroom."

Still inwardly reeling, Peyton allowed herself to be led. They were halfway to her room when she tightened her grip on his arm. Something he'd said replayed itself in her mind. "So...you think I'm heartbroken over Liam because you are, too?"

"Oh, I wouldn't go that far," he said. "In fact, I'd venture to say neither one of us got out unscathed. Certain people tend to leave a mark. But I don't have to tell you that, do I?"

They continued to her door in silence. He bent to kiss her forehead.

"Do I really look damaged?"

"You've been through an ordeal. A bit of damage is to be expected."

"*Matthias.*"

He inclined his head. "Well, there is the fact you flinch almost every time I say his name. It is a bit telling."

Her lips parted in consternation. She hadn't been aware of that. *You better stop before you get home.* For years, she'd struggled to hide her true feelings from Liam. What if he looked at her now and saw the truth? What if Caroline did? Too many people knew and pitied her already. But Peyton couldn't face it if Liam found out.

Matthias rubbed her shoulder. "It's almost imperceptible, I assure you. But I guess you could say I was searching for that sort of reaction when you came aboard."

"I'll have to watch that. Do me a favor—don't hide in your office tomorrow. I want to say goodbye properly. I'm—I'm going to miss you."

Impulsively, she stood on her tiptoes and kissed him on the cheek. Matthias reached up to stroke her hair.

"Peyton, if I'm wrong about everything—if Liam doesn't come to his senses—you can always come back here."

"Wh—"

He held up his hands, cutting her off. "It won't come to that, but if it does, the *Ormen Lange* will be waiting."

He abruptly turned on his heel and walked away, disappearing around the corner before she could reply.

CHAPTER 18

*P*eyton half-expected Matthias to skip breakfast, but he was true to his word. He was waiting in the dining room for her bright and not so early at around ten AM.

However, he didn't touch any of last night's revelations. Whenever she tried to bring them up, he would change the subject, determinedly distracting her with some other topic. The untouchable sophisticate from her first days on the *Ormen Lange* was back.

Despite that, Peyton couldn't help but enjoy herself with Matthias. His conversation may have been deliberately shallow, but it was witty and urbane. The stories were entertaining. She liked that he seemed to enjoy talking to her.

Matthias was such a forceful personality, and it was easy to be carried along in his wake. Almost effortless. But as the meal ended, she was very aware their time was growing short.

"When will we arrive?"

"We docked ten minutes ago. Did you not feel it when the engines stopped?"

Peyton looked around them in surprise. She hadn't noticed at all—a fact which spoke to the power of Matthias' aptitude for distraction.

She must not have appeared entirely happy because Matthias put his hand over hers. "Everything will be fine. I'm not wrong about Liam. He just needed something to shake him out of his complacency. Your kidnapping has done it."

She wished she were as confident as he was, but his conviction was heady stuff. He'd almost convinced her. "What about you? What are you going to do?"

He shrugged. "I'm going to do what I always do. Sail around the world, dividing my time between business and pleasure."

The way he said that last bit made a flash of heat course through her. It sounded as if he had definite plans for the future. "Does that mean you are going to be visiting the mainland to hit a few clubs or something? Are you going on shore-leave?"

He laughed. "Well, I hadn't thought of it that way, but your visit here has sparked a certain...hunger."

Peyton set down her glass. She was glad she'd finished her orange juice or else she would have choked on it.

"I would go pack, but I don't have anything but that awful white dress. I'd sooner burn it. Will you give it a proper burial at sea once I'm gone?"

"Of course, but you're welcome to take any of the gowns I bought you."

"No, thank you. I can't take them. Besides, I wouldn't have anywhere to wear them."

He seemed as if he wanted to argue. "Not even the sweatpants?"

She laughed. "Just the pair I'm wearing. Why don't you keep the gowns for the next damsel in distress?"

His face clouded over, but she didn't take it back. If anyone needed a purpose in life, it was Matthias Raske. "Just because you don't break up sex-trafficking rings anymore doesn't mean you can't help people," she said softly.

He cleared his throat. "I went ahead and sent Liam and the others a message. Told them to expect us after lunch, so you can have some time—"

Loud voices interrupted. Matthias straightened, his eyes fixed on the door behind her. "Or it could be sooner."

Peyton twisted in her seat. Liam and Patrick were rushing through the door, both were talking at full volume.

"Where is she?" Liam said in a near shout, coming up short when Matthias stood to greet them.

Peyton stood, heart in her throat as she watched Liam and Patrick Tyler cross the near-empty room to reach the booth.

Liam was faster than Trick. She'd just opened her mouth to greet them both when he yanked her into his rock-hard arms, crushing the breath out of her.

For a moment, the walls came down. Tears stung at her eyes in contradiction to her soaring heart, but she remembered he was spoken for all too soon.

Fortunately, Trick saved her from herself. The younger Tyler brother tried, unsuccessfully, to get her out of Liam's arms, but when he didn't let go, Trick joined in, embracing her from behind in a Tyler brothers' sandwich.

While it would be most women's dream come true, it was just uncomfortable under the circumstances. She could barely breathe. Sometimes, the guys just didn't know their own strength.

Outside of the muscular prison, Matthias snickered.

Peyton tapped Liam on the arm like a wrestler asking for mercy. "Liam, *my ribs,*" she said in an exaggerated wheeze.

When he released her, she stepped away from him, meeting his eyes for the briefest of moments before glancing to check Matthias' reaction.

Liam didn't cooperate. He grabbed her firmly by the arms, turning her this way and that before asking if she were hurt.

"No," she replied, red-faced. "I wasn't harmed."

"But—" Trick began.

"No, I assure you I'm fine," she insisted, cutting him off. "That would have been damaging the goods."

The relief in Patrick's expression was gratifying. He'd always been a caring friend, but Liam didn't appear satisfied. His face was still dark. He kept a hand on her arm, running his eyes up and down over her body as if checking for bruises or missing limbs.

Matthias cleared his throat. "Gentleman," he said, inclining his head formally.

Their host's aloof demeanor crumpled when Patrick threw himself at him. Peyton almost laughed aloud when Trick lifted him off his feet. It was quite a feat considering Matthias outweighed him by at least twenty pounds.

"Oh my God. I can't believe you're here in the flesh. Thank you— thank you so much. *Again.*"

"Again? I'm sorry, have we met?" Matthias asked as Trick let go. He smiled, taking the overly familiar greeting in stride.

"I'm Patrick Tyler—I played you once."

"You *played* me?"

Trick—a hand-waver when he talked—swept his arms up in a grand gesture, encompassing the room. "I pretended to be you when you lent us your other yacht. It was over a year ago."

Matthias nodded, enlightenment clearing his frown. "Oh, that's right. When you rescued Eva Stone from her captor. A brilliant woman."

"Did Liam tell you about her?"

"No. I met her recently. Common business interests."

"Did you?" Trick's brow raised. He started to say something else when Liam cleared his throat.

"Hello," Liam interrupted, his hand still on her arm despite her best efforts to move farther away from him.

His voice, normally a low growl, sounded hoarse to her ears.

For a moment, the two men stared at each other. Despite the practice she'd had over the years, it was difficult to read Liam's expression. Matthias was much easier. He was clearly amused.

"Hello," he replied, a hint of a smirk on his face. "I wasn't expecting you so soon. I left a message saying we'd be docking later this afternoon."

A flicker of annoyance crossed Liam's face. "Yeah, I had a man watching the harbor," he said, putting a hand on Peyton's shoulder to haul her a little closer.

Trick nudged him away, throwing both arms around Peyton's neck and hugging her to his front. "I don't know how we'll ever repay you. My sister hasn't slept since we found out what happened. She'd be here now, but Liam got the message the *Ormen Lange* had arrived and he peeled out—I had to chase him down the street or he would have driven off without me."

Trick turned to his brother. "Maggie's going to kill you. You know that, right?"

"She'll get over it once she sees Peyton," he said, reaching for her hand around his brother. "Everyone will be able to relax. And Ethan and Jason can finally back off."

"Is everyone waiting at the hotel?" Peyton was simultaneously relieved and a little nauseated.

"We can hold them off if you're not feeling up to it," Trick told her, squeezing her shoulders.

"No, it's okay. I'm fine. It's better to run the gauntlet tonight. Get it out of the way so everyone can see I'm all right."

She tried to infuse her words with more enthusiasm than she felt. As much as she wanted to see Maggie, her friends, and the rest of the Caislean staff—many of whom had been like family since she was a child—she was still feeling drained.

Matthias reached out, his fingers touching her chin. "I did try to buy you a bit more time."

"I don't need it."

They stayed like that for a moment, looking into each other's eyes, when Liam appeared at their side. He gave Trick a hard nudge, jostling her into breaking the contact. "We'll be going then," he said.

Peyton frowned, and Matthias chuckled noiselessly.

Trick threw his brother an exasperated glance. "It's going to be a mess tonight," he told Matthias, "but it'll be a mess with lots of great food and alcohol. The chef has been prepping to cook Peyton's favorites all week. Once the part where my wife and Maggie stop crying about this is over, it might actually be fun."

"Is that an invitation?" Matthias asked.

"*Yes*," Liam abruptly barked. He cleared his throat. "Yes, it is. Will you come?"

Another hint of a smile played on Matthias' lips. "I would love to. Unfortunately, I have plans that can't be changed."

"Are you sure?" Trick looked at him hopefully.

Matthias shrugged with just the right touch of apologetic regret. "I would reschedule if I could, but it's business."

"Well, if you change your mind or can make it tomorrow or the day after, we'd love to have you. Maybe we can gather the guys to come in so they can meet you. We can have a quiet dinner at the hotel. Just say the word and I can have our chef whip up a spread to rival the Feasts of Beasts."

Matthias' smile curdled a little as if the idea of meeting a room full of people who didn't work for him was the last thing he wanted to do. "I'm not sure I can shuffle my commitments, but I can try."

Even Peyton knew that for the lie it was. "I guess we should go. I don't want to keep Maggie and Thalia waiting. In fact, if we take any longer, they'll show up here."

"She's right," Liam said, moving to extricate her from his brother's grasp. He paused right in front of Matthias. "We should get going, but if you can get away, it would be good to catch up."

Peyton watched, wide-eyed, wondering if Matthias would agree to come, but all he did was incline his head in acknowledgment.

Liam started ushering her to the door, Trick at his heels.

"Three days, Peyton," Matthias called after her.

She tripped. Liam caught her easily, keeping her from literally hitting the deck. Getting to her feet, she blushed and tried to pull away, but he didn't let go.

"Not that you will need it," Matthias added with an almost imperceptible nod at the other man, who gently tugged until she started moving again.

Peyton paused at the threshold. It was on the tip of her tongue to tell him not to wait. Instead, she only thanked him. Then she let Liam guide her out the door.

~

PEYTON PULLED the covers over her head, but it didn't shut out the bright sunlight pouring through the windows. The light filtered through the ultra-white down comforter.

Shit, I should have closed the blinds. She squinted at the bedside clock, wrung out despite more than twelve hours of sleep. Over the last few days, she'd been alternately hugged, kissed, and coddled in every way platonically imaginable, and she was exhausted.

Matthias was gone.

He hadn't called to say goodbye…not that she had expected him to. But the three days had come and gone and she was still here at the Caislean, sleeping in the empty suite next to Trick and Tahlia's.

Five days ago, Peyton had left the *Ormen Lange* and had been ushered to the inner sanctum, the top floor of the hotel where the offices and family suites were located. Trick and Liam had fussed over her, insisting she needed time to process her ordeal before she saw everyone. Not that anyone had listened to them. Her friends and surrogate family descended en masse—a little at a time, but then the trickle became a stream. Soon, it was a flood…in more ways than one.

First, Maggie had cried all over her. When she was done, Thalia had a turn, then Maia MacLachlan. Then Maggie had another go.

The staff was slightly more circumspect with their welcome. Only Constanza shed tears in front of Peyton, but several of the other housekeepers had gotten misty-eyed. Then the food had arrived. In spite of the circumstances, it had become a party. A surreal one for her, but a celebration, nonetheless. Their love washed over her. Everyone was so happy and relieved she couldn't help but be, too.

· · ·

"WHAT DID Matthias mean by three days?" Liam had asked her somewhere in between Maia's crying jag and Maggie's round two. His dark eyes bored into hers as he demanded an answer.

Once upon a time, she might have told him what he wanted to know. She used to tell him everything. Maggie used to get so upset that Peyton could never keep a secret from him.

Things were different now.

"Nothing," she'd insisted, turning away to talk to his sister. She'd had to repeat that several times over the next few days—long days where she hadn't been able to go anywhere without him knowing. He'd kept her close. Even though she knew she should, Peyton hadn't complained.

Liam stopped asking after the fourth day. This was the morning of day five. And it was Sunday.

Brunch was a tradition for the Tylers. Peyton showered and pulled on her clothes, still not feeling quite herself. But there was solace in familiar routines.

For a minute, she eyed the charm bracelet on top of the dresser. Liam had surprised her with it in the car on the way back from the docks.

"You forgot this," he'd said in his deep rumble, fastening it on her wrist without another word.

Trick had watched him do it, his shoulders high and tight, but Peyton hadn't fought Liam over it. But she had taken the bracelet off to shower that night, and she'd never put it back on.

Impulsively, she reached for it, about to strap it on, when she noticed a new charm. It was a small computer—a vintage desktop model, just like the one she learned to code on at the old B&B.

Her heart gave a little squeeze, and she put the bracelet on with a smile. Swinging her arm to hear the charms jangle, she went down to Divine, the hotel's restaurant, to join the family for the meal.

Maggie was just sitting down when she arrived, but Trick and Tahlia had plates in front of them. They were scarfing down pancakes like they were going to run out. "Sorry," Trick's wife apologized after she swallowed. "I told Trick we shouldn't start without you, but I was starving."

"Don't apologize." Peyton grinned, waving at her friend's extended belly. "You're eating for two."

"Yeah." Maggie poked her brother in the ribs. "What's your excuse?"

Trick guffawed. "It's called transference or something," he said, waving his fork.

Jason, Maggie's husband, and his partner Ethan had made a quick appearance at dinner the first night, but the two were on assignment. They'd only been able to steal away from the round-the-clock surveillance they had on a Russian mobster for a few hours.

Liam breezed in soon afterward. Peyton perked up under his warm appraisal. His attentiveness over the last few days had been gratifying, if a little suffocating.

Everyone stopped when Caroline Wentworth entered the room. "Darling," she called. She glided to the table on gold-colored heels. They matched her cream suit, setting off her blonde perfection perfectly.

Liam glanced at Peyton quickly before getting to his feet to pull out a chair for his *fiancée*. Forcing air into her lungs, Peyton picked up her fork. But then a cloud of expensive perfume washed over Peyton, making her waffle taste of jasmine. She set her fork down again, unable to eat another bite.

"Peyton, dear," Caroline gushed. "I'm so happy to see you again. Everyone was so worried when you went missing. I swear Liam didn't sleep for weeks."

Peyton studied her, registering genuine concern on the woman's face.

"Sorry for worrying you all," Peyton murmured, reaching for her juice.

"Hey, Caroline," Maggie said with a tight smile. More lackluster greetings from the others came around.

Liam hadn't mentioned Caroline Wentworth for days. For some

reason, Peyton hadn't expected to see the woman again. Which was ridiculous. No one had mentioned Liam ending his engagement. No one had mentioned her at all. But Caroline hadn't fallen through a manhole or off the end of the world. Matthias had been wrong.

"*Peyton.*"

"I'm sorry, what?" Peyton started, glancing around. Everyone was watching her with an array of stricken expressions. Liam's face was pinched, his lips tight, and Trick was visibly wincing. Thalia's eyes were on her plate, and Maggie clutched her fork mutinously.

"I said I can call Pietro for a fitting—if you're willing, that is." Caroline smiled, showing off her blindingly white teeth.

"A fitting for what?"

"Err…for your dress. I hope you won't mind being paired with my cousin Eustace. He has two left feet, but he's been taking lessons so he should be shipshape by then."

"Dress?" Enlightenment came slowly. "Are you asking me to be a bridesmaid at your wedding?" The one to *Liam*?

She'd thought she couldn't feel worse, but she'd been wrong. The pain had grown too sharp. Somewhere in her head, a bubble burst. Blessed numbness followed.

"Yes, I was going to ask before, but then you got that job. But you're back now, and I know it would mean the world to Liam," Caroline rushed on, putting a hand on his arm. "He's been beside himself with worry, but now everything will go back to normal. We can all get on with our lives."

"*Caroline*, now is not the time," Liam growled. "Peyton has been through a—"

"I'm fine," Peyton rasped, finding her voice. "But I can't be a bridesmaid. I'm sorry. It would be…against guidelines."

"Guidelines?" Caroline repeated. She stared, apparently at a loss for the first time since Peyton had known her.

"What guidelines?" Trick echoed.

"The ones where I don't expose myself. There's a whole list. So, no, I can't be a bridesmaid."

"Is this something Matthias Raske told you?" Liam asked with a frown. Caroline's lashes fluttered, but it was her only reaction to the man's name.

"Technically, they're Priya's rules." Peyton took a tiny sip of juice. "I have to keep a low profile, and your wedding would be anything but. I'm sure the pictures will be all over the papers and gossip sites. The slavers might come after me again if they knew I was walking around free. Maybe they'd go after Matthias as well, although that's less likely with his army of staff and security personnel."

There was a pointed silence.

"Oh, of course." Caroline nodded. "I should have realized. Well, perhaps we can find another role for you, something in the background."

"Thank you," Peyton murmured, wondering why Liam didn't say anything.

Brunch ended with her still waiting.

CHAPTER 19

*P*eyton studied the grey late-afternoon sky from her temporary suite as Maggie and Trick fought over who would open the bottle of wine. Neither had mentioned brunch or their brother's *fiancée* for the last few hours. Thalia had fallen asleep half an hour ago, too tired to keep her eyes open. Trick had carried his very pregnant wife next door for an overdue nap, but he'd come back. He threw himself on the couch in front of the television set until it had gotten late enough for it to be socially acceptable to drink. They were starting their second bottle.

She knew neither of Liam's siblings liked Caroline very much, but the funereal air they maintained was almost comical. Not that Peyton felt like laughing. She was still numb. For now, at least. But the pain waited on the other side of her icy shield.

This is it—this is rock bottom.

It won't ever be this bad again, she promised herself.

This was her own fault. She had let herself hope. *Dumbass.* It had been a mistake, and the only person she had to blame was herself. True—Matthias had lit the spark with his baseless conjecture, but she'd been the one who set herself on fire hoping for what could never be.

Trick and Maggie kept exchanging worried looks as if they were waiting for Peyton to burst into tears. She half expected them herself, but they didn't come.

Maybe I've cried myself out. A few years ago, there had been a time when she'd cried herself to sleep on a regular basis, usually when Liam started dating a new woman. His model period had been especially rough. But today, her eyes were so dry they stung. Perhaps she'd shed all the tears she was going to. Wouldn't that be something? She had run out of tears for Liam.

Or I'm dehydrated...

"Peyton, I'm sorry about Caroline," Maggie said, finally bringing up the disastrous brunch. She handed her a very full glass of wine.

Peyton handed it back. "I think I need water, not wine."

Trick went behind the bar, then tossed her a bottle. She caught it one-handed, opening it and taking a swig.

"Do you want to talk about it?" he asked.

"I really don't." She sat on the couch next to Maggie, who threw her arm around her. "But you two do, so go ahead."

"Not if it upsets you," Maggie protested.

"It doesn't," Peyton said.

Trick and Maggie regarded her with identical expressions of skeptical sympathy.

"Well, it doesn't any more than I already was," she said, waving them on. "You don't have to walk on eggshells around me. After the last few weeks, there isn't anything you can possibly say that would make me feel worse. We can only go up from here," she added.

Her philosophical air broke the dam. Soon, Maggie groused about Caroline and her endless plans. "This wedding is going to be the worst."

"Then I guess it's a good thing I'm not going to go." Peyton poked her in the ribs. "What is the bridesmaid's dress like?"

"Can something be elegant and awful at the same time? Cause Caroline's choice manages to be both. It's a genuinely nice fabric and the bodice is all right, but the skirt is a *mermaid train*. I can't walk in it. Sometime that night, I'm going to end up flat on my face. I just know it."

Turning suddenly, Maggie clutched her arm. "You don't hate me for being a bridesmaid, do you?"

"Of course not. It's not like you can say no. Liam would kill you." Peyton turned to Trick. "Are you going to be the best man?"

"No, Calen is. I told Liam I'd be the best man at his next wedding," Trick said with a wicked grin.

"You did not!" Peyton almost smiled.

"I did," he said. "But the only reason he didn't punch my lights out is because I hid behind my pregnant wife. Thalia somehow convinced him that the real reason is she was afraid of going into labor, so I might not be able to fulfill my best man duties. The wedding is near enough to her due date for that excuse to work. She was obviously lying through her teeth, but she's too pretty and pregnant for him to hassle just now, so he let it go."

"Having a woman to hide behind suits you," she remarked wanly, sipping her water.

A buzz sounded from Maggie's phone. She lifted it to read the text displayed on the screen, but then promptly put it away.

"What's that?" Could it be Caroline again? Had she found a suitable 'background' role for her?

"It's just Jason. He thinks he can break away from the surveillance detail for us to go to dinner, but I'm going to text him not to. I told the chef to prepare your favorite meal, and then—"

Peyton held up a finger to interrupt. She took the phone to read Jason's pleading message.

"Don't even think about it. Your hot FBI agent husband, who's been stuck in a van for weeks and weeks, apparently *needs* to meet you for dinner and no doubt a quickie."

Maggie laughed at her brother's curdled-milk expression.

"Maybe it could be a double date?" Maggie suggested softly after a moment. "Ethan was so happy to see you. He's been worried, too."

"If Jason can get away, it's because Ethan is covering for him," Peyton pointed out. "I'll catch up with Agent Thomas some other time. Now please get out of here so I can live vicariously through you."

It took more poking and prodding, but Peyton was able to convince Maggie to join Jason for dinner. Once she was gone, Peyton looked at Trick, wishing he'd leave, too.

"Don't look at me like that," he said, pointing the corkscrew at her. "I'm not going anywhere. Besides, my wife's asleep. If she follows her new routine, she'll be dead to the world for a few more hours."

He sat next to her on the couch, shuffling a deck of cards he'd picked up from the table. "Wanna play twenty-one?"

"Well, I've got nothing better to do."

"Ouch," Trick said, putting his hand over his heart.

She flicked his nose. "Stop. I just mean I can't even work. I don't have a laptop anymore. All my stuff is still in California."

"We can ship it out here."

"No. I...I won't be staying that long."

Sighing, Trick slid a hand over his face. "I know. For what it's worth, I thought Liam was coming to his senses for a minute there when he insisted on putting that charm bracelet on you. But he's a glutton for punishment. I just hope he doesn't regret marriage to the ice queen too much."

Peyton blinked, then snorted lightly. "You're going to have to stop calling her that. She's going to be your sister-in-law."

It hurt less to say it aloud than she thought it would. "And don't let Maggie be mean to her. I think Caroline is feeling sensitive about the wedding."

"How do you figure that? It's all she talks about."

Peyton shrugged. "Maybe that's because she senses everyone's reluctance. It would be hard for her not to. You, in particular, cringe every time she brings it up. And she has to know that's not a man's general wedding-talk aversion. You and Maggie planned your ceremony and reception down to the last detail."

"I guess I have been kind of a dick." Trick's exaggerated sigh reminded her of when they were kids and the cooks tried to get him to eat his vegetables. "You're not going to leave right away? You have to stay until you figure out what you're going to do."

"Whatever that is…Eva called. She held my job open, but Priya is right. I can't go back to my old life. It won't be safe."

Trick grabbed her hand. "We won't let anyone get you again," he promised.

"It's not me I'm worried about," she confessed. "I came out of that mess relatively unscathed. I know I wouldn't be that lucky a second time, but the bigger threat wouldn't be to me. That outfit was professional and well-organized. And they were also careful and ruthless— they wouldn't be afraid of causing some serious collateral damage if they believed I was on the loose and could cause them trouble. I don't want anyone to get hurt trying to protect me. I've got to be smart about this."

She sat up with a gasp. "Oh, my God. I didn't even ask. What the hell happened to Dylan?"

"Don't worry." Trick's mouth turned down. "We didn't let Liam kill him. Dylan's in jail."

"Oh." She sagged against the couch. "I can't believe it. Do you think he'll be safe there? Those dealers wanted to kill him if he couldn't pay up."

"He traded *you* to pay that debt. Don't tell me you're worried about that asshole?"

"I don't know." She sighed. "He was desperate. I won't forgive him or anything stupid like that, but I don't want him dead."

Trick sniffed. "Well, he should be safe enough in prison."

They sat in silence for a little while. "I need a new computer," she said after a while.

"I'll buy you one tomorrow."

"I wasn't angling for a handout, Trick."

He scoffed. "It's not one. And I hate to point out the obvious, but you can't use any of your own money, so you better cut up your credit cards when we get them back. I'm sure that's on the Priya woman's list of dos and don'ts."

"I'm sure it is. She was highly organized. Matthias used the expression *terrifyingly efficient*."

Peyton rubbed the rim of her water bottle contemplatively. Behind that ultra-professional veneer was a brilliant and passionate woman. Matthias had been the bank, but the underground railroad had been all Priya. Peyton couldn't help but admire the other woman's desire to make a difference in this crappy world.

If only she'd had a little more time, Peyton knew she could have cracked Priya. They would have been friends. As for Matthias, thinking about him sent an unexpected wave of longing through her.

He was another missed opportunity. *All that time spent pining for Liam.* One chance after another had come and gone. The worst part was, she'd closed the door on them herself. At the time, she hadn't cared, but that was how she'd gotten to this point—an almost twenty-five-year-old virgin with no job and no prospects of independence. She was going to have to rely on her friends in order to start over. Life had officially passed her by.

"What did you say?"

"Hmm?"

"You muttered something about Matthias." Trick looked at her out of the corner of his eye. "He's an interesting man. More fit and a hell of a lot younger than I thought he would be. That look he gave you when we picked you up…did anything happen between you?"

"Of course not." She was an idiot hell-bent on wasting her life on unrequited love. "And it never will. He's gone now."

Trick glanced at his watch. "Yeah, he should be by now."

Peyton blinked. "Matthias left two days ago. The *Ormen Lange* was pulling up anchor and getting the hell out of Dodge on Friday."

Trick rubbed his nose. "Something must have delayed him because Liam's guy at the port said the yacht was still there this morning. I didn't think anything about it, but Liam seemed anxious about it. I didn't tell him I tried sending Matthias a message, inviting him to brunch, but I'm glad he ignored it now. Caroline does have a way of spoiling things, doesn't she?"

He wasn't watching Peyton anymore, so he missed her parted lips and dumbfounded expression.

He's still here. Matthias was still in Boston. Why? Her lips parted as she remembered the look in his eyes when he almost kissed her. And perhaps the greater revelation—she had wanted him to.

Peyton sprang to her feet, then ran to the window, staring in the direction of the harbor as if she could search for the *Ormen Lange* from here. It was the right direction, but too far. The view was obscured by other buildings.

"Could he?" she whispered. Had Matthias extended his stay in Boston because he was waiting for her?

The deadline had come and gone days ago, but, in retrospect, three days hadn't been long enough for her to reassure all of her friends of her well-being. She was still fielding calls from friends from school and former coworkers who had transferred to Caislean hotels in other states.

She'd barely had a moment to herself—her fault, of course, for clinging to Liam since she'd gotten back, but she hadn't had any time to think. Had Matthias decided to give her more time?

"What's wrong?" Trick sat ramrod straight, watching her reaction with a tight expression.

She took a deep, albeit shaky, breath. "I just realized something."

"What?"

She wiggled two fingers. "Well, it's two things really. First—I'm done feeling sorry for myself. And second, I want you to stop feeling sorry for me, too. Don't be mad at Liam on my behalf. We haven't been fair to him. It's not his fault that he never fell in love with me."

"Peyton—"

She held up a hand. "Trick, I love you, but you and Maggie are too loyal for your own good. But now that Liam is getting married, you have to give Caroline a chance. She was just trying to be nice and include me when she asked me to be a bridesmaid."

He wrinkled his nose. "You don't think she was trying to rub your nose in it?"

She thought about it, but then shook her head. "No, I don't. She's... still an outsider. No one confides in her, and she's not around us enough to guess what I'm feeling. Maybe she suspects, but I don't think so. It was a genuine gesture on her part."

Trick sniffed. "She's not around us by choice. Caroline only ever wants to socialize with Liam and other jet setters. She lives and breathes high society, and she never stops networking. I would call her a social climber if she weren't an heiress herself."

"Maybe, but we didn't exactly roll out the welcome mat. Not for her or any of her predecessors. In fact, we've been assholes to most of Liam's girlfriends," she admitted.

"I wouldn't go that far," Trick grumbled, but he couldn't quite look her in the eye. "It doesn't help he doesn't exactly go for the warm and fuzzy types—the ones with two brain cells to rub together anyway. If they were halfway intelligent, then they were usually cold or self-involved. It was intentional, too. A normal woman would have developed real feelings for him, then he would have had to dump her."

Peyton snorted. *At least I saved Liam the trouble of having to dump me.* She'd broken her heart all on her own.

"I'm not sure they were all that bad," she mused, thinking back on the parade of beautiful women Liam had run through. Some of them had probably been nice enough if they'd bothered to give them a chance. But she hadn't been able to do that. Because of her, his siblings hadn't been able to either...

Then there was Matthias. Closing her eyes, she pictured him—the way his eyes locked on her when he talked and the funny little twist he put on certain expressions...and how alone he was.

But he doesn't have to be.

Peyton laughed aloud, a hysterical tinge making the sound thin but light. Almost happy.

Trick groaned. "Okay, I think all the stress made you crack up."

Peyton didn't answer. She returned to the window, putting a hand over her heart. But the dull gnawing pain that had been a constant companion the last few months had faded.

Was there any chance the *Ormen Lange* was still in port? Her heart skittered and skipped. *I have to find out.*

Spinning on her heel, she went to the bar to grab another bottle of water. She tossed it at Trick. "Drink up. You need to be sober enough to drive."

He frowned, setting aside the wineglass and picking up the bottle that had landed next to him. "Where are we going?"

She inhaled, holding the air in her lungs until she could summon the wherewithal to answer. But she didn't need to.

Trick gasped, his eyes bulging out of his head. "No!"

"Yes," she said, her eyes shining. "Get your keys. *Now.*"

"LIAM IS GOING TO KILL ME," Trick muttered under his breath as his sleek Bugatti prowled through the piles of crates and shipping containers like a spaceship from another world. "And when he's done, Maggie is going to have a turn. She's had enough nightmares about you going missing as it is."

Peyton winced, clutching the Caislean-branded duffel bag to her chest. It held all her worldly possessions—a few changes of clothes and her passport, which had been waiting for her on the desk in the suite. "I promise I'll call her as soon as I can."

She should have promised to call Liam, too, but she couldn't make herself do it. Maybe someday he'd understand.

"You better," Trick sighed. "Are you even sure the *Ormen Lange* is still here? When we asked the guard back there, he didn't seem to know what we were talking about.

"I'm sure," Peyton said. It was crazy, but she did believe it. Matthias was waiting for her. It was the only thing she was certain of.

Trick studied her with troubled eyes. He didn't have to say it aloud. Trick thought the boat was long gone. The gate guard hadn't recognized the name. If a mega-yacht were parked at his work, he'd remember the name, wouldn't he?

Doubt trickled down her spine like sweat. She tightened her grip on the bag. *He's here.* He has to be.

It wasn't until the low-slung Bugatti turned the corner that the *Ormen Lange* came into view. It rose up like a behemoth in front of them, tied to a massive yellow cleat at the end of a long pier.

Peyton lunged forward, inadvertently straining the seat belt too hard across her chest.

"*Holy shit.* It's still here," Trick said as he steered the car closer to the pier. "I was almost hoping it wasn't."

"But it is." Eyes dancing, she gave him a shaky grin and unbuckled her belt.

He bit his lip, gazing from her to the boat and back again. "You're really doing this, aren't you?"

Her heart was beating so loud she was surprised he couldn't hear it. "I am. Are you going to try to stop me?"

"No."

"Why not?"

His smile was sad. "Because I haven't seen you this happy in a long time."

Peyton threw herself at him. The long divider that separated the seats dug into her side, but she didn't care. "Trick, you're the best brother I never wanted."

He sniffed loudly. "I love you, too, pigpen."

Peyton pulled away from him with a watery grin. Trick hadn't called her that in years. He tugged her toward him, planting a kiss on her forehead.

"I'm sorry for the way this ended up. You deserve so much better than my brother, but I didn't warn you off because, well, I guess I wanted you to be my sister for real."

This time, her tears were happy ones. "Trick, I *am* your real sister."

Then she smacked him on the shoulder. "And stop acting like you're never going to see me again. Despite what you read on the internet, the earth isn't flat. The boat isn't going to fall off the end of the world."

He snorted and nodded, his eyes gravitating to the glowing lights of the *Ormen Lange*. "Are you sure he's expecting you?"

Peyton raised a brow, and he chuckled silently. "All right. You're sure. He better take good care of you."

She opened the door. "He will," she said in a matter-of-fact tone. "I'll make sure of it."

Trick followed suit, climbing out of the car and looking at her over the top. Peyton slung the strap of the duffel bag. "Maybe I should go with you. Give him hell like a big brother should."

She tapped the top of the car with the flat of her hand. "Trick, go home to your pregnant wife. I'll be fine."

"You know, I think I believe you." He smiled, but it waned quickly. "I just wish I could say the same for the rest of us."

Smiling, Peyton dipped her head. She started walking down the pier. But, before she knew it, she started running and laughing as she waved goodbye.

Trick still stood at his open car door when she disappeared inside.

THE PORTER at the door of the Ormen Lange took one look at her and stood back, admitting her aboard with a respectful bow. That was the easy part. It was dinnertime, so she searched for Matthias in the dining room, but it was empty. So was the pool, the gym, and, according to one of the steward's, he wasn't in his office.

In the end, Priya found Peyton wandering the second deck. Priya took pity on her by leading her to Matthias' stateroom, which occupied the entire prow of the third story.

"Through there," Priya said, pointing at the deck outside the French door, disappearing like a genie before Peyton could casually ask if Matthias had delayed his departure for business reasons.

Heart pounding, Peyton stepped outside on the deck. Matthias was across the deck at the railing that faced the open sea. He stood still, but there was tension in his posture.

At least he's alone out here, she thought as she inched toward him. Imagine if she'd done this and he'd been entertaining another woman. *Or a man.* Now that would have been awkward.

Her strangled laughter carried in the wind. Matthias started, spinning around, his face slack in surprise.

"What the *hell* are you doing here?"

She stopped short, stricken into immobility. The hurt must have shown on her face because Matthias rushed to her side, reaching out to grasp both her arms. "I didn't mean it like that, Peyton. I'm thrilled to see you. It's just—well, why aren't you with Liam?"

Peyton shuddered, covering her beat-up heart with her hand. The poor organ couldn't take many more of these jolts and shocks.

She cleared her throat. "I assumed the *Ormen Lange* was still in port because you were waiting for me. I'm sorry that was presumptuous."

Matthias tilted his head. "I was waiting for you."

"*Oh.* Good." Peyton stared up at him. Despite the shadows under his eyes, he looked amazing. She scowled. "Then don't scare me like that."

Matthias moved to caress her hair. "I was only going to give you one more day, or so I told myself. I didn't think you would come. Did Liam not call off the wedding?"

"Nope." She smiled.

Matthias seemed genuinely confused. "Why not?"

"Because the stars haven't realigned." Sighing, she shrugged, twisting to put her hand on his arm. "You just have to accept it... He's not coming back to you," she said softly.

He laughed. "That's not what I meant, and you know it."

She dropped her eyes, focusing on the tantalizing bit of his chest visible underneath the small gap at the top of his button-down shirt. "You were wrong."

"I find that hard to believe."

He seemed so certain, but Peyton didn't know how to convince him so.

"What is it they say about one man's trash being another man's treasure?" She grimaced. "Not that you think I'm treasure or anything like that."

His smile was wry. "Well, you were very expensive."

Blushing, Peyton tried to cover her face with her hands, but it wasn't easy. Matthias still held both her arms.

"Peyton, to me, you are worth any price—a prize beyond measure. It's obvious to anyone who meets you. And you can be damn sure Liam knows your value, too. He's just too pigheaded to admit it. I don't know what his problem is, but, and please pardon my language, *fuck him*. He had his chance."

His lips came down on hers—the briefest of kisses. But he raised his head before she even realized what was happening.

Matthias fished his phone out from his pocket. "Captain Nilsen, this is Raske. Pull up anchor. We're leaving. *Now*."

Peyton blinked at his hard tone as he hung up the phone. "What's the rush?"

The corners of his mouth turned up. "You may not believe this, but Liam will come for you. So we're not going to be here. Like I said, he had his chance."

More like a lifetime of them. She would have argued he was wrong, but Matthias tugged her closer, putting both hands on either side of her face. His mouth came down again, demanding and hard.

Overwhelmed by a feeling of gratitude, Peyton melted. The heat between them was real, and it was *fierce*. His mouth slanted over hers, his tongue dipping into her mouth, and she moaned, clinging to him.

He made a little sound and pulled her closer, obliterating all coherent thought. The fire burned away the past. Peyton forgot how they met, and who he'd been with before her. She even forgot she was supposed to be suffering from a broken heart.

CHAPTER 20

*L*iam shoved the stack of china pattern and flower catalogs aside. Why couldn't Caroline keep all this damn wedding paraphernalia off his desk? She had been back less than a day, and they were already taking over again.

Not to mention the fact there was an exceptionally large and empty coffee table at her disposal in front of the couch in the corner. Or better yet, she could leave these with his assistant. It wasn't as if he were going to choose the bloody flowers. He had to work. Caroline knew that, and she'd agreed—repeatedly—to handle all details.

He finally dug up the contracts he was searching for under a stack of upholstery samples. "What does she need those for?" he grumbled before giving up and tossing the lot on the shelves behind him.

Liam settled down to work, but he stopped a few minutes later, unable to focus on the intricate clauses of the deal in front of him.

Yanking at his tie, he all but strangled himself in his haste to get it off. Why was he having so much trouble?

Yes, it had been a hellish few weeks. Peyton going missing had been a nightmare, but he'd gotten her back. It had only taken him betraying his personal convictions to do so, but screw it. Peyton was back, and she was safe. He could sleep again.

So what if he got up a few times a night to make sure she was in her bed? She never woke up when he came in, not even last night when he'd reached out and touched her lips.

I was only checking to see if she was breathing. "Fuck," he muttered, squeezing his eyes shut. He had to stop doing that.

Eyes still closed, he noticed the silence for the first time. He checked his watch and the empty couch. Where the hell was Peyton? For the last few days, she had been camped out in his office, reading quietly in the corner so she wouldn't disturb him while he worked.

Well, you knew it was only a matter of time before she stopped that. Peyton couldn't stay idle long. He'd heard Sam asking for her help on updating the security feeds just yesterday. No doubt she was helping him.

Those small tasks weren't going to keep her occupied for long. Trick was right. Peyton needed more of a challenge. He didn't want her running back to Silicon Valley as soon as the coast was clear.

How was he going to keep her here? A sneaky voice whispered in his head, *You could start by not marrying Caroline.* Liam gripped the pen so hard it broke.

"Damn it, not again." Where the hell was Constanza ordering these pens? They needed a new supplier, one that didn't sell crap.

His brother blew in like a storm gale. Trick grunted a greeting, closing the door. He went straight to the bar.

"Hello to you, too," Liam said, wondering if he and Thalia had a fight.

His brother's bride was the most even-tempered sweetheart Liam had ever met. Thalia was the most perfect sister-in-law he could ask for, but since falling pregnant, she'd developed the distressing habit of crying at the drop of a hat. His brother, an enthusiastic father-to-be, took every unfortunate episode in stride, so whatever was bugging him now was bigger than that.

And that meant the fight was his brother's fault. Liam waited, ready to read his brother the riot act for Thalia's sake, when Trick spilled his favorite scotch all over the table.

Hell. This fight must be a bad one. But Trick settled on the couch instead of running after his runaway bride, so it would eventually blow over. "What did you do?"

"I drove." Trick waved the full glass of Scotch at him.

"Don't spill on the leather," he said, glancing down at the contract he hadn't read.

Trick ignored him, downing half the contents of the glass. "Congratulations by the way."

"For what?"

Tricks' eyes narrowed, but his expression wasn't hostile. More like resigned. "For driving away the only woman who will ever truly love you as you are."

"What are you talking about?"

"I'm supposed to forgive you by the way, but I don't feel like it at the moment, so let's table that until tomorrow." Trick downed the rest of the glass. "I don't know when Maggie will forgive you, but Peyton was right. We have to accept Caroline and move on."

Liam sat up straight. "Wait, what about Peyton?"

His brother rubbed the rim of his glass, but he only succeeded in making a terrible squeaking sound. "She's gone."

"Shit!" Liam bolted upright, grabbing his coat. "Where the hell did you take her? The airport?"

Was she returning to California? Had she not taken Priya's advice to heart? It was too soon for her to reconnect with her old life.

"You can forget that. Where she's gone, you can't follow. Matthias will make sure of that."

Liam froze, then scowled. "Wait, are you telling me Matthias is behind this? Did she ask him to set her up somewhere else?"

Fuck. He should have known. Peyton was too independent for her own good. She hated depending on anyone. After getting kidnapped, she was going be forced to start over, but the hardheaded woman was determined to do it all on her own.

"No, jackass. She left *with* him."

Liam blinked rapidly, a narrow but endless pit opening in his stomach. He couldn't say anything, but his brother didn't require an answer.

"Peyton has sailed off into the sunset in search of a happily ever after—literally," Trick said.

"With Matthias?"

Trick gave him an incredulous look. "What did you think was going to happen when you called in a young and conveniently single Nordic billionaire to come to her rescue?"

Liam stared at his brother, but it was as if his voice were coming from a long distance away. "Not Matthias. That just isn't possible."

Trick threw up his hands. "Un-fucking-believable."

Liam shook his head again, even though it was making him dizzy. "Peyton can't leave."

Disgusted, his brother sighed and stalked to the door, throwing it open.

"Liam, stop being so fucking dense. She's been in love with you her whole life, and you're getting married to someone else. All these efforts to hold onto her are only hurting her. Cut her loose. She deserves a chance to be happy, too."

The door closed behind Trick a moment later. Liam pushed away from his desk, then grabbed his coat. He didn't know where the hell he was going, but he couldn't stay here.

CHAPTER 21

*P*eyton stretched out in the sun under the white sheet, glorying in the luxury of a professional massage under the Caribbean sun.

Hmm, this is the life. It was mid-November and she was basking outside, surrounded by crystal-blue water while being rubbed down until she was almost boneless.

"Please turn," the masseuse said in an accented voice Peyton couldn't pin down.

Approximately half Matthias' staff hailed from Scandinavian countries, mostly his home Norway. But the other half was a mixed bag. Priya was born in Bangladesh, while Polina and Demetre were from Estonia and Georgia, respectively. She thought Ha-eun, the boat's masseuse, mentioned she was Korean, but once the massage started, she stopped talking, only responding to questions with low hums of acknowledgment.

She would ask Priya later, Peyton decided as she flipped over on the table. Ha-eun adjusted the sheet over her naked body, taking care to preserve her modesty in case another staff member interrupted—not that they would dare. When Matthias welcomed her aboard, he made a ship-wide announcement she would be his guest indefinitely.

At first, Peyton had been nervous, concerned the staff would continue to act the way they had during her first voyage. But this time around, they seemed far more relaxed, as if they had realized her return was a sign that the underground—*overwater?*—railroad wasn't restarting.

Oiled-up and deliciously relaxed, Peyton let her mind drift as her body was kneaded and pulled like taffy by Ha-eun's skilled and strong hands.

Speaking of which. Peyton's lashes fluttered open, startled as those hands moved under the sheet, grazing the tops of her nipples. She almost giggled aloud, but then it happened again.

Blushing, Peyton held her breath, but the contact didn't happen a third time. The massage ended soon after. Gathering the sheet close around her, she thanked Ha-eun in a rush, nodding and ducking into Matthias' stateroom just as he walked in.

He looked good enough to eat. His suit was linen in deference to the warm weather, but it was neatly pressed and fresh-looking as if he'd just stepped out of the pages of a high-end magazine, summer edition.

Still red in the face, Peyton turned to peek out onto the deck, making sure Ha-eun had departed before hurrying to him.

"You're not going to believe this." She laughed, her tingling breasts growing heavier at the sight of him. "I just got felt up."

Matthias paused. "Did you get a massage from Ha-eun?"

Peyton gaped. "You *know*?"

"That she has a habit of tweaking certain portions of the female anatomy? I heard a rumor about it, but it's been years since anyone has mentioned it. I thought she had stopped."

"Well, well…" Ha-eun had struck her as proper and self-effacing, but what did Peyton know? She'd just met the woman. Then she wrinkled her nose, scowling at him. "Is she perhaps in the habit of giving *you* a special massage? The kind that end ever so happily?"

"No," he said, laughing.

"And I'm supposed to believe you why?" she asked, the corner of her mouth turned up.

Matthias put his hands in his pockets. "Well, for one, because I don't mess around with my staff. And two, I have someone for that now."

He pulled her close, pressing her almost-naked body against his tall hard form. He pressed a hot kiss to her lips, but he raised his head too quickly.

"Oh?" She couldn't suppress her sarcasm. "Then why am I still a virgin?"

Peyton had been on the *Ormen Lange* for days, but aside from a few toe-curling kisses, Matthias hadn't touched her. Well, he hadn't touched her enough.

"Because I meant what I said that first night. You're special. I want to take things slow, to establish a foundation before we get intimate."

She sighed, disappointed, but she knew he was right. Matthias was a wonderful man, but she didn't know him well. Waiting was the best course of action, especially if she wanted a lasting relationship. It was an exceptionally good sign that he seemed to want one, too.

"Well, don't expect me to be satisfied with some cheap thrills on a massage table. I don't expect you to go all the way, but you can at least put out, mister," she teased, pressing a little closer.

He didn't laugh. Instead, he drew his head back. "Ha-eun didn't make you uncomfortable, did she?"

She laughed. "No, but you may want to warn your guests before she gets them on the table."

He shrugged. "I would only have to warn the women. And not all of them. She only does it to the most beautiful ones."

"She's gay?"

"I don't know. I never asked." He looked down, his eyes drawn to the cleavage exposed by the thin sheet. "I am sorry if she upset you, although I can't say I blame her."

Shifting to hold the sheet up with one hand, she reached up to touch his cheek. "I'm not upset. In fact, it was a little…titillating"

Surprise flitted across his features. Matthias grinned, a hot and deeply sexy smile. He leaned down, a wicked glint in his eye. "Well, well, Miss Carson. I find that remarkably interesting news indeed."

She poked him. "I said titillating, not arousing. Not enough for a repeat performance. So don't get any ideas about a threesome."

This time, it was disappointment that settled on his face. "Well, that nixes my big idea. I guess I can forget the speech I prepared."

"W-what?" Peyton stuttered.

Sighing, Matthias gestured to the bed. "Sit."

Wide-eyed, she hauled up the ends of the sheet, making sure it didn't drag on the floor as she crossed the room and perched at the edge of the massive bed.

He rubbed his chin, studying her for a long moment without saying anything. The silence stretched so long Peyton hunched her shoulders, feeling downcast. "This is where you tell me you don't want me after all and offer to send me home, right?"

"I'm not sending you anywhere," he said.

"But you want a threesome because I'm apparently not enough for you…" Peyton stared at her hands.

"You *are* enough. And I'd be happy in an exclusive relationship. For a while…anyway. But I know myself. Eventually, I'd want more."

Peyton wanted to crawl into a hole. "So you're ending this before it even starts?"

"No!" Matthias hurried over, getting on his knees in front of her. He reached out to grasp her hands. "I'm explaining this very badly, but I do see a future with you. The thing is, I know myself. I told you—I learned the hard way that I'm a man with certain appetites."

"Well, for a man with an appetite, you haven't been indulging much," she pointed out.

"Not yet. The thing is—I sense we could be happy long term in a different kind of relationship."

She filled in the blanks. "You want a long-term threesome."

"Yes, but not with you and another woman. I'd like you to consider adding another man to the mix."

"Huh." Of course he meant with another man. He'd told her about his affair with Liam. And he hadn't been the only male partner. Matthias had mentioned others. No doubt there were plenty of women, too. Some at the same time.

Still, the idea had some extremely interesting benefits to it. Images of herself with Matthias and another man flashed through her head. *Damn, if I were wearing panties, they would be soaked by now.*

Peyton was certain her face was beet red. "Talk about jumping from the frying pan into the fire," she joked weakly.

"I know this is a lot to ask from you, especially given your level of experience. And no matter what you decide, I still want *you*. Nothing will change my mind about that. I've been doing a lot of thinking since you came aboard. The potential for lasting happiness is here. But I wouldn't want to ruin what we could have with an affair three or four years down the line because I wanted a man, too. I won't make that mistake again."

Again? Peyton absorbed that in silence. There was a lot he wasn't telling her.

"So you want to see if I can handle a—a..."

"The word you are looking for is polyamorous."

"Yes, okay. You want to know if I can handle a polyamorous relationship right off the bat?"

"I do...What do you think?"

"I think...um...I don't know. This is kind of a lot to ask of a virgin."

Matthias winced. "I know, but let's look at it this way. You have a lot of catching up to do."

Peyton snorted softly. The man had a gift for understatement.

Bracing his arms on either side of her, Matthias let his weight tip forward, leaning closer. "I may be wrong about this, but I sense you are a well of untapped sensuality. It shimmers behind your eyes. I think you'd enjoy being with two men—a lot. Why don't you take some time to think about it?"

"No."

His face fell, but Matthias hid his disappointment with a self-deprecating laugh. "I see. Never mind. Forget I said anything—"

Her head swam, but Peyton gripped her hands together, interrupting him. "No, I meant I don't have to think about it. I want to give it a try."

His lips parted, but he shook his head. "Are you sure? I'm starting to think it was wrong of me to ask. You're not ready."

Peyton grabbed him by the collar, pulling him close enough to kiss. When he lifted his head, he had the most adorably bemused expression on his face. "I forgot what I was saying."

"You were saying I get final approval on this other man," she said.

His expression didn't change much, but she could tell she'd surprised him. "Negotiating, are we?"

"Damn straight," she answered. "It's my body. And yours. We have to find someone who works for us both. And I get to use one of those black balls now—in advance."

"For who?"

Wasn't it obvious?

"Liam Tyler," she said, raising her brows for emphasis. "I know you have a soft spot for him, but he's off the table, so don't even think about it."

"Not even—"

"I said *no*."

He held up his hands. "All right, I concede. Anyone but Liam," he agreed. "But finding the right man may take a while."

"You're the one determined to take things slow," she pointed out.

He stood over her for a moment, shaking his head in wonder. "I'm going to fall madly in love with you, aren't I?"

Peyton wrinkled her nose. "You say that like it's a bad thing."

She rose on her knees, using his tie to pull him closer. "But until we find and both agree to this third man, there is no sense in waiting, is there?"

If that were the case, then why the hell had she started taking birth control shots? It certainly wasn't for her love of needles. Feeling bold, Peyton shimmied, letting the sheet she was wrapped in slide down several inches, exposing the tops of her breasts.

"*Omegadritt.*" Matthias' lips parted, his eyes growing hot as he ran his hungry eyes over the tanned mounds.

She guessed that was Norwegian, but she had no clue what it meant. "Is that good?"

His only answer was to push her down on the bed. Muscles tensing, Peyton tried to relax as Matthias covered her with his body, lowering his head to take one of her nipples in his mouth.

"*Holy...*" Coherent thought eroded like a sandcastle in a storm. Lifting her head, she watched Matthias' lips move across her chest to suckle at her other breast.

Biting her lip, she willed her racing heart to calm down, but it was hard. Her whole body was flushed. Raising shaky hands, she pushed at Matthias, trying to work his linen suit coat off.

Matthias caught her hands. "I meant it when I said we would go slow," he said, pressing her arms above her head. "This is just a quick taste."

He meant that literally. After ordering her to leave her hands where they were, he tugged the sheet off her legs, leaving her completely exposed to his gaze.

A little growl escaped as Matthias ran his big hands down her waist to her thighs. Embarrassed despite herself, Peyton waited, holding her breath as he slowly pushed her legs open.

Crawling down, Matthias gave her one last smoldering glance before bending his head and licking her heat. She was already wet, but Peyton was surprised by the instant electric shot of pleasure that jolted through her when his mouth closed over her clit.

Soon, his hands joined his mouth. Parting her lips with his fingers, he used his tongue to penetrate her, thrusting deep. Her hips started rocking in unison with his movements, trying to lengthen each burgeoning pulse of pleasure.

Long minutes passed as Matthias worked his magic. As he alternated sucking and swirling her flesh with his tongue, Peyton climbed higher and higher. Nothing had ever felt so good. Each delicious stroke made her channel shiver. Apparently sensing her need, Matthias dipped a finger inside her.

Peyton thought it couldn't get better, but she was in the hands of a master. Working her G-spot with his fingers, he latched onto her clit with his mouth until she broke. Throwing her head back, Peyton moaned, her hips rising off the sheets as she thrashed in a maelstrom so intense she lost control. Falling back on the bed, she squeezed his finger tightly, desperately trying to hold onto the rapture for a few more precious seconds.

When she had recovered, Peyton reached for him, but Matthias reared back, still fully dressed.

"I need a cold shower. Excuse me."

"But—"

He held up a hand like he was trying to ward off temptation. "You were delicious," he called behind as he escaped into the bathroom. A moment later, the sound of the shower starting filtered past the closed door.

Peyton threw herself on the bed. After a moment, though, she grinned, rolling around in luxurious sheets. This was definitely a step in the right direction.

CHAPTER 22

"Are we back here?" Caroline's voice was like jagged glass against the inside of his skull. She threw her purse on the coffee table as he rose to a sitting position from the unfamiliar cream couch he'd been sleeping on.

Liam winced, reaching for the cut-glass crystal tumbler next to him. He sipped the watered-down whiskey, wondering when the hell all the ice had melted. The silver ice bucket next to him was filled with water.

"Liam, are you even listening to me?"

He coughed, wondering why his throat felt as if it had been scraped with a cheese grater.

"Where am I?" The room seemed vaguely familiar, but he couldn't place it.

"Savannah. You're at *my* hotel—the Wentworth Star. Apparently, you arrived last night stinking drunk while ranting and raving."

"Raving about what?"

"That you needed to see me, of course. I wasn't even here, Liam. I was in Boston meeting with the wedding florists. I don't know what possessed you to fly down when I was *minutes* away from you back there."

"I needed to talk to you. But I don't know why I came here. I don't understand what happened."

Caroline crossed her arms, standing over him like an avenging angel. "Oh, I know what happened. You've gone off the rails again. And I don't even need an explanation why. I knew this was going to happen the moment you saw him again."

"*Him?*"

"Matthias Raske," she snapped. "You went to him for help, throwing the door wide open for him to waltz back into our lives, to ruin everything—*again.*"

Liam struggled to think with the cotton wool that had seemingly replaced his brain. "No. It's not about Matthias. I mean, it is, but only because she left with him."

Caroline blinked, giving herself a little shake. "So this is about *Peyton?*"

Liam didn't say anything, letting the silence stretch as the copious amounts of alcohol in his gut roiled. He was in danger of being sick, but he had to keep it together. He owed Caroline that much.

She snorted softly, closing her eyes. "Good God, I've been worried about the wrong one. All this time, I thought if you saw Raske again, you'd relapse and call off the wedding. When, apparently, the one I should have been worried about was perfect Peyton. I can't believe what a fool I was. I should have seen it before."

"We're both fools."

How could he have thought marriage to Caroline would solve any of his problems? It had only created new, even worse ones. And he'd hurt one of his best friends in the process.

"I'm so sorry about this, Caroline. You have no idea how much. But we have to call the wedding off. I can't go through with it."

She sniffed. "Well, obviously," she said tightly. Jerking away, she whirled, her icy shield up so high it chilled the air around them. But the evidence of the pain he'd inflicted was all over her face.

"If it makes you feel any better, this ends badly for me. I…I lost her to him. Matthias took Peyton away on the *Ormen Lange*. They're gone, sailing off into the sunset together."

Caroline's laugh was brittle. "Yes, well, I suppose that's the one bright spot in this entire fiasco. Karma works."

She took a deep breath, picking her purse up from the coffee table in front of him. "I'll have to sue you, of course. For breach of contract."

He frowned. "For calling off the engagement?"

Liam knew some jilted fiancées went that route, but he'd never imagined Caroline would. She was too high class. "I didn't think you'd want to call attention to the end of our relationship that way."

She sighed, rolling her eyes. "No, you *ass*. I'm going to sue you for calling off the merger. Not that I have a choice at this point."

"Oh, Caroline." He hadn't even thought about that.

Gene, Caroline's father, was getting on in years. He was eager to hand over the reins of his business. But the old fart was too much of a sexist to leave everything to Caroline outright.

Caroline had been pushing their union for the sole reason of her father finally being able to retire and give his overworked heart a rest. Plus, the ailing Wentworth chain needed a bailout. Folding them into the Caislean group would have solved a lot of her problems, but now that wasn't going to happen.

He rubbed his face roughly with both hands. "Let me talk to Gene. The merger can still go on. I know you need this."

Disbelief and resentment flashed across her face. "You know that can't happen now. Daddy will never agree to it on those terms. And neither will I."

"But—"

She held up a hand. "Stop. Just stop. I've wasted enough time here. I need to get back to Boston. I have a wedding to disassemble."

I am a shitheel. "Please let me handle it." His people could take care of those details. They did it all the time at the hotel.

"I think you've done enough."

Caroline turned on her heel, heading for the door. Once there, she paused, determined to have the last word. "I would wish you the best and hope you will find what you're looking for, but knowing you, you'll ruin that, too."

CHAPTER 23

The next time, Liam opened his eyes he was staring at the Chrysler building. He groaned, putting his hands on either side of his head. At least the view was familiar this time. He was in his own hotel, the penthouse suite of the Caislean New York.

There was a knock at the bedroom door. "Anyone alive in there?"

Calen poked his head inside. He walked in, wrinkling his nose at the smell. Empty liquor bottles dotted the tables of the room. "Did you drink the entire liquor cabinet?"

"It feels like I did."

Calen shook his head. "I was afraid of this. I knew you shouldn't have called Raske for help."

"Not you, too." He groaned.

"What?" Calen frowned. "It's only natural you'd feel this way after seeing him again—even if it was only for a little while."

Calen was the only person who knew what had happened between Liam and Matthias. He'd been encouraging Liam to come out of the closet ever since.

Liam hadn't had the words to explain it wasn't going to happen because he wasn't *in* the closet. He liked women—and one man. That was it.

But his best friend was tenacious. He'd sworn his support up and down, lecturing Liam about living 'his truth,' telling him he'd be a happier and better-adjusted person if he would just admit he was gay.

Calen's earnestness about his sexuality had been caring and infuriating in equal measure. There had been times when Liam had wanted to strangle him, but Liam didn't have that many friends, so he let him live to bitch another day.

As far as he knew, Calen had kept his secret. But now he was going to have to tell him a much bigger one. "Peyton left with Matthias. She's back on the *Ormen Lange* headed to God knows where."

Calen froze in the act of sitting next to Liam on the bed. "Are you serious?"

"Yup," Liam confirmed with a dark scowl. "They're probably fucking their way through the south seas as we speak."

Calen sank into the chair. It took him a long time to respond. "Huh. I wondered why Maia hadn't heard from her. The wife invited her to dinner night before last, and nada. I figured you were keeping her busy."

Liam snorted. "I should have been. It was stupid to give her time alone. I turned my back for a few hours, and she was gone."

"Ah." Grimacing, Calen scratched his head. "Well, I guess Peyton and Raske got close on the trip back from the auction. Not surprising, I guess. You mentioned Raske swung both ways. He's got good taste."

"Fuck you."

Calen shrugged. "You're not my type."

Liam shook his head, but he immediately regretted it. "I can't believe you're being so cavalier about this. He took *her*. He took Peyton."

Calen appeared at a loss. "Well, it sounds as if she went willingly. And it was only a matter of time. I know you care about her in your own way, but this is for the best. Once you and Caroline marry, forget it—"

He stopped short.

Liam shrugged, not want to live in denial anymore. "Because Peyton's in love with me, or at least she used to be."

"Err..." Calen opted to not to reply. It was something they never discussed. Calen always kept his mouth shut because he thought of Liam as gay and uninterested. That, and he wanted to protect Peyton, not wanting to expose her tender feelings for Liam's callous dismissal.

"And I love her, too," he said.

"I know, man," Calen dared to reach over and pat him on the arm. "In your own way."

Fuck, this bullshit between them was now the size of a mountain.

"No, I mean I *love* her," Liam emphasized. "As in 'I want to fuck her until she's having my baby' love her."

Silence.

His friend looked confused. "And you're sure it's not some kind of transference thing?"

Liam wanted to throw up his hands or hit him with something. "Calen, shut up."

The other man cocked his head. "Do you mean fucking in the traditional sense?"

"Seriously, shut up!"

Naturally, that didn't faze Calen at all. He just blinked a few times. "How long have you felt this way?"

"I don't know. Forever? I tried not to think about it."

"If that's true, then why didn't you do anything about it? I mean, she was right there at your side all this time. Poor Peyton. It was killing her, too."

Liam scrubbed his eyes in a half-hearted attempt to gouge them from his skull. "I—I couldn't. At first, it was because she was too young. Then, when she wasn't, it still seemed wrong. That was around the time I met Matthias. When I was with him, I felt great, but after it ended...I don't know. I didn't feel clean enough to touch her. How could I? She deserves someone normal. Someone decent."

"There's nothing indecent about you," Calen said loyally. "But normal, yeah. We all told her that. She still wanted you anyway."

Or she used to. Liam hadn't taken his shot. For years, he'd ignored and suppressed his feelings until he'd genuinely convinced himself they weren't there.

It took her walking away to crack the veneer around his reality. When she'd disappeared, it felt as if his entire world had shattered.

"I don't think your feelings for her change what was happening with you and Raske, though," Calen observed, still mulling. "Don't forget I saw you two together back then. It was one of the few times you looked happy."

Liam shrugged. He didn't analyze his time with Matthias. It had just been one of those things.

Calen reached for the open bottle, tipping it up to drink from it directly. Finding it empty, he put it down with a thump. "So, let me get this straight. The man you might have been in love with two years ago with has run off with the woman you've secretly been in love with for years but were in complete denial about?"

"Basically." Calen was a succinct bastard sometimes.

"Then can I ask something else?"

"What?"

"What the fuck are you waiting for? Call off the wedding and commandeer a boat or something. Go after them."

"And do what? Ruin Peyton's chance at happiness again?"

Even if he somehow managed to get his head screwed on right, it was too late. Matthias and Peyton were together now. He couldn't mess that up for her, no matter what he wanted. He'd hurt her enough.

CHAPTER 24

*L*iam resisted the urge to batter the phone in its cradle. Instead, he set it down gently, so maintenance wouldn't have to replace it again.

More than a week had passed since he'd talked to Calen in New York. He was back in Boston, barreling through the dissolution of his intended merger with the Wentworth chain. Predictably, it was going badly.

Caroline was really sticking it to him in the backend. But he couldn't blame her. Even Trick didn't blame Caroline when he and Maggie discovered Liam had called off the wedding. But the actual details were dreary and painful. Which was why he had to handle them himself. It was his mess, and he wasn't going to subject his siblings to the aftermath, even if they pleaded with him to be allowed to share the burden.

He half-suspected Trick wanted to celebrate the end of his engagement with a parade, but his younger brother kept his mouth shut. Maggie had been even more circumspect, but he suspected her mind was on Peyton and how she was faring in Raske's company.

If Peyton had gotten in touch with either of them, they didn't share that with him.

The phone rang before he'd finished approving the final changes to the settlement Caroline was demanding for the straggling Wentworth hotels. Ignoring it, he doubled down, determined to finish before someone charged in demanding he put out some other fire.

Liam wasn't giving Caroline everything she wanted. He couldn't— not without introducing some strict austerity measures for his own hotels. But he did want to give the Wentworth chain, a sincerely valuable property, its best chance.

It was a simple matter on paper. In reality, it was a bear. But he had reached the end of the tunnel, enough to feel some light on his face. He just needed to dot his *I's* and cross his *T's*.

Eventually, the continued ringing got the best of him. "This better be good," he barked.

"It's about fucking time you picked up," Calen snapped. "You have to get over here."

"Your penthouse? Does Maia need something?"

"No, at *Helios*, you jackass. I'm at work. It's ten at night."

Helios was the newest club Calen had opened in their hometown. It wasn't a club in the traditional sense. It was more of a cross between an exclusive speakeasy and a cigar bar, but it served exquisite rare wines and small plates. These were prepared by a rotation of excellent no-name chef's Calen managed to keep digging up, all thirsty for their shot at culinary stardom.

Liam raised his head, noting the dark sky and illuminated windows of the buildings around them with surprise. "Oh. I didn't realize it was that late."

"Whatever," Calen snapped. "Get in your fucking car now. He's here."

"Who?"

"Raske."

Liam bolted to his feet. "Is Peyton with him?"

"Nah, he's alone. He's holed up in the VIP room talking to some guy. Looks like a business meeting of sorts. I don't know. Just get over here."

Liam stopped asking questions. He grabbed his coat, texting Trick to go over the contract on his desk one more time before pushing it through legal for him.

He needed to find out why Peyton wasn't with Matthias. What the hell had that man done to her?

IT WAS ALMOST comical how quickly Liam showed up after Matthias arrived at Helios. Matthias had barely finished his convo with Bryce Brogan, the first candidate he wanted Peyton to meet, when Liam burst through the doors of the private VIP salon.

"Where is she?" he yelled from across the room.

Matthias sighed, dismissing Bryce with a *you-better-leave-fast* gesture. Liam charged forward, scowling ferociously as the younger man passed him on the way out.

"I assume you mean Peyton," he offered as Liam threw himself into the winged-back chair facing his.

"Who the fuck else would I be talking about?"

Matthias raised a brow and his glass at the same time. "Language," he chided before taking a sip.

He flicked an imaginary piece of lint off his trouser leg. "And she's not here. She's still on the *Ormen Lange*."

"You left her alone?"

Matthias' mouth quirked, but he was starting to feel sorry for his former lover.

Liam had deeply set dark circles under his eyes. The brackets around his mouth were a little more harshly carved than the last time Matthias had seen him just a few weeks ago. Not that it detracted from his appeal. Even tired and unkempt, Liam was still one of the most roughly elegant men Matthias had ever met. He often wondered what would have happened if they hadn't argued so viciously about the railroad.

"Are you upset because I'm with her or because I'm not?" he asked, affecting a casualness he didn't feel. Seeing Liam again, alone this time, was more impactful than Matthias cared to admit.

"Don't be a fucking douchebag on top of being a twatwaffle."

"A *what?*" He laughed. That was a new one for him.

"It's one of Peyton's favorite swearwords," Liam informed him. "Clearly, you haven't pissed her off enough yet for her to call you that. Perhaps when you get back. I can't imagine she's pleased to be ditched within days of leaving with you."

"On the contrary. When I told her our mutual business was bringing me back to Boston, she told me to come alone. She's still getting comfortable in her new surroundings and I didn't want to derail her with a premature homecoming."

Liam's expression darkened. "What 'business' could you two possibly have together? And please tell me whatever it is, it doesn't involve *Bryce Brogan.*"

He said the name with an audible sneer.

"As a matter a fact, it does," Matthias replied with an expansive gesture. He shouldn't be enjoying this, but he couldn't help himself. "Or it might. I guess it depends on how well he and Peyton get on."

Liam's eyes narrowed to slits. "Bryce is a brainless trust funder who has never done an honest day's work in his life. He considers shopping for a sugar daddy his profession. That and getting laid. All he wants is to get into your pants."

Matthias acknowledged that with a nod. "Well, in this case, that last may be a bonus. But I don't know how well he'll mesh with Peyton. She gets final say, of course."

Dawning horror began to slide over Liam's face. "You better not be implying what I think you are."

"I didn't mean to imply anything—I'm saying it outright. Peyton and I are shopping around for a third. I think Bryce will do nicely."

The explosion wasn't long in coming. Liam almost lunged for Matthias, but he checked himself at the last moment when Matthias' bodyguards, a precaution for the evening, ominously stepped forward.

Settling back into his seat, Liam opened and closed his mouth a few times. "You're not fucking serious," he spat.

"I assure you I am."

"Peyton would never agree to something like that."

He raised a brow. "Are you sure?"

"Yes!"

"Well, that's presumptuous." He sniffed. "As luck would have it, I don't have to guess what Peyton wants, because I have the luxury of being able to *ask* her. So that's what I did. And after a lifetime of… shall we call it misguided chastity…she's eager to explore and try new things."

"But a *threesome*? You and I both know she's not experienced enough for any crap like that."

"If she's not up for it, she'll say so. Peyton isn't afraid to speak her mind. In fact, she's not afraid of a single damn thing. She's brilliant, beautiful, and daring. I think we're going to do very well together."

Matthias stood. "I've done what I came here to do— I've invited Bryce out to Miami. The *Ormen Lange* will be docked there this weekend. If Bryce and Peyton hit it off, he'll stay on for a while. If not, then we'll take a look at someone else. We have time to figure it out."

Matthias started for the door, but he hadn't gotten far when Liam grabbed his arm, forcing him to stop. "Did you really come here to rub this invite in my face or are you trying to tell me something?"

Pleading ignorance seemed the safer bet. "Sorry? I don't follow."

"Did you come here to Boston—to my best friend's club—for Bryce fucking Brogan or were you here to ask me?" Liam rasped.

Matthias could see what the question cost the other man. But he had to tell him the truth…as he saw it. "I came here for Bryce."

"But—"

"I have to be honest, Liam. Peyton only put one restriction on my search for a third."

He watched as Liam visibly braced himself. "What was it?"

"The man can be anyone…except you."

LIAM SAT in the now-empty VIP salon. He stared at his shoes until Calen waved a bottle of something in his face. He took the bottle, ignoring the glass his friend offered with it.

"That was painful to watch."

"Did you hear everything?" He gestured vaguely at the walls, unsure where the discreet security camera was hidden.

"That would be illegal. I don't have the sound on. Of course, it pays to learn how to lip read."

"Is that something your dad taught you?" Liam sneered slightly.

In their youth, Calen's father had been a notorious gangster. But Colman had kept a low profile the last few years. The former menace to society was enjoying semi-retirement, playing with his grandchild and looking forward to the next one.

Calen didn't take the bait. "Some of his lessons were worth learning. So are you going to Miami?"

Liam's mouth twisted. "I can't do that—I can't *share* her."

"Then you're going to let Matthias and some other random guy share her?"

"*Hell no.*"

"So you *are* going to Miami?"

Liam didn't answer.

Calen leaned forward, face serious. "I'm sorry about this."

"Wha—"

His query was cut short by his best friend leaning over to slap him in the face—*hard*.

"*Ow.* Fuck, Calen!"

His friend tsked. "Stop acting like a little bitch."

Liam rubbed his face. "But I can't be in a threesome with those two. How would that even work?"

Calen shrugged. "Hell if I know. But you're going to regret it if you don't at least try."

Liam stared at his best friend, prepared to argue. However, nothing came out.

Why was this so fucking complicated? *Or maybe it's not and you're just making a convoluted mess of everything.*

He staggered to his feet. Calen was right. He would never be able to live with himself if he didn't go. "I need to call my pilot. I'm going to Miami."

Calen threw up his hands as if to say *Hallelujah*. "It's about fucking time."

Liam ran to the entrance, but then stopped to ask, "How am I going to explain this to Maggie and Trick?"

His friend waved that away. "Burn that bridge when you come to it. Now get the hell out of here."

CHAPTER 25

*L*iam waited until Bryce Brogan was alone on the pier before grabbing the smaller man by the collar.

"If you don't leave now, I'm tossing you into the ocean," he snarled.

"What the hell?" Bryce reached up, trying to break his hold. He couldn't.

"I'm serious. You're not getting on that boat, so don't even fucking try." Liam shook him for good measure.

"I was invited."

"No, you weren't," he countered. "Not really. You're just here because Matthias likes pushing my buttons."

And it had fucking worked. He was here, and now he'd be damned if this shithead set one foot on the *Ormen Lange*.

"I don't believe that." Bryce frowned, but he clearly wasn't sure anymore.

"All right, you asked for it." Liam dead-lifted the guy, hauling him inches off the deck and over the water.

"What the hell are you doing?" Bryce yelled.

It should have been obvious, but there was a chance Bryce's parents were cousins. "I'm fulfilling a threat," Liam said helpfully.

"Put me down!"

"Okay." He obliged, lowering his arm.

"Not in the water, you crazy shit," Bryce shouted after the tips of his thousand-dollar Italian wingbacks broke the surface of the water.

"Are you going to leave? Because my arm is getting tired," Liam said.

"Fine. But I'm only going as far as my car. I'm calling Matthias Raske, and he's gonna…"

"He's going to what?" Liam asked, setting the other man on solid wood.

Bryce shook out his jacket by the lapels "He'll do *something*."

Huffing, the man stalked in the direction of the parking lot. He whirled around when he was a safe distance away. "You always were an asshole, Tyler!"

Liam only smirked before facing the covered slipway leading up to the *Ormen Lange's* deck.

Don't run inside. In his experience, people didn't respond well to a man of his size barreling in their direction.

Liam was halfway up the ramp when Matthias appeared on the other end. "It took you long enough."

"SHE'S NOT GOING to be happy to see you," Matthias warned.

That was the understatement of the year. Liam peeked out of the blinds out to the deck where Peyton was reportedly getting a massage. "Is she almost done?"

"I have no idea." Matthias glanced at his watch. "Depends on how long she can take Ha-eun's tender treatment."

Liam spun around, aghast. "You're not letting that pervert touch her, are you?"

"Peyton seems to find it…stimulating. If she didn't, I doubt she'd be going back for seconds."

Unacceptable. "*No way.* If this is going to work, you and I are the only ones who can touch her."

"Isn't that up to Peyton?"

Liam glared at Matthias. "Yes," he spit out from behind gritted teeth.

"She's going to put up a fight, you know. She's incredibly angry with you."

"Has she been talking about me?" If Liam was on her mind, it couldn't be all bad.

"Actually, she hasn't mentioned you at all."

Liam's shoulders dropped. After a moment, Matthias took pity on him. "I'll reassign Ha-eun. She won't enjoy the transfer to the *Sha* since my aunt never invites anyone less than sixty to her outings, but I'll soften it with a pay bump. Peyton can get her massages from Newberg."

"Newberg's the gay one, right?" It was hard keeping track of Matthias' staff, but he'd made the effort to get to know them when he'd spent a lot of time on the boat a few years back.

"I believe so, but you don't have to worry about him hitting on you. You're not his type."

Liam snorted, standing on his tiptoes in search of Peyton, but the deck at the prow was too spacious. From here, all that was visible was an expanse of well-scrubbed hardwood. "Well, you better not be his type either. You know I won't fucking share you with anyone but her, either."

Matthias watched him with an inscrutable expression. Liam reached out, taking the man's arm. "Peyton's not the only reason I'm here. If she were with anyone else contemplating a threesome, I wouldn't have come."

Matthias nodded once. "Thank you for that. I admit this isn't how I saw things going if we ever reconciled—if that's what we're doing."

"If it's only the two of you, I want to be here," Liam confessed. "Here and nowhere else."

"Good." Matthias seemed pleased, but it had always been hard to read him when his guard was up. "However, are you sure you're going to be able to handle *me* touching *her* in front of you?"

How the hell was Liam supposed to know until it happened?

"I guess we'll find out."

They eyed each other. Memories Liam had buried broke loose. He blinked, wondering what the hell he should do now.

The fucking question of my life.

"You're certain you don't want to wait?" Matthias asked after a long moment. "Perhaps you would care to take a nap first?"

Liam blinked a few times. "A nap?"

Matthias put his hand on his shoulder, giving it a squeeze. "Don't get me wrong—you always look good to me—but it's obvious you haven't slept in days. Kudos for showering at least. But do you want to face Peyton at anything less than your best? Plus, it might be a good idea for me to soften her up before we let her know you're here. We can tell her after a fabulous dinner...some wine. Lots and lots of wine."

"Don't you dare get her drunk," Liam growled, his overprotective instincts kicking in automatically. Liam could never let anyone take advantage of Peyton. Not even himself. Especially under these circumstances.

"I wouldn't dream of it. Peyton should be sober when you take her virginity."

Liam had made the mistake of taking a step away from the doors. He tripped, but he caught himself before he fell flat on his face.

He spun around so fast he made his own head swim, shock etching his features.

Matthias smirked at his reaction. "I never told you what I paid to get her back."

"How much?" Liam's brow creased.

"The exact sum is unimportant. Just know I paid a premium for a verified virgin."

Liam's heart stuttered. Flipped. Squeezed painfully. He'd have never suspected... "I didn't chase away *all* her boyfriends."

Matthias raised a brow.

"All right, I did," he conceded. "But only the ones I knew about. Surely there were more. She and Maggie excelled at sneaking out at night when they were in high school. They nearly drove me into an early grave."

"I guess there weren't any men of consequence," Matthias hazarded. "Regardless, I didn't share that very confidential piece of information to gossip. But you need to know what you're getting into."

"Why didn't the two of you, err, consummate your relationship?"

Matthias snorted softly. "Because it wasn't worth my life to initiate her on my own. Peyton's going to be furious, of course, but I knew I couldn't go forward without giving her what—*who*—she truly wants."

"And what if things don't work with the three of us?"

"Then they don't." Matthias sighed. "But I owe it to Peyton and myself to find that out. I owe it to you, too. But, seriously, you need to go for now. Sleep. Meet us after dinner."

Liam wanted to argue, but now that he was here, he was feeling those long, sleepless nights. "Are you pulling up anchor?"

Matthias hesitated. "Why don't we see if Peyton throws you over-board first? It'll be a much shorter swim if we're still in port."

Liam snorted. Matthias was right. After everything that had happened, everything he'd done, Peyton was far more likely to punch him in the face than kiss him.

Liam raised his head, gesturing to the deck. "Um, you know what? I have an idea about that..."

He told Matthias his plan.

The other man was incredulous. "That's the route you want to go with? It'll only buy you a minute."

"All I need is a minute."

He hoped.

153

CHAPTER 26

*P*eyton giggled, resisting the urge to reach up to rip off the blindfold Matthias had insisted on.

"This better be a good surprise." Not that anything could ruin this night. It had been a fabulous evening. Dinner had been light and delicious, served under the stars. Each small course had its own wine pairing, but Matthias had insisted she only sample each to get a quick taste. He didn't want her drunk. Which meant tonight was special.

She couldn't wait. Her time on the *Ormen Lange* had been fun, and Matthias had been great company, but she was getting frustrated. She *needed* more.

"Well..." Matthias hesitated as he guided her down the few steps that separated his bedroom from the deck. "I think it's a good surprise, but taste is subjective."

Somewhere, someone laughed. Peyton reared back, but Matthias' hand on her arm kept her from falling on her butt.

"Who is that?" It wasn't one of the staff. Matthias wouldn't have used a blindfold.

Instinctively, she reached up to the mask, but Matthias moved behind her, putting his hands on her upper arms, effectively restraining her.

"I told you I was going to invite a friend to meet you. This is him."

Peyton scowled under the mask. Matthias had told her all about Bryce Brogan. His picture had been intriguing; however, this was a strange way to meet him. "I'm not allowed to see him?"

"This was a special request of his. It will only take a minute."

"O-kay, fine. Whatever." It better only be a minute.

Stiff as a board, she stood there in her light satin gown. The dress was another recent gift. Peyton had stopped arguing whenever Matthias expanded her wardrobe because he enjoyed the dresses on her more than she did. This one was a gun-metal grey sleeveless number that felt like heaven against her skin. However, it was also very light, and she felt exposed to this stranger's gaze.

Peyton's skin was already tingling when a second pair of hands skittered across her face, touching her cheek. She almost jumped out of her skin. For some reason, the small contact filled her with apprehension. It was electric...

"What the hell—" she began, but a firm pair of lips cut off the rest.

Her head began to spin, but her heart was racing out of control because it knew what her senses were screaming at her. It was his scent. Only one man smelled like this, of spice and leather with a hint of ginger.

Peyton ripped off the mask with one hand, shoving at Liam's chest with the other. *"Absolutely not."* She spun on her heel to glare at Matthias. "How could you?"

Matthias winced. "Peyton, just listen to what he has to say."

"I don't care what he has to say. We agreed on anyone but him."

"But, Peyton—"

"No!" Her voice bordered on shrill. She threw her arms up, knocking Matthias' hands away. "What are you even doing here, Liam? Shouldn't you be planning your honeymoon?"

"I called off the wedding."

Peyton put her arms down. "What?"

Liam didn't answer. He looked amazing and exhausted. The circles under his eyes were darker than she'd ever seen them. But his shoulders were just as broad as ever and his hair was still too long, enough for the ends to curl.

"I called off the wedding. Or to be honest, Caroline beat me to it. But it's over. I'm not getting married."

Her body flashed hot and cold. "That…that doesn't matter. You need to leave."

Whether he was still attached didn't make a fucking difference. He didn't belong here. His very presence was a slap in the face.

"I'm not going anywhere." Liam's voice sounded like he'd been gargling with gravel.

"You still haven't explained what the hell you're doing here," she snapped.

"I'm here for you," he rumbled, stepping closer. Peyton backed up a step only to hit the wall that was Matthias' chest.

Figuratively stuck between a rock and hard place, Peyton froze as Liam's head bent and he took her mouth.

Fire raced up her spine, melting her bones into liquid wax. It went on and on, blistering her soul, then his hand tugged her chin down, his tongue demanding entrance.

Peyton jerked away, slapping him as hard as she could before she lost all her pride. The sound was very loud in the quiet. Matthias hissed in sympathy, but she'd deal with him later.

"I waited years for you. *It's too late.*" Peyton's breath hitched, but she would rot in hell before she cried in front of him.

Damn it, she hadn't meant to tell him that. Yes, it was an open secret, but he didn't need to hear it from her.

"I know." Liam grimaced. "And I lied to myself for years, pretending it wasn't true. I wasn't good enough for you. I'm still not."

"On that we can agree," Matthias chimed in, obviously trying to lighten the mood. Both she and Liam turned to frown at him. "Not the time for jokes, I see. But we're going to look back on this later. While we may not laugh aloud—"

She held up a hand. "There will be no trips down memory lane. Liam is leaving now."

Peyton whirled on the man in question, who was still rubbing his face. "Peyton, I'm sorry."

"I don't care. I'm done with you."

For the first time, the brash and confident Liam she knew resurfaced. He cocked his head, his eyes unreadable. "No, you're not. We're just getting started."

"Unbelievable—"

"I will not apologize for coming here, but I will apologize for cutting your G-string bikini into pieces and throwing out your Gucci perfume."

Peyton drew up straight in surprise, and she gaped at him like the lunatic he was. "*What?*"

Liam gave her a tight smile. "When you were nineteen. We had just opened the Caislean in Boston. It was sweltering and you and Maggie were going to join the guests at the pool, so I made up an errand to delay the two of you. Then I went after your suit with scissors."

"Why?" Matthias asked.

"She was going to go out there in a white G-string bikini. I *had* to. She would have caused a riot."

Matthias laughed, but he subsided after she shot him a dirty look. "And my perfume?"

The first bottle had been a gift from Maggie. Peyton had loved the scent and wore it often, but then the small vial had disappeared.

"I drove you home one night, then asked to go to the bathroom. I nicked the bottle when you were grabbing me a soda for the road."

"But why?"

"Because it made you smell fucking amazing. And you were too fucking irresistible as it was. Maggie was going to give you another one for your birthday to replace it. I had to steal that one, too."

He reached up to touch her, his hand coming to rest on her shoulder. His fingers traced her collarbone, leaving a trail of tingling skin in his wake.

"Later, I told Maggie that particular scent gave me a headache. She bought you a purse instead."

This time when he crowded her, Peyton didn't move by choice. He stared deeply into her eyes. "I haven't slept in days," he admitted,

"I told you to nap," Matthias muttered.

Liam raised his head. "Well, I couldn't."

He returned to Peyton, who was watching him with her heart somewhere around her knees. "And I'm not going to be able to sleep until I'm balls-deep inside you."

"*Holy shit.*" Peyton's voice was little more than a squeak, but she didn't get anything else out before Liam kissed her again.

If Matthias hadn't moved to hold her waist, she would have fallen down.

Peyton could count the number of times Liam had kissed her on one hand. Two were forehead kisses on her birthday and the rest were cheek, except for that one time he'd been tipsy and had missed, pressing his lips against the corner of her mouth instead. She'd cherished that accidental caress for longer than she'd cared to admit. For years, she'd wondered what it would be like to be *really* kissed by Liam Tyler. But her fevered imaginings couldn't compare with the reality.

Heat like she'd never experienced coursed through her body. If she didn't stop this, she was going to pass out. Peyton put her hands up, breaking the kiss so she could get air into her burning lungs.

Liam's face could have been carved from stone. Then he shifted, nodding over her head.

Starting, she glanced at Matthias, feeling guilty for forgetting he was there.

Matthias met Liam's nod with one of his own, then reached to pull the straps of her satin gown down.

The air hit her bare breasts, making her nipples peak.

Liam's eyes widened at the sight. She wanted to explain that this kind of dress couldn't be worn with a bra, but she couldn't find her tongue long enough to speak. Peyton wasn't even sure if she were breathing.

Matthias pushed the dress all the way down. The silky satin pooled at her feet, leaving her standing in nothing but her heels and lace panties. Peyton grabbed his hand—not to stop him, but out of the sudden and irrational fear that Liam might make him leave.

But Liam had other plans. "Get her on the bed," he ordered.

Matthias wrapped his arms around her. The room spun. She landed on her back in the middle of the bed, losing a heel in the process. She kicked off the other one, still trying to catch her breath. Behind her, clothing rustled. She knew Matthias was undressing, but Liam was, too, and she couldn't take her eyes off him.

Always keep your eye on the biggest predator in the room.

She'd seen Liam in swim shorts. Even in his boxers a few times during the old B&B days, but that had been years ago.

Matthias pulled her into his arms, resting her back against his front. His chest was bare, but he might have still been wearing boxers. She twisted at the waist, intent on checking, but he wouldn't let her. His hands held her down, effectively trapping her against him and the mattress.

Peyton thought she was too far gone to panic, but her throat damn near closed up when Liam continued stripping. He stood a few steps from the bed, yanking at the bottom of his shirt. His eyes never left hers as he took off his pants, revealing a pair of dark red boxer briefs.

It was what filled his briefs that made her glad she was being held down—else she might have humiliated herself by running out of the room. Matthias must have felt her tension because he leaned down to whisper in her ear. "It's going to be all right, *prinsessa mi*. Liam's not going to hurt you."

Liam tugged at the shorts, pulling them off and throwing them aside. Matthias coughed. "Well, he'll try not to hurt you," he amended a little too honestly, bending over to press a kiss to her lips.

The caress distracted her, but her attention swiveled back to Liam when his weight depressed the bed. "Be careful," Matthias told him.

Peyton forced her breathing to slow. Liam had been starring in her bedroom fantasies for years. And he was perfect. His chest was a work of art. The number of ridges on his abs seemed impossible. Her fingers itched to touch him, but him holding her down was too exciting to protest.

Matthias had only spent a few weeks flitting through her dreams, but his gold-dusted masculine beauty rivaled Liam's dark and rough elegance. Peyton knew there wasn't a single woman in the world who wouldn't give anything to be in her place at that moment, but her heart was racing too fast for her to be able to appreciate it.

"I don't know if I can handle this." Or at least, that was what she tried to say. Her breath was so short she strangled the words.

"Peyton, look at me."

Almost panting, she obeyed. The look on Liam's face, the hunger and fire, was almost frightening. "I love you," he whispered.

She stared at him, shaking her head slowly.

Liam crawled over her, covering her body with his. His hot skin almost sizzled when it touched her much cooler one. "You heard me. I love you."

Tears stung at her eyes, and Peyton shuddered. She wanted to deny it, but the truth was there for her to see. He wasn't hiding it from her anymore.

Matthias squeezed her arms, and she moved to hold his hands instead. In front of her, Liam reached out to pull down her panties, exposing her to his hot gaze.

Peyton cringed, instinctively moving to hide her secrets, but Matthias forestalled her. His ankles hooked around hers, spreading her legs wide. Liam smiled—a hungry, almost feral, expression.

"You're so beautiful," he breathed, reaching out to part her pussy lips with his fingers.

She strained forward, arching up as he stroked and explored. Peyton's nipples stiffened in response, inviting him to touch. He cupped one breast, leaving the other for Matthias.

Both of their hands on her was sensory overload, but then Liam dipped his head, determined to taste her.

His dark hair brushed the sensitive skin of her inner thighs, and she gasped. "No, no. I don't want you to do that."

It had been different with Matthias. Not knowing him as well had helped her get over her embarrassment, but this was different. This was *Liam*.

His mouth didn't move. Instead, his tongue snaked out, licking her from top to bottom. Peyton whimpered and writhed, but she couldn't move under Matthias' restraining hold. "Just relax, baby. I promise you'll enjoy this."

By the time he finished the sentence, Peyton could barely process words. She was moaning aloud as Liam licked and probed, using his hands and mouth in a plundering invasion.

Peyton whimpered as her pussy began to heat and swell. She lost all sense of time and space as he lathed her clit, tasting her intimate flesh until she was seething and rocking, almost grinding into his face. Long minutes passed. Shameless in her abandon, she gloried in his every caress as the waves built, one upon the other until she was pulsing down there. Aching and swollen, she felt the warning stirrings of an approaching climax.

Liam must have sensed the change. He increased his tempo, but it wasn't until Matthias whispered in her ear, cupping and kneading her breast, that she arched, convulsing in a splintering orgasm as he pinched her nipples.

Liam didn't give her a chance to recover before he moved up her body. Bracing himself with his hands, he shifted between her legs, his thickly muscled thighs coming to rest between her still-spread legs. She felt him against her, thick and hard, and then he was pushing against her.

The burn wasn't unexpected, but the intensity took her breath away.

"Easy," Matthias said as she heaved, her chest pumping up and down a bit too fast.

"Are you okay, Peyton?" Liam's voice was strained. The muscles in his arms shook as he held himself, the effort to go slow and gentle taking a clear toll.

"I'm okay. *Don't stop.*" She had waited too long for this for Liam's innate chivalry and concern for her to stand in the way.

Peyton couldn't move much, but when Liam held himself still, she pushed her heels against the mattress, pumping up and down a little without meaning to. It stung, but the slippery hard heat was too compelling. She wanted more.

"Peyton," Liam groaned. He flexed his hips, and his hard length pushed in another inch.

It was his turn to gasp. "Shit, how are you this tight?"

"Virgin," Matthias reminded him.

Liam swore, muttering something unintelligible as he inched forward, sliding home with a loud groan. Peyton's mouth gaped as her body tried in vain to adjust. The sense of fullness was indescribable.

"Let go of my arms," Peyton begged. Matthias obliged with a murmur, but she didn't let go of him. Waiting until she had wrapped her arms around Liam's neck as he buried his face in her neck, she grabbed Matthias' hand. Both men's breath was hot against her skin.

She was too warm. Being covered by Liam was like being wrapped in a blanket stuffed with hot coals, but she reveled in his heat and the rough satin of his skin too much to let him go.

Liam took her mouth again, his tongue imitating the movement of his hips. Each time he surged, she had to bite back a gasp. It hurt, but the pain was nothing compared to the pleasure.

Her body slowly adapted to the foreign invasion. Peyton flexed her inner muscles experimentally, squeezing his hard cock inside her. Her rhythm wasn't quite right at first, but he guided with little murmurs and a hand on her hip. Soon she was moving in concert with him, taking his entire length and squeezing around him at the right time.

Recognizing the signs of another orgasm, Peyton clutched at Matthias' hands for support as Liam drove deeper, his hips slapping against hers as he took her hard and fast. All too soon, those little flutters became spasms as she let go, surrendering her will and body in an intense climax.

"*Oh hell.*" Peyton arched and whimpered. Her vision blurred, darkening as rapture burned through her.

Liam groaned aloud when she went hot and slick around him. He swore again, his hips pistoling hard before he shouted. Inside her, his cock swelled and contracted as he emptied his heat, pouring his seed into her. He collapsed on her. This time, the tears did come. They broke past the barrier of her lids, sliding down her cheek as she shuddered in the aftermath.

Liam took several minutes to recover, but then Matthias nudged him, and he raised his head.

The way Liam looked at her made her heart contract, but it was over too soon. He rolled off her, stretching out on the bed next to them with a rumbling sigh that almost rattled her bones.

His eyes were drifting shut when Matthias moved, adjusting her until she was lying high against his chest. And then she felt something else.

"Oh fuck," she squeaked as Matthias flexed his hips, driving his hard cock into her from behind. Peyton's arms flung out. She was splayed against him, impaled on his cock.

Laughing Matthias covered her mouth, kissing the soft skin next to her ear as she twisted to check Liam's reaction.

He was still lying motionless next to them, but he was tense as if he were holding his breath. Matthias didn't care, however. He continued to pump, holding her pressed against his chest, fucking her relentlessly as her other lover watched. If Peyton had a chance to think, she would have said her over-sensitized body was too drained for another climax. But Matthias' hands were on her breasts, kneading in time to his thrusts.

Liam reached out, taking her hand. "*Are you okay?*" he mouthed.

Peyton moaned in response, and the concern melted out of his expression. The corners of his mouth turned up as he scanned her body being played by Matthias' talented hands.

Liam wasn't a man known for his sharing, compromising attitude. He'd built a hotel empire through ruthless cutthroat deal making. He was notoriously overprotective of those close to him, and he was more than capable of raining down hell if someone unworthy so much as got near them.

She hadn't had time to think about how he would react to another man's hands on her, but her brain couldn't have pictured him watching her with those burning eyes while another man took her.

Thankfully, all she could read in his expression was lust. It had been briefly sated, but it was growing again. Stronger this time. However, he looked too exhausted to do anything about it.

Matthias pinched her nipple, making her whimper under his hand. He was still covering her mouth, but she knocked it away to suck in a deeper breath. His hand moved down, stroking her clit until she writhed, lost in the storm of a third climax as his member slid and surged, grinding against her as he came at the same time.

When she regained her senses, Peyton was still clutching Liam's hand. Matthias pressed a kiss to the back of her neck before moving away. He climbed off the bed, returning shortly with three warm wet washcloths. He tossed one to Liam, who quickly cleaned up. Too spent to move her arms Peyton allowed herself to be cleaned before he discarded the towels. Liam's eyes were closed, but when Matthias returned, Liam opened them and gave them both a sleepy smile. Tugging her closer, he pulled her into his arms. Matthias cuddled against her back.

Peyton was half-asleep when Liam moved his arm, throwing it across her waist. She cracked a lid to make sure he wasn't pushing Matthias away.

He hadn't.

Instead, he'd grasped the other man's forearm, including him in their embrace before he drifted off to sleep.

CHAPTER 27

*L*iam was a machine. After sleeping sixteen hours that first night, he woke up refreshed and raring to go. His energy replenished, he threw himself into relaxing, his only goal to eat and sleep and to make her scream her head off with multiple orgasms every few hours.

Matthias wasn't much better. He spent those first few days like a hedonist indulging his favorite concubines. If he wasn't holding her down as Liam fucked her, then he was behind her, pumping his thick cock into her body like a gladiator set loose in a harem.

At first, Peyton shamelessly indulged. After a lifetime of living on fantasy and self-pleasure alone, she was in the hands of not one, but two, sex gods. And despite what she'd assumed when she learned the two had been lovers, their focus had been fixed squarely on her and not each other.

Of course, no woman could sustain that level of hedonistic gluttony for long. Especially when she'd been a virgin mere days ago. Though it pained her to do it, she had to ask Liam and Matthias for a day or two of recovery. She was too sore for more sex.

Despite her fleeting concern, both took her news with good grace. In fact, Liam scolded her for not asking for a break sooner.

"I should have realized," he said one morning as he lay next to her in bed, engrossed in stroking the bare skin of her hip. "This was too much, too soon."

"She just needs a brief respite. But that doesn't mean we have to stop all the fun," Matthias said, tugging her away from him and moving down her body.

With creativity like that, her brief period of abstinence passed very pleasantly indeed.

Luxury was a byword on the *Ormen Lange*, but after Liam arrived, everything changed. Now the warm tropical air was brimming with fulfilled sensuality. Peyton was decadently pampered and pleasured to the point of indecency. Her every desire was satisfied, including a few she hadn't even known she had—including the emotional ones.

Once the dam was broken, Liam didn't hold back. He told her he loved her every day. Matthias didn't come forward with a similar declaration, but she didn't mind his hesitancy. It was too soon for him. However, he did seem happy. At the moment, that was all that mattered to her.

Whether they had sex or not, they all share Matthias' massive bed every night. Peyton loved waking up with both of them every morning. But one morning, Matthias wasn't there.

"Relax," Liam told her as he joined her for breakfast on the deck outside the main stateroom. "If he's not here, he's in his office. In fact, if you can't find him, that's the only place you ever need to look for him. The man never stops working."

That hadn't been her experience, but Peyton was familiar with the long hours tycoons worked. The fact Liam was saying that about anyone else was a touch too much irony. She tore apart a flaky and buttery croissant. "Pot, meet kettle," she said sarcastically before dipping a piece of the bread in her coffee.

Grinning, Liam threw himself on the cushioned bench next to her.

"At least I know how to relax. Work hard, play hard. You know it has always been my motto."

"Yes, I'm well aware," she said drily, remembering his many former playmates.

She threw her long legs over his lap in a territorial gesture. Now that she had him, she wasn't going to let Liam Tyler get away. He was hers. He'd always been hers. It had just taken the jerk a long time to realize it.

Happily, he wasn't acting like an oblivious idiot now. He stroked her legs in between bites of breakfast. Sighing, Peyton let her legs part in silent invitation.

"I think we've created a monster," Liam said, but his eyes flared. Coughing, he pressed her legs back together. "But you're still sore and I don't need the temptation, no matter how much I want you—and believe me, after that last dry spell, I'm ready to go."

Peyton was about to tell him she had rested long enough, but she was distracted by what he'd said. "What does that mean?"

"Hmm?" Liam hummed, his mouth full of bacon.

"You said it's been a long time."

He shrugged. "Before this weekend, it had been a long-ass time. In fact, the last partner was with this one," he said, gesturing to Matthias as he appeared on the deck.

"What was that?" the other man asked as he sat in a chair across from them.

"Peyton was asking about the last time I had sex," Liam said.

"And it was with me?" Matthias was incredulous.

Liam shrugged. To him, she knew, embarrassment was for peasants. "Yeah, so?"

"Well, that was like a year and a half ago. Or two even."

Liam dismissed his lengthy period of celibacy with a wave.

Peyton wasn't ready to let it go. "But you got back together with Caroline not that long after. You even got engaged."

She wasn't sure if she would get over that last part.

"I thought I explained all this. Caroline wasn't comfortable with a physical relationship after what happened with Matthias, and I respected that."

Her brow creased. "And you were going to get married anyway?"

Liam put down the fork, clearing his throat. "She and I were planning to do our own thing," he confessed. "Caroline was chiefly interested in the other aspects of marriage—mostly being a hotel-owning super couple. And we were friends…"

He reached out for Peyton's hand. "I feel bad for how things went down with her, but it was my fault for agreeing to marry her."

"So, I was the last sex you had?" Matthias gloated.

"Don't look so smug," Peyton said, raising her glass. "I'm the one who broke his fast."

Matthias laughed aloud, reaching for the coffee pot.

"Broke my everything else, too." Liam groaned. "I am officially ruined for all other women."

"Good," she said. "But speaking of your past…when am I going to see some hot man-on-man action?"

Liam frowned, nonplussed. "I don't know. When the spirit moves us?"

Matthias couldn't seem to tear his eyes away from her legs. "I'm not in a hurry. I think we're both consumed with other matters now. Namely you."

The sun was getting stronger. Peyton reached for the sunglasses she'd left on the table. "Well, I won't complain about that, but I would like to add that I want this to work. And if that means I should make myself scarce so you two can have some private time, just tell me."

"I don't see a need for that," Matthias said, turning to Liam. "Am I right?"

Liam nodded, then laughed. "Also, privacy might be counterproductive. If memory serves me right, this one is a bit of an exhibitionist."

"Only in places where no one can identify us," Matthias replied before turning to Peyton. "Besides, this is about all three of us. Without you, none of us would be here."

"I agree," Liam said. "But to be safe, I think we need to set some ground rules."

Matthias put down his coffee, his mouth tightening. "What did you have in mind? I thought we were all getting on just fine, going where the currents carry us."

"We are, or I am, at least," Liam said. "But it's inevitable that some things will change. We're going to need to make sure we carve out enough time for each other. You and I both have demanding jobs. While Peyton's not working now, I know her. She's going to want to or she'll feel unproductive, which will make her unhappy."

The man knew her well. "I am fine for now, but he's right. Coding is like breathing. I haven't gone this long without a computer—well, like ever." She moved, tucking her legs underneath her. "What I'd like to know is what to tell people. I can tell Maggie about the three of us, right?"

Liam grimaced. "Uh, yeah, of course. But you may want to consider leaving some stuff out."

"Like what?" she asked.

"Like me," Matthias interrupted with a smirk. "That is what you're suggesting, right?"

"He wouldn't do that." Peyton was incensed on his behalf. She turned to Liam for confirmation, but he winced and looked away.

"This won't work if we hide what we are," she said in a clipped voice.

Liam put his hands up. "I know. But I think you're overestimating how accepting and open our family and friends are going to be."

"Who are you worried about? Calen?" His macho best friend was the only one she could see having an issue. But they had been friends for years. Calen would come to terms with Liam's true sexuality.

"It's not him. In fact, Calen's been a butthead for the last couple of years, urging me to come out of the closet."

"Oh." Peyton blinked. "Then we have nothing to worry about. Unless you think it's going to affect your business dealings?"

"Of course not. Besides, I wouldn't work with someone who had an issue with who I slept with. My concern is you."

"Me?"

His glance was a touch condescending. "Do you really think my siblings are going to be okay with this? They're more protective of you than I am. Everyone is going to think I'm corrupting you or worse. They might think you're only doing a threesome because I pushed you into it. Mags will kill me."

Perhaps she was being a little naive, but Peyton was too protective of this budding relationship to compromise. "Maggie will be fine. She'll worry, of course. But she knows I can't be pushed into doing anything I don't want to do."

Liam reached for the as-yet-untouched champagne bottle chilling in a bucket of ice next to the table. He popped the cork, then splashed a liberal amount into his orange juice. "There's still Trick. And let's not forget about Ethan Thomas. Hell, that bastard will probably go after me with his gun."

"Who's Ethan Thomas?" Matthias asked, his head bobbing back and forth like a spectator at a tennis match.

"Ethan is my brother-in-law's partner at the bureau. He's in love with Peyton," Liam said flatly.

"No, he's not!"

Liam lifted a single eyebrow, a corner of his mouth turning up sardonically. "You're in denial."

Matthias snorted. "Do we have competition?"

"The contest is over. We're all set now. Ethan's out of the picture," Liam said with satisfaction. He turned to Peyton. "But you have to be ready for his reaction. You know Ethan's not going to take this well. He hates me, and he's going to *despise* Matthias. I mean, look at him." He gestured to encompass the Nordic man's blond perfection. "He looks like Hercules with a haircut."

Matthias straightened, preening silently.

Peyton narrowed her eyes at Liam. "You're being evasive. Ethan's not going to be a problem. You're worried about Trick, and I don't understand why."

Liam's face tightened.

"I know when you're hiding something, Tyler. Spill it," she ordered.

He set down his glass with a loud clink. "All right, fine. I am worried about Patrick."

"Why?"

He scowled. "Haven't you noticed how different he's been lately?"

"No," she said. "Other than being ridiculously happy now that he's married."

Liam dismissed that with a flick of his fingers. "He's always been happy-go-lucky, with the exception of that time he didn't know where Tahlia was, but now they're together, he's...different."

"You're not blaming her?" Peyton didn't understand. Tahlia was the sweetest, kindest woman she'd ever met, with the possible exception of Maggie. Peyton was lucky to call her a friend.

"No. It's just that since they got together, he's so...so..."

"He's what?"

"Religious. Like church on Sundays rain or shine—and not because Thalia is making him go either." Liam scratched his head. "It's all him. I think she'd rather sleep in on Sundays. He even goes on Wednesdays sometimes, too. It's weird. I wasn't even sure we had all been baptized until Trick checked on it so the archbishop would perform the service at his wedding."

Peyton frowned, checking Matthias' reaction, but the other man simply shook his head. "I don't know the man well enough to comment."

"Well, I do," she protested. "Patrick may have found God, but he's still Trick. He loves you, and he's just as loving and open-minded as he ever was. He would never attend a church that tried to change that about him."

Liam wasn't convinced. "That's easy to say, but I honestly don't know how he'll handle this sort of relationship."

He reached for the champagne bottle again. "But let's worry about that later. We should hammer out a few other details, like a traveling agreement. Sooner or later, I'm going to need to check on our hotels. Trick and Maggie are covering everything adequately now, but Thalia is six months pregnant. Trick is going to want to stay home with her the closer she gets to her due date. And he won't be able to travel at all once the baby is born."

"I'm happy to point the *Ormen Lange* in the direction of whatever continent you need to visit," Matthias offered.

"That'll help, but sailing around on this island isn't going to cut it. We're going to need to fly sometimes."

Matthias expression soured.

"You're not afraid to fly, are you?" Peyton asked.

"No, but I find planes…pedestrian."

"Yeah, yeah." Liam smirked. "The *Ormen Lange* is amazing, but it's too slow. I'd like to make a rule that we don't spend more than a few days apart unless we absolutely have to—a week at the most."

Peyton decided to pour herself a glass of champagne. "I like this rule."

"It's a fine rule," Matthias conceded, patting the fabric of his chair as if he were telling it goodbye. "Very well, I agree. But, sometimes, we may need to take a break from each other, too. I propose that Peyton keeps her stateroom next door, and you get one across the hall. By default, we'll stay in mine, since it's the biggest, but none of us should be afraid to speak up and tell the others we need some time alone when we need it."

"I don't like that rule," Liam growled.

"But it's smart," Peyton interjected. "Thank you for suggesting it," she told Matthias.

"A natural peacemaker," he observed.

"She learned running interference for her drunk of a father."

"*Liam*," Peyton warned. "Do not harsh my buzz by bringing up my dad."

Matthias sniffed. "Why don't we add that one to the rules?"

"Agreed," Liam muttered, watching her out of the corner of his eye. "And we need to discuss something else. Birth control. We haven't been using anything. And since we haven't, I'd like to skip the condom route. I never had anyone bare before, and I don't want to go back—not with you."

He took her hand. "I can assure you that I'm completely clean. Like I said before, it's been a while for me. I got a complete workup after Matthias."

"Thanks for that." Matthias laughed.

"I know where you've been," Liam sniped. "And I'm fine. You're obviously clean, too. Otherwise, you wouldn't run the risk of me killing you for touching Peyton, but pregnancy is still a concern."

Peyton's lips parted. "It's, uh, taken care of."

"It is?"

"I'm taking some shots."

"Oh." Liam settled against the bench.

"You almost look disappointed," Matthias said, voicing the obvious.

"I'm not," he said unconvincingly. "It's too soon for family planning."

"It sure is." Peyton giggled nervously.

"That's fine. For now." Liam leaned forward. The look that followed sent her temperature shooting up several degrees.

"But I want you to know this. Now that I'm in...I'm *all* in. Eventually, I *will* put a baby in you."

CHAPTER 28

*a*s much as Peyton cherished Liam's declaration and his determined stance on their future, in the coming days, she wished he'd kept his mouth shut.

For years, she'd dreamed about marrying Liam and having a family with him. At thirteen, she'd gone so far as to name their three imaginary children—Olivia, Ella, and little Liam Junior. However, ever since Liam mentioned babies, Matthias had subtly withdrawn.

He acted as if nothing were wrong, joining in enthusiastically when she requested they resume their sex life, but, in the morning, he was gone, spending most of the day in his office.

Liam didn't seem overly concerned. Apparently, Matthias spent a lot of time working during their earlier affair. He hadn't minded because it gave Liam the excuse to resume his own work. He set up camp in one of the *Ormen Lange's* many utilitarian conference rooms so he could work remotely.

Left to her own devices, Peyton bought a new computer at their next port. She resumed tinkering on some of the personal coding projects she'd put on hold when she'd gone to work in Silicon Valley.

On impulse, Peyton also signed up to take part in a bug hunt—one of several programs that gave coders behind the scenes access to various websites and programs. The objective was to let white-hat hackers find bugs and vulnerabilities in the software. The programs grew bigger every year. Some coders did it for the prestige and satisfaction of solving a problem that others didn't know existed, but for many—including her—the interest was a touch more mercenary. She was in it for the bug bounties, which was cash awarded for successfully finding a substantial flaw in the code.

Liam or Matthias would have been happy to give her money. In fact, Matthias had set up a bank account for her, but she hadn't touched it. Accepting their gifts was one thing. Most were clothes or items of jewelry they wanted her to wear. It gave them pleasure, so she went along with it. But she didn't like the idea of being completely dependent on them. Plus, she enjoyed coding. Tracking down bugs was satisfying.

Peyton also threw herself into another project—cracking Priya. Peyton was determined to make friends with her. She wanted to make nice with the other staff as well, but Priya was her white whale. When the elegant Indian woman began to agree to have lunch on a semi-regular basis, Peyton was thrilled. She was even more excited when Priya began to confide in her. However, Priya's first major slip about her boss threw Peyton for a loop.

"He's a what?"

"Matthias is a widower."

The delicious puttanesca pasta they were eating was forgotten.

"I had no idea," Peyton said. She wasn't sure how old he was—mid-thirties at the most. He didn't seem old enough to be widowed.

"He must have been married very young," Peyton said after a long pause.

There were no signs of Matthias' marriage on the Ormen Lange. In her time on the boat, she hadn't seen any portraits or pictures of him with a woman. In fact, he'd didn't display any photographs of himself at all. The only portraits were oils or photographs of older relatives.

"It's not a secret, at least not among the staff. It was before my time —before he decided to live on the yacht year-round. It was a terrible accident. She was expecting at the time."

Peyton gasped "His wife was *pregnant* when she died?"

Priya began to look uncomfortable. She pushed away the glass of white wine Peyton had talked her into drinking.

"Yes. It was incredibly sad. Mr. Raske is very protective of his privacy when it comes to the public, but since you're here now on what appears to be a long-term basis, with Mr. Tyler, no less…Mr. Raske was very attached to him at one point. Well, to be honest, I thought you knew."

"He hasn't mentioned it, but don't concern yourself. The one thing I've learned about Matthias is he likes to live in the moment."

While Matthias answered almost any question he was asked, he didn't volunteer much about himself. When a past adventure was mentioned, or a place he visited was discussed, it was usually Liam who brought up the subject. Matthias didn't appear to enjoy trips down memory lane.

She could only imagine how he felt about losing his wife. His pregnant wife. *Christ.* No wonder he'd reacted so badly when Liam brought up babies. Matthias and his wife had been on the verge of starting a family when he'd tragically lost her. He must have been devastated.

Priya's face was tight with guilt, so Peyton took pity on her and decided to change the subject. "Can I ask you something. Is it weird, having Liam and me…err…around? At the same time?"

Priya smiled. "The staff knows better than to question our employer's choices. All I will say is we are enjoying your stay. Mr. Tyler's as well. Most of our employer's guests aren't appreciative of our efforts. Most never bother to learn our names."

That was something Peyton had learned from the Tylers. "Liam always made it a point to learn the name of everyone who worked for him, even when he was an insufferable know-it-all teenager. He has a memory like a steel trap. I haven't nailed everyone's name as well as he has."

"You could have fooled me. From what I've seen, you haven't stepped wrong in that respect at all in the last week." Priya hesitated. "I hope you won't mention I was the source of your new knowledge, even though I don't believe there's a reason to hide it. As I said, it's an open secret on the boat, but it might be somewhat uncomfortable for me if Matthias believes I was gossiping about him."

"He'll never know it was you. I swear."

Peyton was dying to ask her more details about Matthias ill-fated marriage, but Priya was done for the day. She excused herself before Peyton could work up the courage.

Peyton spent the rest of the afternoon on the deck with her computer, coding in between breaks to reapply sunscreen. However, she was too distracted to get much work done. The mystery wife consumed her thoughts.

Matthias showed no signs of mourning, so his marriage must have ended ages ago. *Ended in tragedy.* Peyton winced, picturing a beautiful blonde Nordic goddess, the female counterpart to Thor-lite.

She was going to have to talk to Liam. Peyton needed to make sure he dropped the subject of babies. Matthias was obviously sensitive about the subject—and rightly so. It would also be a good idea to shut down that kind of talk for her sake.

Yes, she wanted children. Liam had laid out her most secret desires with his declaration. But things were more complicated now. Matthias was now a part of her dreams of the future, and she would be damned if she were going to let their third's bluntness threaten their potential.

But Liam was a force of nature. Keeping a man like him in check would be like trying to stop a tsunami.

Well, there's no time like the present. Determined to stay ahead of any problems, Peyton set aside her work to hunt Liam down. It was easy. He was in the northern port-side conference room, his makeshift office.

His eyes lit up when he saw her. He pushed away his laptop—a first in her experience—and beckoned her with his finger.

Flushing, Peyton hesitated. It was almost as if a bright spotlight had been thrown on her. "I came here to talk, not have sex."

Liam threw her a wicked grin. "Why can't we do both?"

Rooted to the spot, her body flashed hot and cold, amazed she wasn't running to tackle him. This had been her fantasy for years. Every time she had walked into his office at the Caislean, she had wanted him to throw her on the desk and ravish her. *Damn his timing.*

She found her voice a beat too late. "Because...I'm not sure it's a great idea to leave Matthias out of our sex so soon."

Liam cocked his head. "As long as we make time for him, too, he's not going to have a problem with it. He said as much during our ground-rules talk. Besides, he's smart enough to know you and I are going to need some one-on-one time. We have years of repressed desire to work out. And yes, I know that's my fault. But he's not stupid. Why else did he wait until I was on board to take your virginity?"

Peyton risked getting closer to him. She leaned against the edge of the wide oval table he'd commandeered. "You have to stop gloating about that. I don't need you strutting around like a plundering Viking."

"Am I not allowed to be happy you waited for me?" Liam batted his disgustingly thick lashes at her.

"*No.* Because I very nearly didn't. It certainly wasn't my intention. You're just lucky that men suck. I can't count the number of times a guy stood me up on the second or third date."

Liam grunted something unintelligible.

She frowned. "What?"

He swore, slumping in his chair. "I said they didn't all stand you up. I may have been...redirecting their attention elsewhere."

Peyton rolled her eyes. "Why am I not surprised?"

She should have been angry, but, frankly, she was past that. Those half-hearted efforts to date had been sad attempts to forget the man in front of her. Now he and Matthias were hers. If she could just keep them both on track, that was.

"Well, just imagine if you'd let one of those guys keep that date. I might never have been kidnapped and sold at a virgin auction."

His eyes darkened, his hands fisting in front of him. "Don't say that. Those monsters would have taken you anyway. A lot of terrible things could have happened to you. Your virginity was the only thing protecting you." Liam straightened, making a visible effort to control his temper. "But that's all in the past. You're safe now, and both Matthias and I are going to make sure you stay that way."

It was almost a declaration of war. "Simmer down, gladiator. I'm under no immediate threat. Except maybe from you."

His head drew back. "Me?"

"I learned something. Suffice to say, you have to stop talking babies in front of Matthias."

He frowned. "Why?"

She rubbed her fingers together, trying to find the right words. "Did you know Matthias had been married before?"

Liam stroked his chin. "Yeah, he mentioned it when we first met. Why?"

"And did you know his wife was pregnant at the end?"

His eyes widened, face clouding. "I didn't know that. All I know is what he told me. He didn't mention anything about a child."

"Well, the baby was lost when she died. Apparently, it's an open secret on the *Ormen Lange*. But that's why your talk of children is premature. We were being insensitive. It's not your fault—we didn't know."

"Um, Peyton, what are you talking about?"

"That you can't charge through and dictate how things are going to be. Not about this."

Why didn't he understand?

"But, Peyton, you're wrong. Matthias didn't lose his wife. He divorced her."

~

"WHAT DID YOU SAY?" Needing the support, Peyton sat on the conference table.

"Lise, Matthias' ex-wife—the woman isn't dead," Liam repeated. "She lives in Paris."

"*Oh.*" Peyton didn't think Priya would have lied to her. "Well, that's what the staff believes. And they think he lost both wife and child in some sort of tragic accident."

Liam pursed his lips. "It sounds more like a patented Matthias misinformation campaign."

"You mean he intentionally lies about his marriage?"

"I don't know. Like I said, I hadn't heard this widower rumor before. But it wouldn't be the first time Matthias let someone believe something about him that wasn't true. And this detail about a pregnancy is rather specific, isn't it? It could be the truth. We should ask him. I wouldn't want to poke an open wound."

Peyton groaned, wondering how their secretive billionaire partner would react to such invasive questions. "You're sure his ex is alive?"

"And kicking," Liam drawled. "I took the liberty of checking her out after he brought her up the first time. After the divorce, she settled in France, in a huge apartment just off the Champs-Elysees. She is a renown hostess, spending her king's ransom of a divorce settlement on parties, art, and *haute couture.*"

"Maybe she's treating her loss with some tried-and-true retail therapy," Peyton suggested. "A lot of couples have a tough time making it work after losing a child."

"Well, should we be so unlucky, we won't let something like that happen to us."

Peyton raised an eyebrow. "The three of us, Liam. We have to be in this together with Matthias."

"Babe, I wasn't excluding him. It's simply hard for me to talk in a way that makes that clear."

"It is clear," a third voice said.

Peyton nearly threw out her neck twisting so fast to face the doorway. Matthias stood there with his hands in his pockets. His expression suggested he'd been there for some time.

"How much did you hear?" Liam asked.

Frowning, Matthias scratched his head. "Enough to know you're both misinformed. My ex-wife didn't suffer a miscarriage. She terminated her pregnancy."

CHAPTER 29

*P*eyton felt as if someone had slapped her. "Oh my God. I'm so sorry."

"Don't be." Matthias shrugged. "I got over it a long time ago. And in the years since, I've learned to appreciate the fact there's not a child being used as a bludgeon by two bitter exes."

Peyton mumbled inarticulately. She didn't know what to say to that.

Liam didn't have that problem. He crossed his arms over his wide chest. "I'm not going to let our kids be used as fodder in any fight."

"*Our* kids?" Matthias raised a brow.

"You're the one who said we have to be up front about what we want. Peyton likes kids. I want at least two. I'd like one or more to be biologically mine, but if they end up being yours—and unless we go the petri-dish route, that's just as likely—I'm still claiming them as my own."

Matthias cleared his throat. "Well, thanks for being clear." He turned to Peyton. "And you're worried about this why?"

"I didn't want him to scare you with the baby talk. He's scaring me a bit." She tweaked Liam's ear. "But that's just how he is. When Liam decides he wants something, he wants it now. However, in this case, he's going to have to wait. It's too soon."

Smile widening, Matthias went to an innocuous-looking cabinet against the wall. When he pressed a button, the door slid open, revealing a miniature bar. He grabbed some glasses and a bottle of something dark gold and expensive looking.

"In the interests of full disclosure, I should add my wife felt justi-fied in getting an abortion. I didn't agree with her at the time, but I didn't have much of a leg to stand on in our arguments."

"Why not?" Peyton couldn't imagine anyone ending a pregnancy out of spite.

"She divorced me for cheating. With a man—not Liam," he added.

"*Ah.*" It was all starting to make sense. Matthias's insistence on a three-way relationship was a result of past lessons learned. He'd said something to that effect earlier. At the time, though, she hadn't had all the details. Now she knew everything.

"That is everything, right?" Peyton needed to be sure. "There are no other secrets or skeletons I need to know about?"

"Of course there are," Matthias said with a little huff. "But none that seem relevant at the moment."

"Good," Liam declared. "Glad we got that out of the way. Can we all have sex now?"

Matthias downed the rest of his drink. "I second that."

Peyton laughed. "I'm going to get my bathing suit. Meet me in the hot tub in five minutes."

She hurried out of the room, but not before she heard Matthias ask why she was bothering with the suit.

"She can't go around naked," Liam protested.

"Why not?"

"Because Peyton in all her glory is for our eyes only."

"I would fire all the staff," Matthias said, following him out the door, "but I'm afraid three people can't man the *Ormen Lange* alone."

CHAPTER 30

*D*espite his best efforts, Liam had been forced to resume traveling for the hotel. The trip was only supposed to be for a few days, but he'd been inevitably forced to extend it to more than a week.

Peyton missed him like crazy. Thankfully, Matthias had kept her busy. So busy she had woken up past noon today. Matthias must have been up for hours. Like Liam, he appeared to only need four or five hours every night. If Peyton didn't get at least seven, she was a grouch for the rest of the day.

However, after spending the afternoon making strides on her bug hunt, she decided to bust into Matthias' office for a little R&R.

If I can find it. She knew it was on the top floor somewhere, but his office was his sanctum. To date, she hadn't been inside.

Well, it's time that changed.

However, she didn't feel as confident a few minutes later. One of the stewards was kind enough to point out the way, but his reluctance was obvious. She could tell he wondered if he should stop her. It made her second-guess the likelihood of a welcome.

A man of Matthias' stature was never disturbed by his staff, not unless it was an emergency. Peyton believed it would take something catastrophic—like the boat sinking—for any of them to knock on that door. Caislean employees had been equally cautious about bothering Liam in his office.

It'll be fine, Peyton told herself as she reached the double doors. It wasn't as if he had warned her not to disturb him. She knocked, then waited for him to respond.

Nothing. She tried again, cracking the door open to peek inside. Matthias' desk was at the end of a large, wood-paneled room.

"Hello?" Engrossed in his work, Matthias didn't even glance up when she entered the room. Even closing the door made no difference.

He was poring over something that looked like a contract. Indoctrinated by years at the Caislean, she almost turned around and left before checking herself mid-step.

Hey, I'm not at the Caislean and Matthias isn't Liam. Even Liam wasn't *that* Liam anymore.

Deciding to have some fun, Peyton dropped to her knees, crawling beneath the front of the big mahogany desk.

She managed to get all the way under without Matthias seeing her. Marveling at the man's singular focus, she bit her lip to keep from laughing. Wondering how far she could go without him noticing, she curled up close to his legs, leaving her hands free...

MATTHIAS DIDN'T NOTICE his pants had been undone until his zipper was halfway down. He glanced down to see a pair of elegantly manicured hands caressing him over his boxers. The short nails should have been a giveaway—programmers didn't wear their nails long— but he was so startled he reacted without thinking.

Pushing the chair out, he shot backward so fast he hit the bookcase behind him with a bang, jarring a leather-bound volume loose. It glanced off his head, landing heavily on his shoulder.

Peyton gasped, poking her head out from under his desk. "I'm sorry! Are you hurt?"

Matthias rubbed his shoulder. "No." He laughed. "I'm just lucky it was a first edition of Salinger and not Dostoevsky."

She threw him an adorably abashed grin. "I thought you'd spot me long before this."

"I tend to get sucked into my work." Trying not to smile, he checked his watch. "I only intended to put in a couple of hours, but a few things have piled up and I lost track of time. My apologies. I didn't mean to leave you on your own for so long."

Peyton cocked her head. "That makes me sound like a guest. I'm your partner. You don't have to worry about entertaining me every day."

"That's very understanding." Matthias blinked, thinking how different Peyton was from the other women he'd been involved with.

"Although..." Peyton crawled out from under the desk, rose on her knees, and put her hands on his thighs. "There's no rule that says I can't entertain you on occasion."

Heat coursed through him as she pulled his zipper the rest of the way down. "Well, as your partner, or one of them, it's my job to make sure you have every opportunity..."

His voice trailed off as she tugged his boxer briefs down, taking hold of his cock with a firm grip.

Matthias swore under his breath, resisting the urge to close his eyes as Peyton's full lips closed over the head of his shaft. He didn't want to miss a second of this. Then her tongue rolled over him, licking the sensitive part under the crest, and he groaned aloud, his head tipping back to the ceiling.

"*Helsike*," he said, swearing in his native tongue.

She stopped for a second. "That's not too hard, is it?"

"No!" He laughed, and Peyton blushed.

"You two never let me practice much," she pointed out.

That much was true. Usually, the minute the three of them started up, Peyton absorbed their attention. She was just too damn beautiful

—her glorious skin, full breasts, and waterfall of dark hair were simply irresistible.

Picturing her body made his cock throb. "Once you get naked, it's hard to focus on anything else."

Peyton bit her lower lip playfully. Slowly, she undid the buttons of her blouse. Heaven help him, she wasn't wearing a bra.

Groaning, he reached to cup the full creamy mounds, but she moved his hands so she could bend over his lap again.

Her mouth flamed over him, moving up and down, alternately sucking and nibbling. Matthias took her hands, showing her how to hold him at the base until she was working him over with both her hands and her mouth. Each stroke was torture. Matthias gripped the arms of his chair, his fingers digging into the plush leather pads as the first warning pulses stirred.

Counting to ten in Chinese, he attempted to slow down his reaction, but Peyton was both gorgeous and a natural talent at everything.

After all those years of repressing her natural sexual desires, Peyton had thrown herself into their sex life with gusto. If she had any inhibitions, she had shed them faster than it took Liam to get her undressed. Now she was indulging every fantasy she'd ever had...and knocking down plenty of theirs, too.

Trying to slow down wasn't working. His hard-on was like steel. Reaching down, he pulled Peyton to her feet with one hand, then shoved the antique pen holder and reports off the desk with the other.

Giggling, Peyton sat on the edge, her arms wrapping around the back of his head. He kissed her hard before lowering until his mouth was level with her breasts. Her breath hitched as he took one of the hard buds, lathing it with his tongue.

The lace underwear Peyton wore didn't stand a chance. One hard tug and they were gone, giving him access to her soft heat. His blood pumped so loudly he could barely hear.

"Please, I want you inside me," she panted, kissing his neck.

He was more than happy to oblige. "Not going to be an issue," he said before kissing her, sliding his tongue in until she stroked back with hers.

Breaking away, he took himself in hand, running his cock against her clit before sliding down to coat the head in her moisture. Already aching, he thrust his hips forward, driving deep into her velvety heat.

"*Shit*," he swore, his lust roaring. Pants down around his ankles, he began to fuck her, pistoning in and out until he established a rhythm that made her moan and pant.

Peyton whispered in his ear, nonsense words of desire and praise. They stoked the fire higher until something inside him snapped. The last vestiges of his control slipped away, his thrusts coming rougher and faster. Every time he buried himself inside her, she squeezed him tightly, rocking in matching rhythm.

No woman before her had ever done this to him. Peyton seemed perfectly attuned to him, her every move like a choreographed dance designed to drive him out of his mind. Matthias was ready to explode. She was way ahead of him—her tight pussy shivered and pulsed around him, her nails breaking the skin against his back as she climaxed with a sob in his arms.

Matthias took her mouth, driving himself to the hilt before he let go, groaning and swearing in Norwegian. His dick pulsed, rapture blinding him as his hot seed poured into her waiting womb.

Too weak to hold himself up, Matthias let himself fall forward, controlling their descent with a hand on Peyton's back. She lay spread-eagled beneath him, her breathing rapid and shallow as she came down from her peak.

Matthias moved as soon as he was able, collapsing into his chair so he wouldn't crush her.

A few long minutes later, Peyton lifted her head. She leaned on her elbows, surveying him with an expression of smug satisfaction. "That'll keep you," she said.

Matthias laughed. He must have looked wrecked, but her flushed face was getting him hot all over again. Either that or her exposed breasts—Peyton was blessed in every way.

He pushed the chair closer, rising to kiss her. "It will—for now."

A flash of guilt flitted across her face. "I know we're not supposed to feel bad about doing this without Liam, but I kind of do."

"Truly?" He stroked the soft skin of her leg, running it all the way up to her thigh. "Because I think I can learn to live with the guilt."

She giggled, but he could hear the tinge of uncertainty in it. "Relax, *elskling*. There will be times when I'm tied up and you and Liam will carry on without me."

"And I'm sure there will be times when I can't partake, and you and Liam will finally get busy with each other."

Her less-than-subtle suggestion made him snort aloud. "Are you still angling for some man-on-man, my little voyeur?"

She smirked. "Can you blame me?"

"Not a bit." He reached up to stroke her cheek. "And don't worry. Sooner or later, you're going to get your wish."

Peyton glanced down at the pile of papers he'd knocked off the desk. "Should I help you clean up?"

"Don't worry. I'll do it." He was only one who could put the mess in order—the contract was in Mandarin, one of the five languages he spoke fluently.

"Any chance of you being able to get away for dinner?"

"Sure…" He'd been downplaying the amount of work he had to do. At this rate, he was going to be here half the night, but if he ate quickly, he could manage some time away.

His tone must not have been convincing, because Peyton hurried off the desk. "Don't worry about it. I understand if you have to keep going."

"I could take half an hour to eat," he suggested.

She dismissed the idea with a wave. "It's all right. Don't forget—I spent years in the upper echelon of the Caislean. All the Tylers work like dogs. Liam is the worst of the lot, so I get it."

"Thank you," he said, relieved. Peyton couldn't get more perfect if she tried.

She bent to pick up her shoe, then hopped on the desk to slip the heel on. "Besides, I slept through lunch with Priya. She claims to have forgiven me, but I think dinner will go a fair way to making amends. Especially if we can raid your wine cellar."

She leaned back with a considering expression. "What do you call a cellar on a boat?"

"The wine closet," he said, his chest tightening as he realized she was going to eat with the head of his staff again.

Priya and Peyton had become confidantes. Priya had mentioned Peyton had been asking about their dealings with the traffickers. At first, he hadn't seen a problem with his new lover knowing the details, but the more he thought about it, the more his misgivings he had.

Peyton was a fiercely determined young woman. In the brief time he'd known her, he'd learned to respect her intelligence and drive. Though it appeared she had come through her kidnapping without too much damage, he knew she was still dealing with what had happened.

Sometimes, she would go noticeably quiet. Her jaw would clench and her fists would tighten, but as soon as she saw him, she would paste a smile on her face and pretend nothing was wrong.

Deep down, Peyton was angry. *And she might be looking to do something about it…*

"Have whatever you like," he said slowly, "but I would appreciate it if you would stop asking Priya about our experiences with the slave trade."

Her surprise was palpable. "I…uh…I mean, I wasn't planning to discuss that tonight, but we have talked about it before."

There was a beat of silence. She gripped her other shoe awkwardly in front of her. "Sorry, you've caught me off guard."

Matthias winced, but he had to be firm with her. "I don't want to censor you, but you don't understand how it was. I don't need the staff reliving the Belarus incident. Priya especially. She took it extremely hard."

"Belarus?" Peyton frowned. "Oh. That's where *it* happened…"

It had been a nightmare. Matthias blinked. Suddenly, he wasn't seeing his lover in front of him. His mind was filled with the grue-some images of all those dead girls. Wincing, he squeezed his eyes shut, banishing the ghosts. He opened them to see Peyton watching him with concern.

There was another sharp silence.

"Just stop asking questions," he said, his voice curt.

The line between her eyes deepened. "Are you sure that's a good idea?"

Matthias scowled, his hands going to his hips. "Why don't you understand?"

Peyton shook her head. "I just meant perhaps you should talk to someone. A therapist. There might be some—unresolved things."

She reached for him, but Matthias jerked back. He fastened his pants and shirt with abrupt movements. "I've asked you to respect my wishes on this matter. I don't need the staff getting any ideas. We are *not* getting back into that business!"

By the time he finished, he was yelling.

Rubbing her arms, Peyton climbed off his desk with slow preci-sion. He didn't like the look she was giving him. Like she could read his very soul.

"You think someone here sold you out."

Staggering, Matthias reached behind him, knocking into one of the small iron sculptures bolted into the bookcase.

"*Fuck.*" He shook his hand out, sucking on his stinging fingers for a second. "No," he assured her, striving for a calmer tone and failing miserably. "My people had nothing to do with it."

His staff was the best of the best. Each one had passed elaborate background checks. Not to mention the fact they had been put through their paces by Priya.

Somehow, Peyton knew he was lying. Matthias hadn't been able to face it, but there had always been a thread of suspicion. George Wheeler, his contact at Interpol, had been a pro—a decorated agent with years of success behind him. It had taken a while, but the man had gained Matthias' confidence. His operation had been airtight.

When the sting in Belarus had gone south, Wheeler had taken full responsibility. It had cost the man his career. But deep down, Matthias had always wondered where the fault truly lay. Wheeler hadn't ever discovered how the slavers had been tipped to the raid.

"Matthias?"

Snapping out of his reverie, he turned away from Peyton. There were so many things he wanted to say to her, but the words choked him.

"I have to take a shower," he rasped, spinning on his heel and leaving the room before she could reply.

CHAPTER 31

*P*eyton felt terrible about her argument with Matthias, but more than that, she was worried—for him and everyone who had been involved in the Belarus tragedy.

Could someone on the Ormen Lange have betrayed Matthias and the others? The idea of it made her physically ill. To make matters worse, he was avoiding her.

After pulling her clothes back on, Peyton hurried out of Matthias' office, intent on finding him. Unfortunately, the *Ormen Lange* was an exceptionally large boat. She wandered around until she bumped into Priya near the bridge. The woman immediately asked what was wrong.

"I'm not supposed to talk to you about it." Peyton sighed despondently. "About Belarus."

Priya put down her clipboard. "Oh."

"You and Matthias never mentioned where it happened. He doesn't want me asking about it. He said it would upset you and the rest of the staff."

Priya sighed. "Then you must respect his wishes," she said, but her tone was one of disapproval.

Peyton pushed the toe of her shoe into the carpet. "If my questions upset you—"

Priya held up a hand. "I did not mind. I found it beneficial. I still have some questions about it myself. I believe the operation was compromised."

Peyton reached out to take her arm. "I can't believe this. You think there was an informant, too?"

"Absolutely," Priya said.

Peyton shook her head, marveling at the woman's calm demeanor. "And you're not worried about having someone like that on board?"

The other woman's sooty lashes fluttered. "Are you suggesting the mole was a part of *our* team?"

Straightening, Peyton realized that wasn't what Priya had meant at all.

Lover number one will just have to stay pissed at me. She needed to clear this up. "That's what Matthias thinks. He didn't say so, but by the way he shut me down a little while ago, I think it was pretty damn clear."

Priya leaned against the railing. "I hadn't realized he believed that. I can assure you none of our people had a hand in it."

"So if there's a mole, it's someone in Interpol?"

That made a lot more sense. It was a much bigger organization. She didn't even know who oversaw them. Did Interpol operate like the police, with their own internal affairs unit?

Well, as horrible as the idea of a mole there was, Peyton found it comforting. At least there wasn't a traitor running around on board with them.

"Do you have any idea who it might have been?"

"No, Matthias kept the reports on Belarus. I suspect he destroyed them after. But I don't believe Mr. Wheeler, the agent who oversaw the operation, was involved. His career ended soon after. Belarus completely derailed it."

Peyton rubbed her temple, which was tight, the incipient sign of a headache. "It must have been someone else."

Peyton mulled what she had learned for the rest of the night. The next day, Matthias had sought her out on the deck, inviting her to dinner and taking her to bed as if nothing were wrong. He studiously avoided the subject, talking about anything and everything else—including the possibility of having children.

That was when she realized just how damaged and desperate he truly was.

After a painfully awkward meal, Peyton decided she couldn't live with this between them. She resolved to find out what had happened in Belarus, even if she had to do it behind his back.

Unfortunately, there was only one person she could think of who could help her with that. And he might not want to talk to her.

PEYTON SWAM ten extra laps in the pool, trying to dismiss the niggling guilt she felt after talking to Ethan Thomas on the satellite phone.

He hadn't been upset when she told him where she was. Jason had filled him in, telling him all about Matthias Raske. Ethan had opened the conversation by teasing her about making rebound history.

"I have to hand it to you—a mysterious billionaire is a damn good take. Tyler must be eating his heart out. Did you hear he broke up with Caroline?"

"I did. Liam told me."

"He did?" Ethan sounded surprised.

Peyton grimaced. Why was she doing this now? And over the freaking *phone*?

But she did it anyway.

"Um…yes," she continued. "He's here. Well, he's not here at the moment, but he'll be back soon."

Ethan paused. "I'm not following."

And he didn't follow for a long time. It took Peyton a few minutes to make him understand the nature of her new relationship.

When he finally did, Ethan whistled. "I didn't give you enough credit. I guess I'm not the only one who likes a challenge."

"Promise me you won't say anything to anyone else yet."

"Maggie doesn't know?" Now she had really shocked him.

"No one does," she said." Not yet."

Peyton had sent Maggie and her other friends dozens of emails, assuring them of her well-being and happiness, but she couldn't seem to find the words to tell them about her new relationship. Every time she tried, it came out so stilted and odd, so she'd given up, vowing to tell everyone in person.

Ethan's awkwardness grew. "No offense, but why exactly do I have the honor? Not that I'm sorry I did. We're friends," he ended weakly.

"I'm going to tell them soon," she swore. "The next time I see them, I'm going to tell them everything, but I had another reason for calling you."

Fidgeting with her charm bracelet, she inquired about his friend Mason Ward. Ethan had mentioned him several times. Mason was an Interpol agent.

Settling in one of the *Ormen Lange's* many deck chairs, Peyton told Ethan all about Belarus and Matthias' work rescuing victims of the slave trade.

"That was how he knew how to find me. He posed as a buyer in that world for so long, he was able to track me down when Liam asked."

Ethan *hmphed*. "You're sure this guy is on the up and up? That sounds pretty damn convenient to me."

"I assure you it wasn't. Priya, his right hand, had a hell of a time finding me."

Priya had detailed the search over lunch once. Peyton realized how close she had come to being lost forever…

Consequently, her dreams had become substantially darker.

"I guess money talks." Ethan sniffed. "Out of curiosity, how much did this Raske guy pay for you?"

"I have no idea. He still won't tell me. It's driving Liam crazy because it means he can't pay him back."

Ethan laughed, the sound grudging. But he wasn't an FBI agent for nothing. He asked a million questions, most of which she didn't know how to answer. After learning what few details she did, he promised to put her in touch with Mason.

"Be forewarned. Mason's kind of a hotshot at Interpol, and he didn't get there without knowing how to play the game."

"Meaning?"

"That he won't help without getting something in return. Be prepared."

ETHAN HAD BEEN CORRECT. Mason did want something—her. Specifically, he wanted to recruit her for Interpol.

When Mason called, he'd already been over all the records his agency had on the Belarus incident. He'd even spoken to George Wheeler, the retired agent in charge of the operation.

Mason insisted he wouldn't discuss such a sensitive subject with an outsider were it not for the fact Ethan had vouched for her.

"You know, I thought he was wasting my time insisting I look into this thing," he told her after they had exchanged overly polite greetings.

"And you don't now?"

He sighed. "No. Wheeler insists there was a leak somewhere, but he couldn't track it down. But Ethan says you're pretty sure it wasn't anyone on Raske's crew."

"Priya, Matthias' assistant, is certain. She vetted everyone very thoroughly. Also, there's the fact they're all still a part of the crew. If they had been responsible, I think they would have left."

"Hmm. I think the only way Wheeler sleeps at night is telling himself it wasn't one of our own," Mason shared, rifling papers in the background.

"Does that mean you're going to look into this more?"

"It does, but I'm going to need some help. Your help."

Ethan had told Mason about her coding background, including some of her lesser-known exploits on the dark web.

Peyton hadn't realized Ethan had known about her time as a hacker. She had been strictly white hat, but she'd done enough to make something of a name for herself—or she would have had she signed her work.

"There are mountains of records to comb through," Mason informed her. "I'm not even supposed to have some of these, but I traded in a few favors. Discreetly, of course. The investigation on the group took years. There's a pile of communications I need back-tracked and cross-referenced. I need to know if anyone intercepted those messages. According to what Ethan told me, you have the kind of background that could cut through this shite like it was butter."

"I see." Peyton held the phone closer, checking her surroundings to make sure no one could hear the conversation.

She had some misgivings about getting involved, but Peyton knew she could help—up to a point.

"I might be able to help comb through the data, but without access to Interpol's servers, I can't promise I can trace any eavesdroppers."

"That's all I can ask," he said, promising to send her the information. He began to give her instructions with the intention of setting up a secure drop. She interrupted, directing him instead to a private encrypted server she had set up in college.

"I must warn you," he said after taking down the address. "The records I'm going to send will include photos of Belarus. You might not want to look at those."

"I'll take that under advisement," she replied before hanging up.

Both Matthias and Priya had seen those pictures. Poor Agent Wheeler had lived through the nightmare. Peyton didn't want to punish herself, but if she didn't find something for Mason in the reams of memos and surveillance, she'd do what she had to. Matthias and Priya needed peace of mind. And the victims needed justice.

She just had to get it for them in secret. Peyton rose from the deck chair, heading inside to get ready for dinner.

Relax. Whatever Matthias doesn't know won't hurt him.

CHAPTER 32

*A*fter a tense few days alone with Matthias, things with him returned to normal—mostly. He avoided his office, spending a lot of time with her, dining and watching movies in the ship's private theatre. They even swam, racing each other in the pool.

Peyton tried to bring up their argument, but Matthias had gently taken her hand and said he didn't want to talk about it. He wasn't angry or upset, just…firm. She didn't have the heart to try again.

Still feeling unsettled, Peyton was thrilled to see Liam when he returned from his business trip.

And he was *incredibly happy* to see her, too. He found her on the deck outside Matthias' stateroom mere minutes after the helicopter landed on the platform.

"I missed you so much," Liam panted, trying to simultaneously pull up her dress while pushing her panties down.

Humming nonsensically, Peyton pushed her backside against him. "I missed you, too. Six days is too long."

Liam had arrived just in time for a glorious sunset, which he had completely ignored in favor of stripping her naked.

Peyton grabbed on the rail for support, going weak-kneed when

Liam thrust his hand into the bodice of her gown. He covered her breast with his large hand, kneading it until her nipples peaked so hard they almost hurt.

"Now that you're here, we should wait for Matthias," she said in between panting breaths.

"He's had you to himself for almost a week. He'll catch up." His mouth ran up and down her neck. Peyton moaned aloud, leaving one hand on the rail and using the other to press his head closer.

When her panties slid down her legs, Peyton kicked them aside before they tangled in her heels. The night air hit her bare backside, but the breeze was gone as soon as Liam pressed against her. Velvet-covered heat pushed at her backside as his other hand pressed against her pussy.

His fingers stroked and probed, entering her with the aggression she'd come to expect from him. Peyton closed her eyes, clenching her jaw to keep from crying out. He made that damn near impossible when he entered her with a single slow thrust.

Grabbing the rail with both hands, Peyton held on for dear life as Liam started pumping, sinking into her wet heat and then withdrawing, only to rock back before she could recover.

His strokes were short and fast. It wasn't enough. Peyton pushed against him, trying to hold him longer, drive him deeper.

Liam's hand came around her neck, gently holding her to him. "So impatient."

"And you're a tease."

His laugh was low and dirty. Kissing her neck, he pressed deep, driving himself to the hilt inside her. "Is that what you want?"

"*Yes,*" she panted, despite the very real threat of spontaneous human combustion.

Liam made a low sound in his throat—something between a growl and a purr. "Never say I don't give you what you want."

He pumped harder and fasters, lingering on the spot that made her shiver. Peyton's skin felt alive, tingling in the cool wind. The heat of Liam at her back felt decadent, but it was nothing compared to the fire he was stoking inside her. Endless waves of pleasure built. She felt so tight, so hungry. He was silk and fire, like a picture of a Djinn she had seen before—not the cute cartoon kind, but a creature of heat and dark magic. Shuddering, she reached behind herself to clutch him to her. She needed more, but she was torn because she never wanted this moment to end.

"Don't hold back, baby," Liam hissed in her ear. "I want to hear you scream."

"Not-gonna-scr-scream," she ground out, eagerly pushing back to meet his thrusts.

The feel of him was too good to believe. His thick length plundered and possessed as if he were trying to brand her.

"You will," he promised, turning her cheek gently so he could kiss it. His mouth left a trail of heat across the sensitive skin below her ear. Peyton moaned again, giving herself over to the glorious push and pull of him.

It was like riding a storm. She could barely see straight. All she could do was feel, his strength and fire contrasting with the colder metal of the rail under her hands.

Her orgasm broke over her like a wave. She tensed, her entire body pulsing. Despite her best efforts to keep her mouth shut, she cried out, rearing backward into Liam's embrace, trusting him to hold her upright. If he hadn't, she would have crumpled to a little heap on the deck.

"I see someone started without me." Peyton twisted, spotting Matthias leaning on one of the beams next to the dining table.

He was dressed more casually than she had ever seen him, in jeans and sweater. His hair was a little wet as if he'd just come from the shower. Most likely, it was from the pool. He spent a lot of time swimming lately.

Liam wrapped his arms around her, rocking her in a carefree and affectionate gesture. "I didn't think you'd mind seeing as you've had her to yourself for ninety-one whole hours."

"You counted in hours?" Peyton pulled away, making sure the hem of her dress was down where it was supposed to be before sitting on the padded bench next to the dining table.

Liam shrugged, surprising her by walking over to hug the other man. Their heads stayed close together for a murmured exchange she couldn't hear. Then Liam laughed at something Matthias said, just before he leaned over and kissed him on the lips.

Peyton wasn't aware she was holding her breath until her lungs protested. Matthias broke the kiss first, rubbing Liam's shoulder and asking how the trip went.

Relaxing, she lay against the cushions, watching the two men interact without listening to their conversation. It was enough to have seen their moment.

To say that both men were handsome, or even beautiful, was too inadequate to describe the sight of the them together. They were both so different. Liam was dark, his features angular and bold as if they had been carved from granite. Matthias' features were finer, a touch prettier, but he, too, was hard, his masculine virility just as potent and as intoxicating as his counterpart.

Liam pivoted, his eyes flaring. "You're wearing an anal plug?"

Peyton giggled. "Oh, uh…yeah. Matthias showed me his sex toy drawer. Rather, his cabinet. It was before you left. Anyway, there was plenty of interesting things inside. Long story short, I took some of the new things for my own personal use. Surprise!"

"Damn, I should have known." Liam seemed impressed. "I thought you felt…different. Tighter."

"She wanted to prepare," Matthias said, sitting next to her. "She wants to take us both at once."

"Are we sure that's a good idea?" Liam pursed his lips. "We've been doing all right as we are. I certainly don't mind taking turns. Neither of us wants to push you into something you're not ready for." This last had an added edge, but it wasn't directed at her.

Matthias held his hands up. "The plug was *not* my idea."

"It was mine, so you can relax," Peyton interjected. She picked at her skirt, certain her face was beet red.

"I'd be lying if I said I didn't want to be inside you at the same time he is," Liam began, gesturing expansively, "And I applaud your foresight and willingness to prepare—"

"Stop talking as if you're addressing a shareholders meeting," Peyton interrupted, tossing a pillow at his head.

Matthias snickered as Liam caught it and dropped his arms. "Fine..." He sighed, but his lip twitched as he tossed the pillow aside. "I still think it's too soon."

Peyton tried hard not to pout, but it was difficult to hide her disappointment.

"However..." Liam trailed off, reaching to take his tie off with exaggerated leisure.

"Do you have something to share with the group?" Matthias asked, amusement crossing his features as he watched the slow-motion striptease.

"I do. Peyton wants to be closer to us, but she isn't ready for what she's proposing." Liam moved, circling Matthias like a lion eyeing a juicy antelope. "But there is someone here with more experience who could fill that role she wants to play—and will later."

Rooted to the spot, Peyton watched wide-eyed as Liam pressed his mouth to Matthias' neck. The Nordic man appeared startled, but after a moment, he closed his eyes and swayed slightly, slack with his arousal. Then Liam reached around him, starting to undo the buttons of Matthias' shirt.

Peyton put a hand over her mouth, overwhelmed. She'd never seen Matthias that unguarded. The expression on his face was her undoing —it was filled with longing, lust, and something she could only call love. True, that love had been a bit damaged, but it was still there after all this time.

They shed their clothing with haste, but Liam was faster. His hard, golden body emerged from its confining suit. It was a touch paler since leaving a week ago, but his chest and arms were just as chiseled and defined as ever. Taking a second, he rifled through Matthias' pant pocket, pulling out a miniature bottle. Peyton recognized one of the small bottles of lube from the sex cabinet. Matthias had put in his pocket with a big wink when he'd shown her his cache of pleasure accessories, but she hadn't seen it since. Apparently, Liam knew it would be there, presumably taught by past experience.

Her heart started to thunder in her chest, anticipation and nervousness mingling low in her belly.

Matthias was tugging at his zipper when Liam took over, undoing it with a slow, sensuous movement. Peyton held her breath as Liam pushed Matthias' shorts down, revealing his already erect shaft. Gazing at her over Matthias' shoulder, Liam met her eyes as he slid his hand down Matthias' hard chest and grasped his cock. When Matthias moaned deep in his throat, Liam started to move his palm up and down until the other man bucked his hips, fucking into Liam's large hand.

Holy heavenly fuck. Liam's expression was hot enough to singe her skin. Instead of joining them, though, she stayed fixed in place like a fool. Not that she could have made it to them—her legs were too weak to carry her.

Thankfully, that didn't matter. They came to her. A blink later, Matthias and Liam loomed over her.

Peyton didn't need them to tell her what to do when Liam continued to stroke Matthias' hard shaft in front of her. Breaking free of her stupefaction, she leaned forward, Matthias' familiar musk filling her nose. Putting her hand over Liam's, she paused long enough to press a kiss to Matthias' shaft before opening her mouth to take him inside.

"Shit," Matthias hissed, his hands fisted in her hair. She skipped the preliminaries, swallowing him down as much as she could with Liam's hand sharing her space, before retreating and doing it again.

Liam set the pace. He kept his hand gliding up and down Matthias' thick cock, feeding it to Peyton on every downward stroke. His groans egged her on, pushing her to suck him harder and deeper.

She peered up, wanting to see Matthias reaction, but he pulled away. "Stop," he begged. "I don't want to come yet."

"No, we don't want that..." Liam murmured. Kissing Matthias' neck again, Liam pushed the other man's back so he bent at the waist. Eyes hooded with carnal desire, Liam stroked rough hands over Matthias' ass, then flipped open the top of the lube bottle with one hand.

Peyton watched with parted lips as Liam coated his fingers with the silky liquid, her mind racing—anticipating and rejecting scenes from her most vivid fantasies.

Nothing in those fevered imaginings compared to this reality. When Liam spread Matthias' cheeks and murmured, "Going to get you ready for me, Matthias, but it's going to be quick and dirty," Peyton shivered, her tingling skin a contrast to the molten warmth between her legs.

A broken gasp escaped Matthias' parted lips when Liam slid one lube-covered finger inside the man's ass in one smooth forward movement while keeping his gaze on Peyton. Roughly pistoning it until Matthias rocked his hips, seeking more, Liam withdrew only to sink two fingers back in.

Pupils blown wide, Matthias rode Liam's fingers, incoherently groaning what sounded like *more*. Peyton stared in fascination. Unable to resist, she clamped her hand between her own legs, trying in vain to ease the ache of her arousal. She had never seen anything so beautiful, so virile, and they were all *hers*.

Peyton tugged at Matthias' hands, urging him down on top of her when Liam pulled his fingers free. "Fuck me," she pleaded. That Liam had blown her world to smithereens with a mind-bending orgasm at the railing didn't matter. At this moment, she wanted Matthias inside her so badly she ached.

He obliged, pressing her onto the bench. Kissing the soft skin next to her ear, Matthias cradled her to him before adjusting to work his length inside her satin heat.

Peyton threw her head back, nearly boneless, as he slid home. Liam knelt next to them, then cupped her head with his hand, leaning over for a hot openmouthed kiss as Matthias began to pump inside her.

Matthias wasn't as thick as Liam, but he was a bit longer. Taking him inside her was just as overwhelming, but in an utterly unique way. However, she didn't have time to catalog the differences because Liam moved, climbing onto the bench behind them with an air of sinful determination.

Taking a cue from recent experiences, she grabbed Matthias' arms, holding him still as Liam lubed his cock, put a hand on each of Matthias' ass cheeks, and spread them. Biting into her lip, Peyton watched the play of emotions across Liam's face as he moved closer to guide his shaft to the place he'd unveiled—lust, tenderness, raw need, and dominance. Everything he was feeling was there on his face, the revealing display so precious and private it made her heart swell.

She couldn't see Liam's cock disappear inside Matthias, but she wished she could. Knew she'd demand a chance to witness it and soon. But she *could* feel Matthias' tension, the way his body trembled and jerked when Liam pressed into him until there was no space left between them before sliding back. And then again when Liam thrust his hips, deepening the penetration.

Matthias' lips parted on an exhale, and he opened his eyes. The turbulence and heat reflected in them took her breath away.

Peyton put her hands on either side of his face. "I love you," she said.

She hadn't planned to say those words. Loving Liam was different. That had started so long ago it had become one of her pillars—part of the structure on which she'd built her life. Her attraction to Matthias had been there almost from the start. Until now, she hadn't been aware it had grown, evolving into so much more.

Matthias pressed his forehead against hers. "I love you, too," he whispered.

Bubbling over with happiness and relief, Peyton kissed him, slipping her tongue between his parted lips. She hadn't been sure what he was going to say. She didn't think he'd known either.

When she broke their kiss, Liam started moving, slowly at first, but then faster and faster. Matthias was driven forward, taking the hard thrusts without leaving her body. Each time Liam stroked into him, leaning over his back, Matthias penetrated her deeper, hitting a spot that made her writhe and pant.

Reaching up, she ran her fingers over him and Liam, touching their muscular arms and shoulders, feeling them flex and slide, like steel covered with satin.

"Fuck," Liam groaned. "You're so fucking tight, Matthias." His pumping grew a little rougher, and he swore again.

Peyton clenched her arms around them both, holding tight as Liam retreated, surging forward to drive his entire length inside Matthias. In turn, it made their Norwegian lover plunge so deeply inside her that his tip rubbed the entrance of her womb. Matthias' broken gasp was echoed by Liam's moan—the sound so low and deep it was as if it vibrated down her spine.

High above her, Liam threw his head back, his body wracked by a bone-deep shudder as he obviously reached his release.

"I do love you," Matthias groaned, his cock swelling inside her. Stars exploded in her head when he flexed his hips a few more times, her orgasm detonating like a shockwave that crashed over her just as his climax flooded her with warmth.

When Peyton opened her eyes, Matthias had collapsed on top of her.

Liam rolled off Matthias to lay naked and flushed on the wooden deck next to them. "Isn't somebody going to say they love me?" he asked, perilously close to pouting.

Sluggishly, a spent Matthias reached over to swat him on the head. "You know we love you, too. Don't be greedy."

"Fine." Liam chuckled. His head lolled to stare up at the night sky. "*Damn.* If that's the kind of welcome home I'm going to get, I should leave more often."

"Bite your tongue," Peyton said, hugging Matthias' head to her breasts. "If this is what a Wednesday night looks like with you two, I refuse to let you leave again."

Matthias huffed out a laugh before stretching and adjusting so he wasn't crushing her anymore.

"You know, I take that back. I'm hoping you'll both come to Sydney with me at the end of the month," Liam said.

"Sydney?" Matthias lifted his head, frowning. "Why do you need to go back? I thought you were just there."

Liam grunted. "Yeah, I did a fly-bye after Bangkok, but they're going to need me there longer. Our renovation hit some paperwork snags with the city. A manager misfiled some licenses. I smoothed most of the issues over, but I should be on site when the construction work resumes." He winced. "I'm guessing I'll be stuck there at least three weeks. But before that, I need to visit Paris and Milan for a few days."

He broke off, rising and heading to the table to pour himself a glass of wine, still gloriously naked. "I'm afraid the work in Sydney isn't something Maggie could handle. It's not her area. I would ask Patrick—"

"We know. With the baby coming, Thalia needs him at home." Peyton turned pleading eyes to Matthias. "You know...I've never been to Paris. Or Milan."

Matthias' expression turned wry. He ran his teeth over his lower lip as she watched him. She knew her hope had to be written all over her. Finally, he sighed. "I'm never going to be able to say no to you, am I?"

"Welcome to my world." Liam laughed. Matthias stood as well, his softened member still impressive. His and Liam's comfort at being nude was a revelation, but she couldn't let the awesome sight distract her.

Peyton threw a pillow at Liam. "You said no to me all the time."

"Not as often as I should have," he scoffed.

Incredulous, she raised an eyebrow.

He wagged his finger. "You didn't need a ten-core processor to upgrade the hotel's website. And you definitely didn't need all that extra RAM. Or the server upgrades." He stopped to sip his wine. "Your huge screens were a bit excessive, too, and, coincidentally, you just had to have them before the last *Assassin's Creed* came out."

He elbowed Matthias in the side. "Eventually, everyone realized if they wanted some high-ticket item approved, all they had to do was get Peyton to ask me."

She narrowed her eyes. "You never gave me what I *really* wanted."

Liam raised a brow. "In my defense, you never actually asked."

"He has a point," Matthias said with a snort. Liam gave his ass an appreciative pat, and the two men smirked at her, looking entirely too pleased with themselves.

"Hey, that's not how this works." She laughed. "We gang up on *Liam*. It's not the two of you against me."

"Really? Because I thought you two were just ganging up on me, trying to get me to agree to travel more," Matthias teased.

"Does that mean you will leave the *Ormen Lange?*"

Matthias' sigh was long and drawn out, but Peyton knew he'd thrown in the towel. "I suppose. A few days here and there is one thing, but it sounds like Liam is going to be on the road for the better part of a month. That's too long."

Peyton jumped up, squeezing him tightly.

He hugged her back before heading to the double doors. "Why don't we move this show inside? I think we've entertained the seals and dolphins long enough."

"Why don't you start the shower?" Liam suggested. Matthias, still coming down from the sexual high, obligingly staggered inside.

Liam waited until they were alone. He took her hand, keeping her from following. "Is everything all right?" he asked, the line between his brows deeper than usual.

"Yes," she said, confused about why he asked. "This isn't because I told him I loved him, right?"

"No, of course not. I think that's good—*he's good*. For both of us."

She nodded in agreement, but Liam continued to frown. "I just sensed something when he came in. You seemed nervous... Did you guys get into a fight?"

Damn. Peyton never could hide anything from him. She ducked her head. "Yes. But it was days ago. We made up before you got home."

"What was the fight about?"

"Nothing. Just a misunderstanding. Don't worry about it. We're all good now."

She started to head inside, but Liam hadn't let go. "Are you sure nothing else is wrong?"

Taking a deep breath, she considered about telling him about her conversation with Mason and the materials he was going to send her. It was only a split second of madness. Liam would shut her down faster than Matthias.

Which is why you're not telling either of them. Peyton bit her tongue, tugging away with a smile. "Everything else is fine. Absolutely perfect," she lied.

CHAPTER 33

"You can't hold this against her," Liam pointed out as he whipped off his tux jacket.

He tossed it on an armchair, a contemporary piece so space age Peyton half-expected it to fly.

"If she wasn't so damn beautiful, this wouldn't keep happening." Matthias grunted, throwing himself down on the couch, another modern masterpiece that complemented the stark beauty of the Caislean Paris.

Peyton ignored the exchange between her lovers, deciding to kick off her heels so she could enjoy the plush carpet under her feet as she danced. Skipping around a high-backed ottoman, she began to hum strains of the waltz they'd played earlier at the ball.

Over a month had passed since she and Matthias had started flying to Caislean hotels to accompany Liam while he worked. They had spent two and a half near blissful weeks in Sydney. After that, they tripped through Milan before arriving in Paris a few days ago, much to her delight.

In the brief time they had been here, Peyton had visited Petit Palais, the Musee Dorsay, and spent hours lost in the Pompidou. She was saving the Louvre for the weekend when she could devote an entire day to the museum's extensive art collection.

Aside from one short trip to Barcelona with Maggie after she turned twenty-one, Peyton hadn't traveled much. Money had been a big issue when her father was alive. His alcoholism and gambling had been a constant drain on her finances. She could have traveled for free with Maggie, but it would have been a violation of her self-imposed rules. Peyton hadn't wanted to take advantage of their friendship that way.

This was different, she told her drunken self. Now Peyton got to indulge her curiosity about all the places she'd read and dreamed about visiting while in the company of the two most important men in her life. *Both of whom love me.* She twirled again, this time in celebration.

"Are you seriously complaining that Peyton is too attractive?" Liam poured himself a drink before reaching for a second Waterford tumbler.

Matthias looked as if he'd swallowed a lemon. "I don't know how you can be so fucking calm. That jerk was practically mauling her."

"And she took care of it, didn't she?" Liam laughed. "It was smooth, too. I almost thought he fell on accident. He probably thought he did, too."

"You actually tripped him?" Matthias asked her.

"As a matter of fact, I did," she replied, waving her arms like a dancer in first arabesque. The many glasses of wine she'd drunk made her as graceful as a cloud, although it was more than likely she resembled that hippo in a tutu from the old Disney cartoons.

"I taught her that trick," Liam gloated. "Those heels can be effective weapons when used properly."

"Wrong. Trick taught me that trick," she corrected as she wound a path around the coffee table like a drunken ballerina. "You don't get to take credit for everything I do, you know."

"I wasn't." Liam laughed. "But I will take credit for your right hook.

Pity you didn't get to use that tonight. I would have liked to see that guy flat on his ass after getting decked instead of his face."

"What happened to your Zen attitude?" Matthias smirked.

Liam sat next to him, handing him a very full glass of whiskey. "Oh, make no mistake. I'm not Zen when it comes to Peyton and other men. But I learned early on if I mix it up with her many admirers, I'm inviting a lawsuit. That's why I made sure she could take care of herself. Unless they get too handsy, of course. Then all bets are off. But trust me. This is something you are going to need to get used to."

Matthias grunted. "I may get used to it, but I don't have to like it."

"At least someone understands my pain now," Liam murmured, his eyes growing warm as Peyton hiked up her skirts and jumped over his legs. "Doing all right, honey?"

"I'm good." She was better than good. She was great. Paris with her men was everything she had dreamed of.

Deciding there was enough room between their legs and the coffee table, she attempted to celebrate with an old yoga move. Shifting her weight, she balanced herself on her forearms before resting her head on the ground and raising her legs straight up in the air. Then, she parted them, doing the splits.

"Holy shit," Matthias swore, sitting up abruptly. "Did you know she could do that?"

Liam set his tumbler on the table behind him with a thunk. "If I had, I guarantee she wouldn't have still been a virgin at twenty-four."

Peyton clenched her jaw to keep from giggling. She had some concerns about getting out of the pose, but she needn't have worried. A few seconds later, she was flying through the air, supported by a pair of strong arms. Matthias gently lowered her on Liam's lap, tugging at the zipper of her dress.

She lost track of time after that. One heartbeat blurred into the next as she was undressed. Hands covered her skin, stroking and caressing every inch of her body. Heat and silk surrounded her. Pleasantly lethargic, Peyton gloried in every touch.

Somewhere in the back of her mind, guilt jumped up and down, trying to get her attention. *Pleasure like this should be illegal...* But with the help of the artificial alcohol bravado, she was able to ignore it, relaxing and giving herself over completely to the hands of these two masters.

Liam's mouth covered hers while Matthias' slid up and down her neck and someone's hands removed her panties. She was so wet it would have been embarrassing had she been sober.

Matthias' hands skimmed up her bare thigh, his fingers running over her heated lips before pressing inside her, teasing and stretching her until she gasped aloud, arching her back to deepen the penetration.

Peyton moaned when his fingers were replaced by something much larger. She opened her eyes, wrapping her arms around Liam's neck as his thick shaft forged insider her. With nothing but a few thrusts, she was almost there, panting and crying out as the first pulses of a powerful orgasm began. But he and Matthias had other plans.

Liam pulled her close to him, his grip like iron. Peyton rested her heated forehead against his as Matthias rubbed her ass with his palm. A cool wetness trickled between her cheeks, then there was pressure and pleasure pain as he slipped his finger inside her rear, then added another before widening the space between them.

It burned a little, but it was a good burn. Weeks of wearing a plug —albeit haphazardly—had been enough to make her comfortable with the move. Nevertheless, when she was probed by something else, Peyton had to suck in a hard breath.

"Don't hurt her," Liam said over her head as Matthias pressed his length against her rosette.

"Never," he promised, stopping as the head of his cock widened her. "Should I stop?"

Peyton clutched Liam's shoulder, her lips parting. "*No.*"

He murmured something in what sounded like Norwegian, his hips pressing forward until the flared end breached the tightly constricted ring of muscle, popping inside her with a groan.

"That's it, baby. The worst is over. Are you okay?" Liam asked.

Okay didn't describe it. "Yes, now please just *fuck me*."

"You heard the lady." Liam laughed, but it turned into a hiss as Peyton flexed her muscled, squeezing him tight.

That was all the encouragement they needed. Matthias and Liam began to move, slowly at first but building fast. They established a counterpoint where one was entering her body just as the other was leaving it. She could actually feel their cocks sliding against each other, only a thin barrier of skin separating them.

The sensations were almost too much. The fullness and pleasure were decadent, tinged with darkness, as Matthias pistoned behind her and Liam surged into her, their thrusts building in speed and strength.

All Peyton could do was hold on, moaning as the tight tingle of an orgasm crept ever closer. Breasts swollen, she cried out when Matthias' hands covered them from behind, his finger pinching her nipples.

It was too much. Peyton's rhythm broke. A keening wail escaped her as she gyrated, grinding against Liam's cock as Matthias groaned. Panting, he shuddered and moaned his release.

Her climax followed, storming through her. Nirvana tightened every cell of her body. Nearly blind with pleasure, she sobbed as Matthias withdrew, the stinging pain only another nuance of the kaleidoscope of sensations colliding inside her. Then Liam was alone, bucking and lunging up to thrust into her pussy with ragged, rough strokes. Always a bit louder, he came with a shout, plunging into her one last time while he gripped her hips so tightly he was probably going to leave bruises.

His seed was so hot it almost burned. Unable to hold herself up, she collapsed forward, falling on his chest and fighting to catch her breath.

"*What the hell?*" a new voice said.

Liam jerked, recognizing the intruder. Peyton jerked her head in the direction of the door.

Trick stood there, his face red, hands up as if he were in a stick-up.

His eyes were wide as he took in the bacchanalian scene in front of him.

Even Matthias, who was sitting on the carpet nearly naked, didn't seem to know what to say. Everyone just froze, staring at each other.

Peyton found her voice first. "Oh, *hey*," she mumbled, still too weak to get up.

Trick shook his head as if to banish the vision in front of him, but it didn't appear to work.

He cleared his throat. "Maggie has the flu," he announced, as if that explained his presence.

Matthias stood, zipping up his pants as he went. He whipped off his shirt, throwing it over her as he helped her to her feet.

Liam's face gave nothing away as he pulled his pants up. "Is it serious? Has Tahlia been given a flu shot?"

"Uh...no and yes," Trick said, his mouth twisting. Peyton couldn't tell if he was restraining a scowl or trying not to laugh.

Matthias coughed, taking one of Peyton's hands. "I think we should leave these two alone to talk."

Clutching the halves of his dress shirt together, she smiled awkwardly—more of a grimace, really—as she let him lead her out of the room.

"You're sure Maggie is all right?" Liam was embarrassed, but any health concerns in the family trumped his discomfort. Nevertheless, he checked to see if his fly was done before he waved Trick over to the dining room table.

His brother hesitated, rubbing his eyes as if he were trying to scrub certain memories from his brain. "It's just the flu. She doesn't even have a fever anymore."

"Oh, that's good," he hedged. "Does she need me? Should we fly back together?"

His sister was rarely ill, but when she did fall sick, she went down hard. Normally, Jason, her husband, would be at her side, but his work at the FBI sometimes prevented that.

"No, she's fine. She's resting."

Liam ran rough fingers through his head. "And Tahlia and the baby are okay?"

Trick threw him an incredulous look. "Yes, they're fine…and stop avoiding the fucking elephant in the room. What the hell is going on here?"

Trick covered his eyes. "I think I need to sit down because it feels like I walked in on Maggie and Jason—only ten times worse."

He staggered toward the chair, sitting heavily.

Liam's neck was corded so tight he wouldn't be able to turn his head without hurting himself. "It's very important you remember Peyton is *not* our sister."

Trick threw up his hands. "But…but that's how I think of her. I thought you saw her that way, too."

"No." Liam slowly shook his head. "*Never.* I've wanted her for a long time."

"But *how?*" His brother looked lost, as if the entire foundation of his life had been realigned.

Liam went over to the sideboard, pouring them both a drink. "Here."

Trick accepted the glass, but he set it on the table untouched. "I don't understand how this happened."

Shit. This was harder than he had imagined it would be. Talking about his feelings wasn't something Liam did, not even with his brother.

With one recent exception. "I told Peyton I loved her."

Trick's eyes widened. "So did I…when she left. But I guess you and I don't mean the same kind of love."

"Fuck, I hope not." Liam snorted. "Especially since you're happily married."

Rising, he pushed the glass of whiskey at his brother with a meaningful glance. Sighing, Trick picked it up and took a large sip.

Liam sat back down. "I do *love* Peyton. I love her so much it hurts. And I mean the way a man loves a woman. I know that doesn't make sense, but I was in denial about it for a long time. You don't know how close I came to fucking it all up. But there were complications..."

Trick whistled. "Damn, your gift for understatement is surreal. I take it you are referring to Matthias Raske?"

"Yes. He's a part of this...like one-third of it."

Trick inhaled, scrubbing his face. "And you and he are *both* sleeping with Peyton? I wasn't having some sort of twisted Freudian hallucination?"

Liam swallowed. "We are," he said, barely managing the words over the weird lump that had taken residence in his throat.

There was more he wanted to say, but explaining it properly felt utterly impossible.

"But, Liam, how can you do that? You *hate* sharing. When we were kids, you used to break your toys rather than let me use them."

Liam closed his eyes, laughing as he remembered what a little shit he'd been before his parents had passed. *That's not you anymore.* Well, it was, but there was way more to him now. At least, he hoped there was.

"I don't just share her. She shares me. And we share Matthias."

"Huh?" Trick stared without comprehension.

Liam put his hands under the table, clenching and unclenching his fists several times. "I'm bisexual," he said shortly. "I was involved with Matthias a few years ago. Right after we met, then for several months after."

"Oh." That was all he got. Trick lapsed into silence, apparently at a loss for words.

"But I'm not gay, no matter what Calen says," he said.

"Calen knows about this?" His brother's expression grew irritated. "You told him about Matthias, but you didn't tell me?"

Liam put up a hand. "Actually, he was around when Matthias and I met. Caroline introduced me to him a couple of years ago at the launch of one of Calen's European clubs. Long story short—Calen is too fucking observant. He put two and two together when I started spending all my free time with Matthias. Things were intense between us. But we ended our relationship after a few months…"

He stopped, rubbing the back of his neck. He didn't like recalling the last fight that had ended their affair. Both Liam and Matthias were cutthroat in arguments. They had said things that were hard to forgive. Or so he had thought at the time. But now he knew them for the excuses they were. His resolve to walk away had been based on his insecurities about being with a man.

"After it was over, there didn't seem to be any point in mentioning it to anyone else," he said after a minute. "I thought being with a man was a one-off. I'd never been attracted to any others—not in any way I'd recognize. Calen didn't think it was an isolated incident, though. He kept pushing me to come out of the closet."

"Except you are in love with Peyton," Trick supplied. "You *are* in love with her, right? I don't have to kick your ass for getting her involved in this, do I?"

"No, you don't," he said repressively. "My feelings for her *are* real. Although I didn't call it love back then. But I was in some hardcore denial. My focus was on our business and building an empire. Then I stumbled into something with Matthias, and it was surprisingly great…until it wasn't. For a long time afterward, I thought there was something wrong with me. I felt wrong. Dirty. Definitely not clean enough for Peyton."

"Wow," Trick croaked. "So when she ran off with Matthias, that must have been hell."

"I deserved it," Liam conceded. "I did everything wrong. I cut Matthias off, or at least I bottlenecked our communication to almost nothing. And I ignored my feelings for Peyton until I drove her away. I almost married a woman I didn't love for fuck's sake. I'm just lucky that when Peyton ran, she ran to Matthias—and that he was willing to give me a second chance to make things right."

"Wow."

Liam needed another syllable. "You said that already. What do you think?"

He held his breath, waiting.

Trick winced. "Are you sure Peyton is doing this multi-partner thing because she wants to or because she wants to be with you?" He leaned forward, his eyes intense. "Could she be indulging you? What if she's giving you what she thinks you want so she can be with you?"

Liam sighed, but he couldn't fault his brother's overprotectiveness. Patrick *did* see Peyton as a sister.

"I considered that, but I think if I weren't in the picture, she'd still be with Matthias. He has his foibles, but he's a good man. In many ways, he's a better one than me. It may have torn my insides to shreds when I wasn't here in the beginning, but he's the only man I can think of who might deserve her."

"Except for you," Trick argued loyally.

Liam huffed. "Oh, I don't deserve her. I have no illusions about that. But I won't give her up. And I can't give him up either. Matthias is a part of our relationship. I know that may be difficult to hear. I'm not asking for your approval—"

"My what?" Trick scowled. "Why are you worried about that?"

Liam considered him, taking in all the changes he'd noticed. Trick had the Tyler looks and charm, but his easygoing nature was a cover. Inside, he was a man of deeply held convictions and drive.

"I know polyamory isn't mainstream, no matter what the TV shows portray. My relationship would never be sanctioned by the Church, and that's something that's important to you right now."

"Wait, hold up." Trick got up, moving down the table before taking a seat next to him. "Is that why you didn't tell me about Matthias? Or about your three-way with him and Peyton?"

"Well..."

"*Damn it,* Liam. I go to church because I had the crap scared out of me when Tahlia was in trouble. It hasn't changed my view on the world or how I feel about you."

This was old territory. His brother had been exposed to a hefty dose of opium and God knew what else during an unfortunate episode with Tahlia. He'd had a vision—one he couldn't explain at the time. But Liam could.

"You were hallucinating, but that's beside the point. You didn't know all this about me. I didn't know how you were going to react."

Liam hesitated. "You don't think me being with a man shows...weakness?"

Trick frowned as if he didn't understand.

"There are some in our business who would think that," Liam pointed out. "They might not want to do business with us if they knew. It's not exactly conventional."

His brother made a *pft* sound. "Those people can go fuck themselves. We've built our business doing things our way, and we've done a damn fine job so far. That's not going to change because you finally found someone—or someones—you care about."

Suddenly, Trick leaned forward. "But you do have a problem. A big one."

Liam's heart sank. "What is it?"

"You're the one who has to tell Maggie you're sleeping with her best friend. And that there's another man in the mix."

Liam coughed, choking on a guffaw. "You know, I think I'm going to let Peyton handle that."

Trick tsked, shaking his head pityingly. "Coward."

"Guilty as charged." Liam laughed, standing and clapping his brother on the back. "Let me check if Matthias and Peyton are dressed. I want you to have dinner with us."

"Sounds good to me."

Smiling, Liam left the room with a spring in his step. He felt lighter and more relaxed than he'd been in a long, *long* time.

CHAPTER 34

*P*eyton forced a smile at the lecherous creep trying to see down the front of her dress. Fortunately for Iver Kuznetsov, he was too short to get a particularly good look, although she was almost sorry about that. If only he would make his lewdness a little more obvious, she would feel justified in decking the man.

Except he's your host and that would ruin Matthias' oil deal.

They were in the short pervert's penthouse in London. It was one of the creep's many properties, or so he claimed in a misguided attempt to impress her. However, neither that nor his extensive collection of nude Renaissance paintings made a dent in her estimation of him. The man had all the appeal of a yeast infection.

I wish Liam were here. Lover number two had taken the Caislean jet for a quick trip to Miami, but he was due back early tomorrow. Of course, that meant she had to handle this crowd on her own. Matthias was being monopolized by a cluster of Middle Eastern oil tycoons.

There had been a muffled gasp when he entered the room. Apparently, lover number one rarely did business in person. The excitement when they spotted him had been palpable. And like a good partner, Peyton had mixed and mingled, taking part in the conversation until it became obvious she needed to make herself scarce so a deal could be finalized.

Regrettably, their host had someone to negotiate on his behalf, which meant he could trail her through his abominably decorated apartment.

Iver was a class-A turd. Peyton shuddered as he put his sweaty hand on her arm to guide her over to a slightly obscene Roman mosaic hanging behind glass.

Peyton's smile grew brittle as she avoided looking directly at the out-of-proportion phallus proudly jutting from the man in the mosaic.

"It is genuine, I *assure* you," Iver said, stressing his favorite word with a hiss.

She nudged his hand away, wiping away the spittle that landed on her cheek.

"I'm sure it is," she said, desperately seeking an escape. It came in the form of a waiter holding a tray of canapés.

"Would you excuse me? I am starving, and I'd like to get a bite to eat."

"Allow me to accompany you," he said, his unctuous smile nausea-inducing. "I can select the choicest morsels for you."

Peyton pictured him trying to feed her, then suppressed a shudder.

"Bathroom," she blurted, clutching her stomach. "Excuse me, I need to find it. *Now.*"

She turned on her heel, not bothering to ask him where it was. *The longer it takes to find, the better.*

Wandering about the room, she weaved and dodged around guests until she was sure she wasn't being followed. She stopped short in front of another sexually charged painting—a graphic modern piece that bordered on obscene. Grimacing, she decided to find the restroom for real. Anything to escape the decor.

At least the bathroom will be free of naked people.

She was wrong. The bathroom had an antechamber with a long settee in front of a lighted vanity mirror with an ornately painted fresco overhead. But at least the cherubs depicted on it were prepubescent. Or was that worse?

Shaking her head, Peyton washed her hands and left, falling on Matthias' neck with melodramatic relief when she found him waiting outside.

His muscular arms wrapped around her in a tight embrace. "I'm checking in. I know this party can't be fun for you."

He wasn't kidding, but she didn't want to discourage him from bringing her with him to business events. With his and Liam's busy schedules, she wanted to make sure he didn't try to exclude her in an effort to spare her. But she had to be honest about the art.

"You know, I never thought of myself as a prude, but the paintings and photos in this place are *gross*."

He smiled sympathetically. "I know, and I apologize. If you like, I can have Aksel drive you back to the Caislean."

"No, no. I'm fine," she said. "Unless you are done here, in which case, let's get the hell out of Dodge."

Matthias leaned down, pressing his forehead against her. "Believe me, I'd love to leave Dodge far behind, but I'm afraid I'm not quite finished. Regrettably, this deal is intricate and requires some face-to-face negotiation."

"You poor thing. I know you'd rather deal with stuff from the comfort of your mega-yacht," she teased, softening her tongue-in-cheek response with a hand on his stubble. "And don't worry about me. I'm f-fine."

Peyton jerked and stumbled, her eyes fixed on the blonde walking past them with her eyes down. It was a girl wearing a low-cut yellow gown, one with a familiar face.

"Are you sure about that?" Matthias pressed close, his arms around her waist the only thing keeping her upright. "Do you feel lightheaded?'

Blushing, Peyton straightened. "I'm fine," she lied. "There's no need for concern, although you had a good idea. I may leave a bit early to soak in the tub for a while."

Matthias' laugh was deep and low. "Is the art bad enough you feel the need to bathe? Because if so, I get it. I feel dirty, too...and not in a good way."

His carefree grin was usually enough to make her drag him off to the nearest closet, but she couldn't think straight.

Peyton's heart was pounding, but she couldn't say anything. *I could be wrong.* She might not know that girl. But she could be right, too.

"Are you certain everything is all right?"

She blinked, snapping out of her distraction. Matthias studied her, concern dampening his expression.

"I'm fine," she said, her voice a touch too high. Peyton patted him on the shoulder. "Go back and finish your business. With any luck, we can both be in the tub by midnight."

With that as a lure, Matthias nodded and left, accepting her upbeat attitude a little too readily. *He doesn't know you as well as Liam.* Not yet.

Peyton's hands shook. She hurried in the direction of the girl in the yellow dress—the one who bore a remarkable resemblance to the one she'd seen in the trafficker's dungeon.

FOR THE FIRST time in her life, Peyton was outright rude to a host.

When Iver offered to show her the private pieces he kept in his bedroom, she 'accidentally' crushed his toes with her stiletto. She topped the move by tripping and falling against him, soaking him with her full glass of champagne.

"Oh, no! I'm so sorry," she cried, waving over a waiter and asking him for a napkin. "These stupid shoes are too high."

"Eh, well, accidents happen," Iver sneered, dropping the unctuous tone and showing his irritation. He took a step and winced.

A flash of guilt assailed her. Peyton helped him to a chair. "I think we need some ice, too," she suggested when the waiter returned. A few other guests clustered around them. Taking advantage of the bustle, she snuck away, resuming her scan of the guests.

Why are there so many people here? Shouldn't big oil deals be brokered in the privacy of boardrooms? Muttering under her breath, Peyton pressed her clutch to her stomach in a vain effort to stop the butterflies wreaking havoc there.

The salon was a bust. Ditto for the kitchen, which, unlike her friends' parties, was devoid of guests. The only people in there were a small group of harried catering staff who didn't appreciate the interruption.

The living room was full of milling guests, but no girl in yellow. Peyton was starting to think she had imagined the young woman until she spotted her on the arm of a short and thin man almost three times her age. Possibly four.

Please be her father. Skirting the crowd, Peyton circled the small group by the fireplace. She pretended to examine the volumes on the shelf next to the door so she could cast covert glances at the pair.

She couldn't decide if it was the line of her jaw or the expression of absolute misery on her face, but Peyton was almost certain she was right about the girl's identity. She became convinced of it when the sweaty man in the suit shifted to cup the girl's ass.

The poor thing's lips tightened with embarrassment and shame. The girl lasted a few more minutes before murmuring something to the man and excusing herself. Peyton straightened, dodging a man who appeared to be about to ask her a question. She hurried through the foyer, following her quarry down to the bathroom.

By the time Peyton was inside, the girl had locked herself in the stall in the back. Her stifled sobs broke Peyton's heart.

She tapped on the door. "Hello? Can I come in?"

"I'm fine," the girl said in a shaky voice.

But I'm not sure I am.

"Um, I think we know each other, and I'd like to help you." Peyton lowered her voice to a whisper. "Is it you?"

The door opened slowly. The girl's mascara had run all over her cheeks. "Is it me who?"

Peyton took a deep breath, fishing a tissue out of her purse. "Do you recognize me?"

The girl shook her head.

"Not from the—" Peyton hesitated. If she were wrong, she was exposing herself, but her gut told her this was the girl and she was in trouble.

"From...from the prison," Peyton finished in a rush.

The girl's eyes widened. "You're a criminal?"

"No, I meant when we were held captive," Peyton said, the realization she had been mistaken setting in. "You don't know what I'm talking about, do you?"

This wasn't the teenager from the sex-trafficker's dungeon.

"No," the girl said in a low voice. "I'm sorry you were kidnapped. But I don't know you. We've never met."

Peyton wanted to sink through the floor. "Yeah, I realize that now. It's just that your face was so familiar. I apologize for freaking you out."

"You didn't. I'm sorry for what happened to you." She stopped, then swore in an unfamiliar language. "I thought I had it bad, but it is nothing compared to your situation."

Peyton waved dismissively. "I'm fine now. Better than I have any right to be, but I mistook you for someone else partly because of how sad you look. Err...is that man you were with your boyfriend?"

The girl shrugged. "I don't think I can call Omer that. But I do have sex with him."

"Oh." Peyton shifted awkwardly, wondering what she should say, but, apparently, the dam had broken.

"He has many other girls, or at least he used to," the girl continued. "My mother was one of them, but she left a few months ago. He gave her a lot of money to leave me behind."

Fuck. "I'm so sorry."

The girl shrugged, drying her tears. "It could be worse. One of my mother's other boyfriends liked sharing her. At least Omer doesn't make me do that."

Peyton swore aloud. "Honey, how old are you?"

"Eighteen. Well, almost. My birthday is in two weeks."

Peyton swallowed hard, forcing her hands to her sides. She wanted to march into that living room and beat the shit out of sweaty little Omer. *Or better yet, I can drive my stiletto into his eye socket.*

Except public and bloody murder would only get her arrested, and this girl would still be in trouble.

Peyton put her arm around her. "What is your name?"

"Anisa."

"Okay, Anisa. I'm Peyton. It's nice to meet you." She waited for the girl's nod of acknowledgment before continuing. "Can I ask you something? Is your mother coming back for you?"

It took Anisa a long time to answer. "I think not. Now that I'm an adult, I don't think she will return. She's been on her own since she was thirteen, and she always said I was spoiled because she stayed so much longer than that."

"And do you want to stay with Omer?" Peyton asked, finally getting to the point.

Anisa hesitated. "I do. He's not so bad."

"Is it because he treats you well or because you have nowhere else to go?"

The girl stayed silent.

Peyton took both Anisa's hands in her own. "If you're afraid to leave him because you have no resources, I can help you."

She hadn't ever used the allowance Matthias had provided her, but she could now. There was more than enough to help fund this girl's escape.

"It's more complicated than that," Anisa confessed. "He has my papers—my passport. Also, he would be angry if I left. He paid a lot of money for me, and he doesn't like to be cheated."

Son of a bitch. Peyton thought quickly. "I think I can fix that, too. I know a woman with experience giving people like you a whole new life. If I'm right, that means a new identity and new documents. I can also float you some cash to get you started."

Priya would do this for Peyton. She was sure of it. Anisa needed help. Matthias, on the other hand, might not be so sanguine. He didn't want anything to do with rescues anymore.

"I—I'm not sure," Anisa said in a low voice. "I don't know how to do anything. A loan is not an income, and I have no skills. I never finished school."

Peyton cocked her head, considering. "You know, without that makeup, you would look years younger. I bet we can get you into high school just by shaving a few years off your passport."

"You can do that?" A look of dawning hope began to light Anisa's eyes.

Please God don't let me be making promises I can't keep. No. This was on her. She had to make this happen.

"I think so," Peyton promised. "Can you get away from Omer whenever you want?"

Anisa nodded. "He knows I can't leave the country. He thinks I'm too afraid, but he lets me go shopping on my own."

"Good," Peyton said, taking out a pen and a receipt. She wrote her phone number on the back, then typed Anisa's into hers.

"I'm going to leave now to get started, but as soon as I can, I'm going to text you to set up a meeting. I will have everything you need to leave. And don't bring anything unless it's small and fits in your purse. No favorite clothes or books. If you're serious about leaving Omer, you can buy anything you need after."

Anisa swallowed, her eyes tearing up. "Thank you."

Peyton wanted to add a million caveats. She had no idea if she could deliver, but when Anisa took her hand, all the warnings died on her tongue.

She *had* to do this—even if it meant blowing up her relationship with Matthias.

CHAPTER 35

Convincing Priya to help her only took an hour. Convincing her that she could get Matthias on board proved to be an abject failure.

"Peyton, I believe we should keep this between us for now," Priya advised. "After what you told me, I suspect he is traumatized by what happened at Belarus. I know the mistake was not on our end, but I don't think he can bring himself to accept that."

Peyton sighed, glad Matthias was still at that heinous party. "I know, but I don't like keeping this a secret from him."

"Whether or not you want to disclose it is your decision, but perhaps you should wait for Mr. Tyler's return to do so?"

"Do you think I need a buffer? Because once Matthias gets over the shock, he will understand why I couldn't look the other way."

"Yes, of course. But Mr. Tyler could provide…insurance."

Peyton couldn't help but laugh. "All that muscle does make an effective shield."

Except what Priya didn't know was Liam wasn't getting here any time soon. He'd called her while she was in the car to let her know he'd been unavoidably delayed in New York. He was terribly sorry and more than a little irritated, but he promised to make it up to her and Matthias with something special.

She wanted to be excited about whatever he had planned—he'd sounded both nervous and gleeful, which was atypical for him, but Peyton couldn't help but worry about the task at hand.

Maybe she should keep it a secret. Once the new papers arrived, Peyton could deliver them to Anisa with a cashier's check.

They talked more, formulating plans.

"Don't worry about making travel arrangements for Anisa," Priya said eventually, more than a hint of enthusiasm in her tone. "The less you know, the better."

Peyton hung up shortly after, relieved the ball was in someone else's court for the moment. *I just hope I'm not getting Priya in trouble.*

That was the least of Peyton's worries. She could protect Priya. If Matthias found out, Peyton would do whatever she had to, including falling on her metaphorical sword, to save her friend's job.

No. Matthias would know who to blame. *Stop thinking about it*, she ordered herself.

She had her own plans to make, and one of the things on her agenda was reviewing the case file and other documents Mason had just sent.

THREE DAYS LATER, Peyton met Anisa at a crowded shopping center. Or at least, she was supposed to. Anisa was over an hour late.

Peyton sipped a smoothie, half-wishing she hadn't ordered one. Drinking anything had been a huge mistake. She had been twisted in knots ever since the fake passport had come in the mail.

Anisa's not coming. I should have known...

Peyton had hashed and rehashed her plan a million times, but her biggest concern was that the girl would back out. Anisa was young and scared, but staying with Omer, as repugnant as he was, might be less frightening to her than striking out on her own.

Or Omer had discovered his almost-legal girlfriend was leaving him, and he'd done something terrible to her. *Don't borrow trouble.*

Peyton took a deep breath, trying to calm down. She craned her neck, scanning the crowd, but there was no sign of Anisa. She took another ill-advised sip of the smoothie, cursing her upset stomach.

It's not just that. Your breasts are sore.

She pressed her hands hard against her thighs. That didn't mean anything. Both Matthias and Liam paid a great deal of attention to that area. No doubt that was why her breasts ached. She wasn't pregnant.

Pushing her misgiving to the back of her mind, she debated whether she should leave. Deciding to risk another text to Anisa, she reached for her phone.

A big hand settled heavily on her shoulder. She opened her mouth to scream, but she choked it – down when she recognized the man looming over her.

"*Peyton.*" Matthias flushed, his eyes narrowed on her face.

"Hi!" she squeaked. Jumping out of her chair, she gave him a tentative hug while giving her purse a good kick. Unfortunately, it didn't make it under the table, catching on the heel of her boots instead.

Matthias bent, frowning as he snatched the bag up. "Why did you sneak out of the hotel?"

"Uh…"

He straightened, his back ramrod straight. "I know you're hiding something. You've been behaving strangely for days. Did you think I hadn't noticed?"

Peyton briefly considered bluffing, but one look into his troubled and bloodshot eyes and she didn't even try. Hanging her head, she sat in the uncomfortable cafe chair. "I'm sorry. I know I've been acting strangely."

She had been so worried he would notice her anxiety and preoccupation she'd been actively avoiding him, even going so far as to spend the night in one of the suite's other bedrooms. Her excuse had been weak—she'd told him she had a headache.

The hurt on Matthias' face was like a dagger to her heart.

"What is going on?" he asked. "I don't understand what all this cloak-and-dagger secrecy is for. Have you been recruited to the CIA?"

He glanced down at her purse. "And what is in here that you don't want me to see?"

Peyton gripped her hands together. "It's a package. Some documents."

Matthias let loose a short bark of laughter. "So, I was right? You are a spy now?"

His accent had thickened so much she could barely understand him.

"No. The papers are from Priya," she said. The need to confess all was overwhelming, but Anisa had appeared at the end of the food court.

The girl was walking fast, turning her head every which way as if she were both looking for Peyton and checking to see if she'd been followed.

"Oh, *crap.*" She grabbed Matthias arm. "You have every right to be suspicious because I did keep a secret, but you must trust me now. I need you to leave."

Matthias' lips parted in protest, but she tightened her hold. *"Please.* I think she'll leave if she sees you, and she needs help."

Desperate, she gave him a little push. He went, but not far.

Shooting her a supercilious glare, Matthias straightened his jacket with a snap. He walked to the left a few feet, then settled at the table next to her with a defiant air.

Trying not to cringe, Peyton forced her features to smooth. The last thing she wanted was for Anisa to see her mid-panic.

The girl finally spotted her. She hurried over, then sat in the chair Matthias just vacated. "Thank God you are still here," she said, out of breath, her English more stilted than usual. "I'm so sorry I'm late. Omer's afternoon meeting was canceled, and he wanted to, um, you know..."

"Yeah, I know," Peyton said, gritting her teeth.

"I had to wait until he fell asleep." Anisa's face was tight, but there was a resolution there Peyton hadn't seen the first time they met. "Was your friend able to get me a new passport?"

Peyton nodded, hyperaware Matthias sat just behind her. Her hands shook as she took the thick envelope out of her purse.

"Thank you for sending that picture so quickly. It was perfectly lit for the ID. There's also a birth certificate with the same name and a social security card. The typewritten sheets include a plausible back-story you can tell people if you can't make up one on your own. We also wrote up a list of schools with flexible admissions policies if you decide to finish high school. You'll have to work on softening your accent, but you can always say you spent your childhood abroad."

Leaning over, she pressed the envelope into Anisa's hand. "I've also included a cashier's check. It will be honored at any major bank. There's more than enough to pay your tuition for a few years plus living expenses. Are you ready?"

Anisa's head bobbed up and down. She gave the contents of the envelope only a cursory glance before clutching it to her chest. *"Yes."*

"Good. There's an Uber waiting at the south entrance by the cart with the sunglasses. It will take you to the Chunnel. You'll fly to the States out of Paris, not the UK."

A tear ran down Anisa's cheek. "I don't know how to thank you."

Peyton had all but forgotten Matthias' presence. "You do that by getting away from that creep and having a nice life, one where you get to choose who you are with," she said fiercely.

The girl's chin quivered, but she didn't cry. Anisa launched herself out of her chair, throwing her arms around Peyton. Then she straightened abruptly, wiping her eyes with the heels of her hands.

The gesture, so distinctive of youth, brought tears to her own eyes, but Peyton fought them. They wouldn't help Anisa. Murmuring words of encouragement, she hugged her goodbye.

Anisa hesitated. "I think I was careful, but if Omer finds out you helped me, he will do something bad. He has a temper—a bad one."

"I'll be careful," she promised, aware Matthias had twisted in his seat. She couldn't see him, but she could feel his eyes boring a hole in the back of her head.

She waited until Anisa had disappeared before slowly turning to face him. Or rather face his shoes. Peyton was having trouble looking Matthias in the eye.

When she did, she wished she hadn't. He stood with his hands on his hips, his expression so dark it made her want to run and hide.

"Please don't look at me like that."

A muscle in his cheek twitched.

"Matthias, I'm sorry I didn't tell you—"

"Was that one of Priya's new-life packets?" he interrupted.

"It was, but I made her help me." Peyton shifted her weight from foot to foot, almost dancing in her anxiety. "Please don't fire her."

Silence.

Oh, this was bad. She'd screwed up so badly. "Matthias, please talk to me."

He held up a hand. The commanding gesture was so imperious and cold she quailed despite herself. It certainly drove home the fact Matthias headed a centuries-old empire.

This must be what his Viking ancestors looked like before they sacked a city.

When he spoke, his voice was hoarse. "*Stop.* Just stop."

This was excruciating. "I have to explain."

"Not now, Peyton," Matthias said, averting his give and shaking his head a little. "I have to go."

"But—"

He looked at her, his brown eyes glacial. "I can't talk to you right now."

Stupefied, she stood there rooted to the spot as he turned on his heel and stalked away.

CHAPTER 36

$\mathcal{L}$iam could hear the argument all the way down the hall. He frowned, closing the jeweler's box he'd taken out to admire.

He slipped it into his pocket as Matthias burst into the hotel suite. Peyton trailed behind him, almost chasing him.

"I can't believe you're giving me the silent treatment," she was saying, her voice pleading. "Just yell at me if you have to. I know you want to."

Matthias ignored her.

Liam could tell by the look on his face that it was bad. He had only ever seen that expression once before—after Matthias had heard about the deaths in the ill-fated trafficker's raid.

Liam had already broken things off when the Belarus massacre had happened, but he'd flown out to the *Ormen Lange* when Priya called. They may not have been lovers then, but his friend had needed him.

Matthias had been pretty broken up at first, but he seemed to recover quickly. *And then he'd asked me to leave.* Back then, Liam had taken it as a confirmation their relationship had run its course.

He didn't think that now.

Liam was about to say something to alert the pair to his presence when Peyton forcibly stopped Matthias, grabbing his arm. "I had to help her."

Matthias closed his eyes before gently pushing her away. "I said not now."

Tears began to stream down Peyton's cheeks. "Liam would never walk away from a fight."

"I am not *Liam*," Matthias yelled.

"No, I *am*," he said, breaking his stunned silence. "What the hell is happening?"

Matthias and Peyton turned to him. The tears streaming down her cheeks gutted him—they always had. He walked over, attempting to put his arm around her, but she shied away.

"I don't deserve to be comforted. He should be mad. I lied to him. By omission, but I still lied."

The whole story came spilling out in fits and starts, but Liam soon understood exactly what had happened. To his relief, Matthias stayed for the entire explanation as well, but his determined silence was not a good sign.

Suppressing a groan, Liam sat on the couch, rubbing his temples in an attempt to ward off the headache starting to build in the front of his skull.

Peyton perched at the edge of the armchair. She stared at her hands, completely downcast. Matthias held up the wall opposite her. Liam sat in between, instinct telling him to appear as neutral as possible even though he wanted to crush them both in his arms until they started looking at each other—and him.

"I understand that Peyton was wrong not to tell you, but I also understand her trepidation in delaying the truth given your history with this sort of thing."

"Are you seriously trying the role of peacemaker?" Matthias asked with a sniff.

"It feels weird for me, too," Liam grudgingly admitted.

Liam was usually the one who needed a mediator. Maggie or his brother usually took turns cleaning up after him. When he fought, it tended to get messy. There had even been one time when a competitor lunged at him across a conference room table after he'd destroyed him in a negotiation.

Something told him this was going to be so much worse than that. Where the hell did he start?

"Matthias, I know you're upset, but I also know Peyton. There's no way in the world she would have turned her back on someone who asked for help."

Peyton cleared her throat, her hands twisting her skirt into knots. "Technically, I offered and she accepted."

Liam's smile grew tight. He surreptitiously made a slashing movement across his neck, one that Matthias caught.

The other man rolled his eyes. "I understand that. What I don't understand is why she didn't tell us."

Peyton was going to tear a hole in her skirt. "I was worried you would stop me," she said. "Time was of the essence."

Matthias threw up his hands. "You still should have said something. You heard the girl—her boyfriend is dangerous. He could have had her followed, then your part in this mess would have been exposed. You might have been seriously harmed."

"It was not a mess," she argued. "My plan worked. Anisa got away! And that man was her *molester*, not her boyfriend. She was a child—I don't care if she was almost eighteen. She is not even legal, and her mother sold her to that pervert. Can you honestly tell me you wouldn't have done the same thing?"

"Of course I would have—but I wouldn't have done the drop and evacuation in person," Matthias snapped back. "I would have sent trained personnel to do it. The pervert would have never even known I was involved. And if you'd only told me what you had planned, he wouldn't know you were!"

Liam passed a hand over his face. "To be fair, we have no idea if this Omer knows anything. And now that Peyton has come clean, we can take steps to protect her."

"I was going to tell you. Despite my precautions, I knew there was still a risk. I don't know much about Omer or his resources—I didn't find much, but Priya is still looking."

"Priya knows?" Liam asked.

"Yes, and please don't fire her," she said, peeking at Matthias from under her lashes.

"Priya did not compromise her security. Her job is not in jeopardy."

Despite Matthias' clipped tone, Peyton visibly relaxed. "Thank you. I know you wouldn't have wanted me to do this—"

"I never said that," Matthias interrupted. "But you should have read me in from the start. That way, we could have planned and made it safe for you."

She frowned. "You mean cut me out of it entirely."

Matthias was close to sneering. "Isn't this the part where you tell me Liam would have never turned his back on a woman in distress?"

"I would never say that," she shouted. "After all you've done to help people, how can you even think that?"

This was getting out of hand. "And we have to turn our back on people in trouble all the time," he said with a sigh.

Peyton flinched, a question in her eyes as she studied him. Even Matthias looked confused.

Liam let himself fall back against the cushions. "Stuff happens behind closed doors. And when you're in the hotel business, that's hundreds of doors."

"Liam, you help women every day. The gold star rooms—" she began, referring to the program they had set up to help women on the run from abusive partners.

"Those do help," he acknowledged. "But those are clear-cut cases. You, of all people, understand we run into a lot of situations that aren't clear. People are good at hiding things they don't want others to see."

He addressed Matthias next, who was still leaning against the wall. "You don't know how frustrating it is, knowing in your gut that someone is in trouble, but you can't do anything about it because there is nothing—no sign or evidence that anything is wrong."

Liam broke off to get up and pour himself a drink. He tossed half back before resuming. "I get the impulse to leap into the fray. It's an admirable trait—one you share. It's one of the reasons I love the two of you. This won't be the last time something like this comes up. But in the future, we can do it together. We just have to agree on how to go about it from now on."

"That's what I want," Peyton whispered, her heart in her eyes as she silently pleaded with Matthias.

"Agreed," he said, still terse, but Liam could tell he had softened.

Thank God. "Good. Do you think we can get past this now?"

"No."

Liam shifted to Peyton, his breath catching as he recognized the signs of another bomb about to drop.

"No, we can't," she continued, her face creased. "Because there's more."

This time, Liam did groan.

"What is it?" Matthias' voice was flat, devoid of any trace of emotion.

She flattened her hands, straightening her skirt out. "I have the Interpol file on the Belarus disaster."

"Since when?" Matthias was aghast.

"How did you get it?" Liam demanded, even though he was fairly sure he knew.

Peyton took a fortifying breath. "I asked Ethan Thomas to put me in touch with his friend Mason. Mason has been at Interpol for a while, but he didn't know the details of what happened. Needless to say, he was upset when he investigated it and decided to look into it further. He—he also sent some confidential internal communiques."

"*Why?*" he and Matthias said at the same time.

"I think he wanted a second opinion from a hacker."

"You're not a hacker," Liam objected.

"Not in the traditional sense, but I've spent enough time in backchannels of the dark web to recognize what he wanted me to find."

"I can't believe this." Matthias scrubbed his face hard with both hands.

She stood. "I know you blame yourself for what happened in Belarus. But it wasn't you or your staff."

"Peyton—"

Shaking her head, she put up her hands. "Matthias, I have read the case file and Priya's records over and over again. You shut it all down because, deep down, you believed someone on your staff leaked the information and sold the operation out to those traffickers, but you were wrong."

That was something Liam had suspected, but given Matthias' refusal to discuss the subject, Liam had never articulated it.

Peyton moved to stand in front of Matthias. "It wasn't your fault."

The cords in Matthias' neck were far too prominent. "That is very easy to say, but—"

"No, I mean it. Neither you nor your staff was responsible for those deaths. But there was a leak. Matthias, you need to hear this—those girls were already dead when the agents got there."

Matthias shuffled back a step, blinking. Liam could feel his shock. He fucking shared it.

"How do you know that?" he asked when Matthias seemed at a loss for words.

"Because the girls you were trying to save died *before* you received the message giving you the auction's location. So your message to Interpol disclosing that couldn't have been intercepted by a mole in your staff. The liver temperatures established a more precise timeline, but they were doctored after the fact. Someone had tipped them off hours before you or anyone who works for you knew where they were."

"How do you know that?" Matthias asked.

"Mason. He found the circumstances suspicious. To him, the layout of the bodies had a staged quality. And after talking to him, I understood why." She broke off, rubbing her arm as if she was cold. "They were exceedingly difficult to look at, but once I forced myself to, I could see it. The bodies did appear posed. But the time of death was determined by those temperature readings. Mason discovered they had been changed by comparing the ones in the file and the handwritten notes by the forensic personnel who took them. The communiques he had me look at prove someone warned the slavers about the raid. Someone in *his* office."

"The mole is in Interpol?" Matthias staggered to the couch, collapsing next to Liam. "All this time, I thought I missed something— that is was one of my people who leaked the information."

Liam finally caught on, feeling like an idiot. He rubbed Matthias' back. "And to be safe, you shut down your whole operation."

"For a brief time, Priya shared your opinion," Peyton continued. "But her personal investigation didn't turn anything up. And she questioned *everything* your group did a thousand times. Probably more."

Matthias stared at his hands. "I realized she was double and triple checking everything, but, for some reason, I couldn't absolve myself of the responsibility."

"At least you had a therapist come in for the staff," Liam pointed out. "You did support them."

"Only to deal with the trauma right after the fact, but just because I wanted to bury everything doesn't mean Priya or the others did." He inhaled audibly. "I didn't do right by them."

Liam put his arm around him. "That's debatable. I think you did the best you could under crap circumstances."

Matthias was quiet for a long time. Peyton knelt in front him, taking his hands. "I don't want you involved in the Interpol mole hunt," he told her. "It's too dangerous."

Liam leaned forward until he could touch her, too. "I agree. Whoever was responsible had no problem with the deaths of almost a dozen young girls and two bodyguards. They're a monster."

"My involvement is over," she promised. "I told Mason I would write up a report on my findings, but while they prove the existence of a mole, there's no way to identify him or her, not with the data he gave me. I would need more. Even then, there's no guarantee I could track the mole down."

"Don't let this Mason guy push you into that," Matthias said in a tone that brooked no argument.

Peyton let her head bang on his knee with a despondent thump. "I won't. I've done enough to damage this relationship."

"You haven't done that." Liam nudged Matthias in the ribs. "She didn't, did she?"

Liam held his breath as the other man maintained a stoic silence.

"No," he finally said.

Peyton burst into tears as Liam collapsed on the cushions in relief.

Liam grunted aloud. "Can we maybe wash away this fight under a hot shower? I've been on a plane for hours."

"That sounds good to me." Peyton gave them a watery smile.

Matthias stood. He seemed a little wobbly, but so much calmer. Bending, he offered his hand to Peyton, helping her to her feet.

Liam's relief wasn't complete until Matthias bent to nuzzle Peyton's hairline.

"Why don't you two go ahead?" he suggested. "I need to reply to a text from Trick."

With matching nods, Peyton and Matthias headed off to the suite's bathroom arm in arm.

Sighing, Liam took off his coat, feeling as if he'd dodged a bullet. *More like a ballistic missile.*

With a grimace, he took out the small black box from his left pocket. Unable to resist, he flipped open the lid, admiring the gleaming set of rings.

There were three, of course, but he'd have to wait until another week or two to see if the exclusive jeweler had the sizing right.

They'll say yes, he told himself.

Granted, those two had blindsided him tonight, but in a couple of days, things would go back to normal. Once it did, he'd be able to lock this down.

Probably... As long as there were no other bombshells waiting to blow him out of the water.

CHAPTER 37

*M*atthias spared a passing thought for eavesdropping on Peyton's conversation, but his guilt was short-lived. If she hadn't wanted him to listen, she would have closed the bedroom door.

Besides, this Mason Ward was the reason she had been keeping secrets for the last few months. Well, Ward was part of the reason, he amended.

Peyton had started investigating the disaster in Belarus to find a way to assuage *his* guilt over what happened. And then she kept lying to help that young girl get out of a horrible situation. Anisa was now attending a boarding school in southern Colorado. Much to everyone's relief, she was thriving there.

He leaned forward, straining to hear what Peyton was telling Ward. He caught the words 'cafe' and a time. Checking his watch, he guessed Mason was coming here in a few hours.

By sheer coincidence, he decided he needed a more up-to-date prospectus on the acquisition he was supposed to make this afternoon. Texting Priya, he had her move his meeting to the following afternoon. And perhaps Mason would appreciate lunch catered by a

Michelin-starred chef.

Peyton would see through his schedule rearrangement in a heartbeat, but she was being very indulgent at the moment. She still felt bad about hiding her investigation from him.

Besides, he'd done a background check on Agent Ward. Though there was nothing objectionable in his background, the photo Priya included pictured a young and handsome man. On impulse, he called the Caislean's kitchen to arrange the special lunch, hanging up with a mild flash of contrition.

Normally, he'd feel like shit for throwing his weight around. Emotional blackmail had been his ex-wife's specialty. After they had broken up, Matthias had taken a good long look at himself and the way he behaved in relationships. But in this particular instance, he wasn't above playing on Peyton's guilt. It was for her own protection.

Liam wouldn't have had any qualms about it, he reminded himself. Which was why it was good their other partner would be tied up until this evening. Peyton would be much more tolerant of any interference if she weren't getting it from both sides.

Now there's a much better idea. A flood of sensual memories flooded his mind. He smiled, planning to make many more.

Peyton came into the room just then. She responded to his grin with one of her own. "What has you in such a good mood?"

"My meeting got pushed back, so I thought we'd have lunch," he replied easily, taking advantage of the moment.

"It was?" There was a thread of suspicion in her tone, but Peyton's benign expression suggested she wasn't going to make an issue of it. Clearly, growing up around the Tylers had taught her when to pick her battles.

"Lunch sounds great, but I may not be able to make it. It depends on the timing."

"Agent Ward can join us."

She bit her lip, obviously to keep from laughing. "So you *were* eavesdropping?"

"Not guilty," he said lightly.

Peyton narrowed her eyes skeptically. "You're denying it now? After admitting you know Mason is on his way?"

"Oh, no. I was listening in. I just meant I don't feel guilty."

Peyton reached over to tweak his tie. "You are shameless."

The phone on the side table began to ring. Peyton excused herself to answer while he went to get his laptop. When he returned, she was frowning. "No, that's fine. I'll come down. It should only take a few minutes."

"What's up?" he asked, his eyes on his computer.

"A small development that will please you. I just have to run down to the front desk for a minute. Be right back," she called behind her, already halfway to the door.

Matthias settled on the couch with his computer, quickly losing himself in stock reports. He worked steadily for a while until a knock at the door roused him. A quick glance at his new watch confirmed he'd lost an hour.

Peyton must have been waylaid again. Liam had warned him about this, too. She made friends everywhere.

"Lunch should be here in ten minutes. I hope you're hungry," he said as he opened the door.

The auburn-haired man on the other side didn't bat a lash. "I'm starving, actually. What's on the menu?"

Taken aback, Matthias blinked. "Agent Ward, I presume?"

Ward held out his hand. "You're not Liam Tyler. I guess you're the other one."

"Matthias Raske," he introduced himself in a flat tone, hesitating before standing aside and gesturing the man to enter. "Peyton went downstairs, but she should be back any minute. She must have been held up."

Agent Ward circled the room with an appraising scan. "I guess as a former Caislean employee, she probably has friends among the staff."

"Peyton has friends everywhere," he said dryly. "You're very well-informed, Agent Ward."

"Well, I was curious about her before she got in touch. Ethan has mentioned her a few times over the years."

"I see," Matthias said, deciding not to waste any more time. "Have you had any luck hunting down your mole?"

"*Ah*...so Peyton told you about that?"

"She doesn't keep secrets from me." His tone strongly suggested Ward not ask her to keep any in the future.

The agent's brows rose meaningfully. "*Oh*. Well...I think I see, too. Sorry. I guess I was read in wrong. I thought she and Tyler were—"

"You thought she and I were what?" Liam asked as he barreled through the door, tugging off his tie. He was carrying his suit jacket over his arm.

Liam ignored the man next to him, pausing to toss his jacket and briefcase on the nearest chair. "I need to call maintenance. The fucking elevator to the penthouse is out. I had to take the stairs."

"Ten flights?" Agent Ward looked him up and down. Liam hadn't even broken a sweat. The only giveaway was the color in his cheeks.

"Yeah." Liam stopped and pressed a quick but hard kiss to Matthias' lips, making the agent's eyes widen a fraction.

Noticing it, Liam scowled at him. "What?"

Agent Ward shook his head. "Nothing."

Liam crossed his arms, staring him down.

Ward shrugged. "I just figured out why Ethan was never able to land his white whale. Poor bastard would have had to clone himself... or find a friend," he said.

"I'm not surprised that last wasn't possible." Grunting, Liam turned on his heel, dismissing the man. He reached for the phone. "I'm calling Phil about the elevators. Where is Peyton?"

"My guess is she's stuck downstairs since the elevators are out," Matthias surmised. She had been wearing her favorite stiletto heels, which would have made the ten flights nine too many.

Liam growled something as a second knock on the door heralded the arrival of lunch. Gerard, the butler, sweated profusely as he clutched a heavily laden tray. Feeling guilty but unable to do anything about it, Matthias waved Gerard inside, directing him to set up the meal in the dining room.

The agent trailed after him. Matthias waited until Gerard had left to speak. "Peyton will tell you herself when she gets up here, but she's decided to decline your offer of working for Interpol, even off the books. She doesn't want to get any deeper in your mole hunt."

Agent Ward smiled wryly, standing next to the chair instead of sitting in it. "You mean *you* don't want her to get in any deeper."

Matthias waved him to one of the chairs at the formal oak dining table. "Peyton is no pushover. She came to this decision on her own. Liam and I just back her up as needed. But while she's a superb programmer, there are many more who specialize in what you need."

Ward rubbed his temple, betraying the strain he was under for the first time. "Yes, well, she's the best I've found outside the agency. And, as luck would have it, she got in touch with me. I would be lying if I said I had a better option at the moment."

Matthias nodded in understanding. "I want to get to the bottom of this as well. The Belarus incident was extremely hard on me, not to mention the staff who helped me arrange it. We have a vested interest in bringing this man or woman to justice. But it can't be Peyton."

"I can't blame her for that. It's a very unpleasant business," Ward said, his crisp English accent sharpening to a knifepoint.

An unexpected shaft of sympathy shot through Matthias. "It must be difficult, knowing someone around you—perhaps a trusted colleague—is responsible for such carnage."

Ward stared off into the distance. "I'm quite chuffed about it," he lied. "Keeps me on my toes."

"You'll find them," Matthias assured him in a quiet tone. "And in her way, Peyton will continue to help."

"How's that exactly?" Ward raised a brow.

"I was prepared to search for an elite hacker to take over for her," he explained. "I employ several knowledgeable coders, but she already had someone specific in mind."

"Are they any good?" He reached for a bread roll.

"Peyton didn't give me a name, but she did call them a rock star," Matthias supplied. "And if she says they can do the job, then they can."

"If that's the case, then—" Ward began.

"It's in the fucking *basement?*" Liam's raised voice could be heard two rooms away.

They turned as Liam stormed into the room. "Is there a problem?"

Liam responded by swearing a blue streak. Ward didn't flinch, but his eyes widened at the particularly colorful string of epithets.

"Peyton is late because the penthouse elevator is stuck in the basement," Liam ground out. "According to maintenance, the last time it was used, it went straight down there instead of the lobby. To top it off, the mechanic has been out to lunch the whole time. I have to go down there and find her."

"Is she stuck in the elevator cabin or is she wandering the basement?" Ward asked.

"I don't know."

Frowning, Matthias threw down his napkin to join him.

Ward stood and followed, adjusting his holster. Matthias was about to comment that a gun wasn't necessary, but he kept his mouth shut. His life had become something of a rollercoaster over the last few years. An armed guard would be a sound financial investment at this point.

The trip down the stairs was nowhere near as arduous as one in reverse would be. But by the time they reached the basement level, the three men were huffing—mainly because Liam started running down the last four flights. He and Agent Ward followed suit.

They hit the basement like the bulls running in Pamplona. Liam didn't need to acknowledge his worry aloud for Matthias to sense it. Even Ward seemed to feel the tension.

The mechanic and his assistant had just arrived, and they were unpacking their gear. But the question of whether their partner was trapped in the elevator car was answered immediately—the door was wide open. There was no sign of Peyton. Neither man had seen her.

Matthias had never been down to this level. It was surprisingly crammed down here—the laundry, storage rooms, and enough water heaters to ensure half the city could take a hot shower.

"Are we sure she didn't go to the cafe in the lobby to wait?" Agent Ward questioned, following as he and Liam started stalking through the warren of corridors in the basement.

"She would have texted," Liam replied, peeking around the corner.

"What if she forgot her phone?" Ward continued, opening and closing a closet.

"Peyton doesn't go anywhere without her phone," Matthias said. She had even kept it with her on the *Ormen Lange*, in the middle of the ocean, where she had been nowhere near her service provider.

They kept searching. Matthias started to sweat. There was no way Peyton accidentally locked herself down here. She'd worked at this hotel chain for her entire adult life, and she knew her way around spaces like this. And she'd been aware Agent Ward had been on his way to meet her...

"Does Peyton like wearing very high heels?" Ward asked.

"Not particularly," Liam admitted, throwing open another door. "But she knows we like them, so she puts up with them sometimes."

Matthias frowned. "Do you see heel marks or something?"

"Not exactly." Agent Ward bent, then fished something out from under a shelf stocked with linens. The distinctive red sole of the Louboutin was like a flashing neon light.

Matthias took it from his hand. "That's one of the shoes Peyton was wearing today."

CHAPTER 38

*P*eyton's head throbbed. A tear escaped her eye as she struggled to focus on her surroundings. She was sitting in a sunny wood-paneled room. There was an antique table in front of her with a pristine leather blotter and one those ugly painted ducks.

Where did my other shoe go?

The pocket of her dress lay flat. The flash drive was gone…and her hands were bound behind her back with hard metal rings. Handcuffs. Ropes were wrapped around her middle, securing her to a wooden chair.

"Welcome back."

Narrowing her eyes against the too-bright light, she turned her head as slowly as possible. Two men watched her from the other side of the table.

"Apologies for the knock to the head. It was necessary to facilitate your departure from the hotel. The Caislean has better security than most."

Still fuzzy-headed, Peyton belatedly realized the table was a desk. One of the men, the older one, sat behind it in a leather chair. The other one, his countenance that of hired muscle, stood to his left as if he were waiting for orders.

Neither was wearing a mask to obscure their features. *That's a bad sign.*

She didn't bother with stupid questions. "I take it I'm meeting Interpol's mole."

The older man laughed. "I see the information we have on you is spot on. You're a very bright woman, Peyton Carson."

The man was English, which didn't surprise her. Most Bond villains were English. However, the prominently displayed wedding ring was a bit off-putting. Did his wife know what kind of bloodshed her husband had been responsible for?

"Not that bright actually." She sniffed. "I have no idea what your name is. I didn't discover your identity in the files Mason sent. You kidnapped me for nothing."

The man drummed his fingers on the disk, a considering light in his eyes. "Well, that remains to be seen. Just because you can't identify me from the breadcrumbs you've gathered doesn't mean Agent Ward can't. The man is tenacious. I should know. I trained him myself."

The man next to him rolled his eyes, but Peyton didn't say anything. She was too sick to her stomach. Mason hadn't mentioned the name of his supervisor at Interpol, so she still couldn't put a face to a name, but the overwhelming wave of betrayal on his behalf choked her.

The Englishman leaned forward. "As you've no doubt surmised, we learned of your meeting with Agent Ward. Travis here has been keeping tabs on him ever since we discovered he was looking into the Belarus matter."

And they had found out she was handing off her report in person at Mason's insistence. No doubt they had pored over all the data on the flash drive.

"Ms. Carson, is there another copy of the report?" the Englishman asked.

"Of course."

"She's lying. Mason would have warned her not to make one," Travis muttered, speaking for the first time. His accent was American. Peyton didn't know why that bothered her so much.

"He did tell me not to make one, but I'm a coder," she said, wishing her voice didn't sound as weak as it did. Her head still pounded. "I always make a backup—that shit is engrained. It's in my private safe at the Caislean. Only I know the code to open it."

The Englishman laughed. "How charmingly transparent of you, Ms. Carson. But you and I both know you are not getting out of this room alive. Not even to retrieve a copy of the report, which, by my estimate, has only a fifty-percent chance of existing."

"It exists," Peyton said, infusing her voice with as much bravado as she could. "And I will be getting out of this room alive and well."

More laughter. "Well, you do have—what do you American's call it? Moxy?"

"Balls. I have balls," Peyton corrected, trying and failing to ignore the pounding of her head. "And I may not know your name, but I have a good idea of your motivation for helping those traffickers. In fact, I suspect Belarus is just one in an extensive list of crimes you're responsible for."

"Do tell..."

She sighed. *This guy is the lamest Bond villain ever.* "It's obvious. You did it for the money."

"It's hardly an original incentive, I will admit, but Interpol couldn't secure me the kind of retirement I had in mind. I had to get creative. It's only fair. They've profited from my connections for decades."

"Then I have good news. Now you get to profit from mine," she said.

The man's lips compressed.

"She means Raske and Tyler."

Irritation flashed across the Englishman's face. "I *know* that."

"Both men are quite wealthy," she elaborated needlessly.

"And you think those two faggots will cough up any cash for you?" Travis sneered.

Peyton's nostrils flared. This piece of shit wasn't worthy of wiping Matthias or Liam's shoes, but she swallowed her fury. Her priority had to be getting out of this in one piece. Then she'd pour gasoline on this fucker and light him on fire.

"I do," she said as evenly as she could.

"I realize Raske paid a high sum for you before—"

"At Liam Tyler's behest. I'm important to him. Always have been," she interrupted, trying her damnedest to sound calm. "Since then, I've also become significant to Matthias. But I am nowhere as important to either as *he* is…"

Peyton looked down, gesturing to her flat belly with a significant nod that made her head surge with renewed pain.

Travis wrinkled his nose. "You're knocked up?"

"Yes," she lied. "It's in the early stages, obviously. But a doctor has confirmed it."

Hadn't those traffickers suggested she would be used as a breeder? Was that why the idea to lie about a pregnancy had popped into her head?

"Pregnant with a billionaire's baby…" the Englishman said, templing his hands under his chin.

"It could be Tyler's kid. He's not a billionaire. Not if he has to split his wealth with the brother and sister," Travis said.

"He's pretty damn close," Peyton snapped, wishing her hands were free so she could slap the sneer off Travis' face. She turned to the Englishman, mentally blocking the other man's presence. "Neither man cares who the biological father is. Both are thrilled—we're going to name him after Matthias' grandfather."

The lies had never flowed so freely. But then her life had never been at stake.

The Englishman tipped his head back to Travis. "We have to consider this."

"No, we don't. She could be lying about this, too."

The Englishman looked her squarely in the eye as if trying to read the truth there. "It doesn't matter. She's right. Pregnant or not, she's worth millions."

Peyton bit back her sigh of relief. He stood. "Keep an eye on her. I have to make a few calls."

Travis grunted as the man left the room, swinging back to stare at her with hostile eyes. Suddenly, he smirked. "Even if I were a fag, I'd fuck you, too. You are that hot."

"Thank you," Peyton muttered, praying silently for his swift and bloody death.

CHAPTER 39

*L*iam braced himself in the backseat as the car turned fast, whipping and weaving through traffic. In front of him, Matthias grabbed the bar above the passenger window in an effort not to be thrown against the door. Agent Ward drove like a maniac.

"I can't believe you have your girlfriend microchipped like a dog," he said.

After arguing who should drive the Lotus Evora Liam kept as his London car, Agent Ward grabbed the keys, arguing he had the most training and the least emotion invested.

"The objective is to get us there in one piece to rescue Peyton," Matthias pointed out as Ward straightened the car, gunning toward the next light.

"I don't have her chipped," Liam protested. "I have a GPS tracker on her charm bracelet."

"The bracelet? That was smart." Matthias twisted to look at him. "I put mine on the diamond pendant I gave her, but she never wears it."

"*Wow*," Ward said with a strangled laugh.

"Fuck you," Liam spat. "She was taken by human traffickers earlier this year. I'm not going to justify putting a tracker on her to you, the man currently responsible for her *second* kidnapping."

Ward kept his eyes fixed on the road, wisely remaining silent.

"Turn left up at the light," Liam ordered, checking his phone before addressing Matthias. "And yes—that necklace was a mistake. It's is far too ostentatious for Peyton. You have to go simpler. She'll only wear that sort of thing if you give her a nudge."

Matthias frowned, turning back to the road. "And here I thought it was very discreet. It's only four carats."

Ward snorted. He took the next corner a bit more sharply than was necessary. "Well, since your overprotectiveness is enabling us to find her now, I'm not going to call you both crazy—even though you're both mental."

Matthias looked at him out of the corner of his eye. "You've never been in love, have you?"

Ward lapsed into silence, following Liam's direction without question, but he held his breath when he saw Matthias glance down a little too long at the Vacheron Constantin watch Liam had gifted him last month. But, luckily, he didn't ask if it, too, had a GPS tracker.

It's only for emergencies. He'd never used it to spy on Matthias. It was just insurance in case something happened.

A chime sounded from his text messaging app. "The security specialists have examined the cameras and elevator," Liam announced, his voice hoarse with strain. "The security feeds were altered. The servers were hacked, and the footage was erased."

"Have them contact the local police for the CCTV footage from the area. There have to be at least a dozen on that block," Ward suggested, referring to the high per capita number of cameras in London. "I would call the office to get that fast-tracked, but I can't trust anyone there just now."

Liam swore under his breath. "When we get our hands on this mole, you're going to shoot him, right?"

Ward grunted something unintelligible. At first, Matthias thought he was avoiding the question, but then he deciphered the swear words the man was muttering under his breath.

"Hell yes, I am."

~

PEYTON GOT to work the moment Travis left the room. He had received a text that made him smirk. Muttering that she wasn't going anywhere, he'd left against orders.

She had no idea how long he'd be gone.

Let it be forever because he died in a freak accident. May he be stung to death by a pack of Africanized honeybees, she prayed. Better yet, his phone could explode in his pocket, injuring a vital organ.

Focus, Carson, she ordered herself. She had to get out of the Englishman's office and out of sight From the décor and furniture, she guessed it was in a house and not an apartment. Maybe the creep had taken her to his country home. There had to be at least one good hiding place. She just had to find it.

Her wrists were scraped and sore from trying to slide out of the cuffs. As for the ropes around her middle—tensing and relaxing to loosen them wasn't working.

Enough of the women in her circle had been in trouble that she'd taken the time to look up some tips on escaping bondage. Unfortunately, she hadn't been conscious when she'd been tied up, so tensing in advance hadn't been an option. If she had, there would have been a bit more slack to her ropes now.

After a few minutes, Peyton acknowledged they weren't going to budge. *Damn.* According to the internet, most people didn't know how to tie a proper knot. These knots were secure but not painfully tight. Additionally, the cuffs were taut, but they weren't cutting off her circulation. Interpol must have a class on how to restrain a suspect without permanently damaging them.

Peyton hung her head, trying to take stock. She was going to have to escape without those internet tricks.

Maybe the English jerk had a particularly sharp letter opener? She craned her neck, shifting this way and that until she almost toppled over. The chair was heavier than she would have guessed from its size.

What if I just stand up? She wouldn't be able to get the cuffs off, but maybe she could get out of this damn chair.

Peyton hadn't attended a Yoga class in months, but it was surprising how flexible one could be when one was the partner of two virile men. Contorting and wiggling determinedly, she leaned forward until she was balancing on the balls of her feet.

She kept shifting and twisting until the chair slid down a few inches. Then a few more.

Peyton was about to get the damn thing off when footsteps sounded on the other side of the door. Freezing, she considered diving to the floor behind the desk, but she thought better of it at the last second. It wasn't as if she could make herself invisible. She'd just end up bruised for no reason.

The footsteps receded. Heaving a sigh of relief, she worked the chair past her feet, jumping up and down to get the ropes off. Without the added width of the chair, they slid down easily. The handcuffs were another story. Her wrists were probably bleeding by this point.

Ignoring the pain, she bent, crouching to run the cuffs down her legs. Her arms ached with the effort, but Peyton was able to move her bound wrists over her feet.

"Shit," she said, examining the deep grooves under the metal. They weren't bleeding much, but she was going to carry these marks for some time. Tentatively, she tried the door, but it was locked.

She hurried across the room, looking out all the windows to try to determine where she was. The office was in the corner of the second story, overlooking a well-manicured lawn. In the distance, she could see fences and tiny four-legged animals—sheep presumably. They were white. There was no driveway or road visible from these windows, so she guessed she was facing the back of the house.

Craning her neck to see past the drainpipe, she searched in vain for any other buildings. Damn, it looked isolated out there…

She pictured herself running across those bare hills toward civilization only to be gunned down amongst the sheep. *Maybe they wouldn't shoot.* Not if they bought the lie that she was pregnant.

If it is a lie...

Peyton didn't believe she was pregnant. Those birth control shots she had taken had a next-to-nothing failure rate. But she'd experienced some breast tenderness and nausea. *You're just stressed out.* It had been a difficult couple of weeks. Still, she would take a test as soon as she was able—just to be certain.

Peyton pressed her head against the glass, trying to see the roof without opening the window. How many stories was this place? Could she climb that drainpipe? What if she didn't go down but up?

But there was no way she'd manage that trick in these cuffs. Cursing under her breath, she started hunting for something to pick the lock. One of the videos she had watched had shown her how to do it, but now she wished she had practiced. *Why didn't I practice, damn it?*

*Metal. Must find metal...*Two of the desk drawers were locked. The rest were filled with papers. Inconsiderately, all conveniently small and bendable pieces of metal had been removed from the room before her arrival. She kept searching until she stumbled on a box on the shelf behind the desk. There was an ornate fountain pen inside. It wasn't a cheap one, either. The tip was very thick, and it had obviously been used.

How pretentious was this guy? Even Matthias didn't use a fountain pen.

This was going to have to do it. Peyton fiddled with the pen, trying to get it into the lock, but try as she might, she couldn't hold it well enough to manipulate it.

Time for plan B. If only she had one of those...

Peyton racked her brain, but no genius ideas came to mind. She groaned. She was going to have to carry out plan A cuffed. *Shit.*

She needed to buy herself some more time.

Kneeling, Peyton examined the keyhole. To her eyes, it looked weak and flimsy—another antique like the rest of the house. Her second attempt to pick a lock didn't go any better than the first.

Brute force it is. Praying there was no one near enough to hear, she rammed the pointed end of the pen into the lock with as much strength as she could muster. Then she used the heel of her only shoe to hammer it in as deep as she could.

When the door swung open, Peyton was shocked, but she didn't stop to dwell on this small victory.

Travis or the Englishman could have heard that. She had to hurry.

LIAM SWORE as he spotted the broken charm bracelet on the floor of a van. They had followed the signal for hours, tracing it to a spacious house nestled in the rolling hills of the English countryside. According to online maps, it was the only home for miles.

Afraid they would be spotted before they could get close, they had abandoned the Lotus a half-mile away before trekking over a wooded hill to get close to the house. The van was parked in a converted barn, next to a classic Rolls Royce.

"Calm down," Mason said. "It doesn't mean anything. They probably took it off to tie her hands."

Matthias groaned, and Liam shot the agent a dirty look.

"Sorry." Mason coughed, turning to look around him. "But I'm sure she's fine. They brought her here for a reason."

Slipping the remains of the bracelet into his pocket, Liam straightened, scanning the house and its various outbuildings.

It wasn't the palatial estate people saw in English movies, but it was a well-maintained and comfortable house, the kind a reasonably wealthy family would have as a country retreat.

"We have to find out who this belong to," Matthias said, keeping his voice down. "I'll call Priya. She'll hunt down the owner."

Mason, who'd been half-listening to their conversation, stopped short in front of them. "Don't bother. I recognize the bloody Rolls."

Liam grabbed his shoulder. *"What?"*

The agent grunted. "I said I know the vehicle. It's hardly standard issue, but the bastard claims to have inherited a hefty sum a few years back. That's why he's taking early retirement."

Matthias' snapped toward Ward. "Then you know who owns this house?"

Ward exhaled wearily. "Yes, it belongs to one of my supervisors."

PEYTON WAS TOO afraid to turn over. *I don't believe this.* On top of the risk of getting shot, she was going to get a bad sunburn.

Somehow, she had managed to climb the drainpipe to the slate-covered roof just over the office, using the unevenness of the stone walls to give her bare feet purchase. However, once she climbed up, she realized there was nowhere to go. There was a cluster of small buildings scattered around the house, but no other signs of life as she'd hoped. Just hills and trees.

The terrain didn't look rough. Peyton didn't think she'd be able to get far in her bare feet—especially since her escape had been discovered. Travis and the Englishman were arguing about it as they searched the other buildings.

"Where the hell is she?" the Englishman shouted.

"I don't know," Travis yelled back. "You were the one who tied her up."

"You were going to scratch the chair. It's a Queen Anne!"

"Whatever. We have to find her."

"Fine. But remember—don't kill her. She's worth a lot of money to me." The Englishman's voice had grown nasal.

"You mean to *us,* you prick."

Stomping footsteps followed, their tempo increasing until she guessed they were both running, throwing doors open and them slamming them shut in their efforts to find her.

Peyton decided her best course of action was to stay where she was. Lying flat, she held her breath, the sun beating down on her. She couldn't even risk turning around in case she knocked one of the slate pieces loose and gave away her location.

They're going to find me anyway. It was only a matter of time before they realized she hadn't hidden somewhere on the grounds, but she'd deal with that when it happened. She just had to remind them she was more valuable alive than dead.

An ominous thump sounded nearby. Risking movement, Peyton shielded her eyes, turning her head to look behind her. She half-expected to see Travis climbing the roof, but there was nobody there.

"Hey." Another thump. Peyton recognized the sound this time. It was the distinctive crunch of a fist hitting flesh.

Her vision blackened momentarily as panic and adrenaline flooded her body. More sounds of fighting followed. Getting on her knees, Peyton crawled to the end of the roof in the direction of the fight.

She almost sobbed in relief. The Englishman was down. Mason held a gun on him. Liam and Matthias were there, too. They fought with Travis.

The younger villain was vicious. He fought like a cornered wolf, snapping and snarling, his fists and feet flying in a series of kicks and punches that would have taken down ninety-nine out of a hundred men.

But Liam wasn't an average man. Her lover fought like a warrior, grappling and returning punches with such speed and fury his movements were a blur. She'd expected no less.

Matthias *was* a surprise. She knew he was fit and strong, but she hadn't expected him to fight like that. He wasn't as skilled as Liam, but it was obvious the man had extensive self-defense training. Travis didn't have a chance against them as a team.

Peyton flinched as Matthias landed a punch across the man's jaw with a sickening crack. Travis staggered to his knees, his head lolling. He fell to the floor, slumping over.

Moved to tears by relief, she put out her hand, starting to call out, when movement just below caught her eye. The top of another man's head moved into view, coming around the corner. He was holding a gun. And neither Liam nor Matthias had seen him.

She didn't stop to think. Screaming bloody murder, Peyton threw herself over the edge, aiming for the asshole's head.

MATTHIAS WAS NEVER GOING to forget the moment he turned to see the assailant pointing a gun at Liam. He died a thousand deaths in that split second, but it was nothing compared to the jolt he'd experienced when he saw Peyton flying through the air, tackling the bastard and knocking the gun out of his hand.

"It was two fucking stories, Peyton," Liam snapped as the female EMT poked and prodded at her ankle. The swelling was obvious. The only question that remained was whether it was broken or merely sprained.

"I wasn't going to let him shoot one of you." Peyton sat up on the gurney to scowl at him. She was shoeless, her hair was a mess, and her face was red from too much sun, but she had never looked more beautiful.

"Two stories—" Liam began.

Matthias didn't want to think about what might have happened if Peyton hadn't decided to play Superwoman. He pulled his partner toward him, kissing him hard—almost desperately—before resting his forehead against his. "Just say thank you."

"I..." Liam cleared his throat as tears pooled in his eyes. "You're right. Thank you, Peyton."

Matthias leaned over to kiss her, too, surprising the hell out of the EMT.

Peyton cocked her head to the side. "Yes, they're both mine," she bragged to the woman.

The EMT blushed. "Wow," she said, putting her hand out for a high five. They clapped hands before bursting out laughing.

"Always making friends, this one," Liam observed, leaning against him for support before scanning the crowd that had gathered in front of the house.

Mason was off at the other end of the yard, talking to the other agents. Not only were high-level Interpol directors present, but reps from MI5 *and* MI6 had shown up. He snorted. God knew how many other agencies were milling around out there...

The EMT excused herself to check on her partner. He was treating Travis's injuries before they transported him to a holding cell.

Peyton rubbed her wrist. "I think they took off the charm bracelet when I was being transported here. I was so worried they had dropped it at the hotel, and you wouldn't be able to find me."

Matthias blinked. *Oh, shit.*

"You knew about the tracker?" Liam flushed guiltily.

"Of course I knew," Peyton said weakly, gingerly touching the sore spot on her head. The EMT had wanted to do a scan for a concussion, but Peyton had insisted on waiting for Mason to give them an update.

"How?" Matthias asked.

"How do you think?" She laughed.

Both men shrugged.

Peyton cleared her throat, straightening her skirt as if readying for a long lecture. "See, there are these things called GPS bug detectors. I own several—"

"Why?" Matthias frowned.

"To scan your cars. I've been doing it for years. I started at the Caislean in Boston. I used to have all your vehicles scanned at least once a week. Maggie and Trick's, too."

"You did?" Liam looked stunned.

"Of course," she said with a dismissive wave. "Well, technically, security did it, but since we've been traveling so much, I decided it would be a good idea to take over."

They stared at her with identical expressions of disbelief.

"What?" she said. "I love Maggie and Trick like family. I couldn't risk anyone kidnapping them—although, honestly, the groupies were the biggest threat. They used to lie in wait at the hotel, ready to ambush you and Patrick."

"Liam had groupies?" Matthias asked incredulously.

"Well, that's what happens when you are a bachelor with money and don't hide away sailing the seven seas," Liam said tersely.

Matthias lowered his head, trying to hide his chortle.

"You didn't love me like family?" he heard Liam ask.

"I think for all concerned, that's a good thing, especially as I was madly in love with you another way."

Liam huffed. "Amen to that," he muttered as Agent Ward joined them.

"Is the baby okay?" Concern made the man appear as if he had smelled sour milk.

"*The baby?*" Matthias sputtered

Peyton held up her hand. "I told those creeps I was pregnant to make myself seem more valuable, but I'm not."

"Are you sure?" Matthias was dizzy, feeling as if he were the one who'd been hit over the head. He could only imagine how Liam felt.

"I'm certain. But it was a long wait up on that roof, and I got my— well, never mind. Let's just say I know for sure."

"*Oh.*" Liam's disappointment was palpable.

Matthias took both their hands. "I know I've been saying I'm not ready for children, but it's not true. I was just afraid of things going to shit again, but that's not going to happen. If you two want to start trying—"

Mason smile was a trifle awkward. "Perhaps you'd like to postpone this conversation until later?"

"Yes, *please*," Peyton said, widening her eyes for emphasis. "I want to know the English bastard's name."

"It's FitzGeorge—Clyde FitzGeorge, the twelfth Earl of Osbourne," Mason said, slipping his hands into his pants pockets.

"Really?" Peyton asked, clearly skeptical. "He's an honest-to-God earl?"

"Oh, yes." Mason sighed. "But the earldom has been bankrupt for some time. Nevertheless, FitzGeorge has connections at the highest levels of society all over Europe. They furthered his career quite a bit. When he started spending more lavishly, he claimed to have found a cache of family antiques that he was selling to finance an early retirement. He even waved some auction catalogs around the office, pointing out things he was supposedly selling to establish a backstory."

Matthias leaned forward. "I don't care if he's the fucking king of England. Be aware—I'm going to be using *my* network of connections to make sure the son of a bitch pays for what he has done."

"Have at him," Mason said. "I'm not going to stop you."

"Is Travis at Interpol, too?"

"Not to my knowledge. He seems to know the ins and out of the agency. However, he came up as an independent contractor. So did the third man you clobbered." His weary air dropped away. "Well done, by the way. It appears you broke his collarbone by dropping down on him like that."

"Hmm. I thought they were both agents," Peyton said, ignoring the praise. "Do you think you'll find proof of FitzGeorge's involvement with the Belarus incident?"

"I think I can do you one better," Mason said, smiling for the first time. "He's already talking, trying to broker a deal. He's giving up everyone and their grandmother. If the intel is good, we may be able to trace the group if we move quickly."

"Then what the hell are you waiting for?" Liam snapped. "Go get them."

He tossed the keys to the Lotus to the agent. "Return these when you can."

Catching the set in mid-air, Ward grinned like it was Christmas morning.

"Will do." The agent hurried away before Liam could change his mind.

"But Mason just saved us," Peyton pointed out. "We should at least invite him to dinner."

"He didn't save anyone," Liam countered. "You saved yourself, then you saved us. Now we're going to the hospital to get your head scanned. Then you're going to stay in bed for a week," he ordered.

Matthias didn't argue with him. He, too, wanted to make sure Peyton didn't have any permanent damage. "Don't worry," he added. "I'm sure we'll see Agent Ward again."

"Yeah, you can invite him to the wedding," Liam said as he signaled the EMT to come back.

"What wedding?" Matthias asked, feigning ignorance as his heart sank. It had only been a matter of time before Liam decided he wanted to make his union with Peyton official.

The other man's mouth opened, but nothing came out.

"*Liam?*" Peyton was trembling.

Liam straightened his shoulders, whipping something out of his coat. He held up a ring box, opening it to reveal three platinum rings. One had a large emerald, Peyton's favorite stone. All were engraved.

His hand shook as he reached out for the one with the most letters. *MFLR.* Those were *his* initials.

"I didn't think—"

"What?" Liam frowned. "You didn't think I was going to leave you out in the cold while I married Peyton, did you?"

Matthias wanted to respond, but he found that his throat was a little too tight. Peyton was watching him with her hands clasped in front of her.

"It won't be legal," he said when the lump in his throat finally let him. Neither Norway nor the United States recognized polyamorous unions.

"So?" Liam scoffed.

"I don't care. It doesn't have to be legal to be real," Peyton said. "Now give me that damn ring!"

They laughed as she wobbled to her feet, throwing her arms around both of them and squeezing tight.

Clapping broke up their embrace. Matthias shifted to see the EMT holding her hands in front of her, her eyes shining.

"Pardon," she said, flushing in embarrassment. "I'll drive you to the hospital now. But congratulations!"

"Thanks," Matthias said as she shut the door. A minute later, the ambulance pulled away.

Squealing, Peyton lay back on the gurney, holding up her hand to admire her ring. Liam put on his. Both eyed him expectantly.

"Oh." He held up the ring, then slipped it onto his finger. "This feels weird," he said with a laugh.

"You'll get used to it," Peyton promised.

EPILOGUE

*P*eyton pried her best friend's hands from around her neck. "I can't believe we're legally sisters now." Maggie sniffed, crying all over her neck.

"Well, strictly speaking, the union isn't legal in America. Or Europe," Peyton pointed out with a laugh. Sipping champagne, she leaned on the balustrade next to the stairs that led to the beach, admiring her two gorgeous husbands as they talked and laughed with all their friends.

She hadn't seen most of them since her ill-fated graduation party. But today, the only tears she was going to shed were tears of joy.

Peyton had married the two loves of her life in the gorgeous court-yard of a brand-new Spanish-style villa. Matthias had built it espe-cially for their new family. It was on the private island he had purchased during his partying days over a decade ago—a decision he'd regretted immediately until recently. He'd never done anything with the place, but the formerly uninhabited isle was being repurposed now.

"Screw that," Maggie said, swiping a fruit-laden cocktail from a passing waiter. "You're my sister now. No damn court will ever convince me otherwise. But I can't believe Matthias bought this whole island just so he could declare it a country."

Neither could she, but her Norse god lover had declared that if they were going to marry, it would be legal *somewhere*.

"Well, it's not actually the reason he bought it, but I'm pretty damn happy he never sold it. The island was the impulse purchase to end all impulse purchases... Can you believe it was easier and faster for Matthias to set up an entire country with its own judicial system than it was for you to pick the flowers?" she asked, her face deadpan.

Maggie pretended to punch her. Peyton grabbed her hand instead, twining their arms. "Everything is perfect. I don't know which is better—the flowers or the food."

Trick and Maggie had outdone themselves. The entire villa had been transformed. Every room had been filled with fresh flowers and candles with the most interesting antiques nestled in between. The courtyard had been built around tall proud palms that had been there for hundreds of years. New flowerbeds filled with native blooms provided the finishing touches.

The food had been prepared by Kari Jones, the celebrity chef Liam had hired to work at the Caislean New York. The restaurant there had just earned three Michelin stars, the highest honor possible, so the food was amazing.

"I think that dress is the best thing," Maggie said, eyeing Peyton's gown. The silk confection was stunning, its light gossamer skirt perfect for the heat of the island.

"Then thank you for choosing it." Peyton laughed.

Maggie leaned forward. "I'm glad Ethan is here. I didn't think he was going to come."

"I knew he would," Peyton said. Ethan might have been a little disappointed since she had announced the engagement, but in the months that followed, he hadn't shown any signs of a broken heart. And she would know. For years, Peyton had considered herself the world's foremost expert on them.

But not anymore. It was a title she was happy to relinquish.

"I should go say hi to him," she said, spotting the dark-haired FBI near one of the hors d'oeuvre stations.

"Want some backup?" Maggie asked.

"Not necessary," Peyton assured her with a smile.

Ethan was wearing his ever-present Aviator sunglasses, so it was hard to gauge his reaction as she approached with two champagne glasses in hand.

He accepted the glass, studying it briefly. "Got anything stronger?"

"I have always believed in having a full bar, regardless of the occasion," she said. "Some of the bat mitzvahs we had at Caislean got very colorful as a result."

Smiling, Ethan sipped the golden brew. "I'm glad to see Tyler finally got his head out of his ass," he said with a nod in her grooms' direction.

"Me too," she said with a grin. "But seriously, I'm so happy to see you. Thank you for coming all this way."

"Well, this was something I had to see—I mean, attending a wedding on a new country, not your...err...arrangement," he said, raising a brow as he gave Liam and Matthias a once-over. "Although, I gotta ask. How will this kind of marriage work exactly?"

"Exactly the same as the kind between two people," she said, then reflected it wasn't the whole truth. "Just...*more*."

"More what?"

"Everything."

Ethan chuckled. "That's what I like about you, Peyton. You never do anything halfway. Congratulations on the expansion of yours and Thalia's program by the way."

Ethan was referring to the vocational training program she and Trick's wife had set up the previous year. Their focus had been on women who had escaped abusive relationships, but now they were growing beyond that.

She nodded in satisfaction. "Yes, we've partnered with some well-respected charities that help sex-trafficking victims. We've been focusing on the States, but we have started rolling it out in other countries—all known trafficking hotspots. The vocational training programs are going strong, but my new learn-to-code course has already discovered some genuine talent."

"That's great. And it's good to know you're putting your new husbands' cash to good use. They have enough of it."

"I'll hit them up for donations soon enough. For now, though, I'm using my own funds," Peyton corrected.

"Sorry, I didn't realize you had any." Ethan's expression filled with chagrin.

"It's new." She smiled. "Some of the irons I had in the fire paid off recently."

"Bank heist?" He waved the waiter over, then requested a whiskey.

"No." She giggled. "I just hit five hundred K in bug bounty rewards," she said, explaining the various program designed to help white-hat hackers fix software and websites.

"Five hundred K as in half a million *dollars*? Damn, girl." He shook his head. "You are unbelievable—in a good way."

"Thanks," she said, tapping his glass with her own to toast her achievement.

Liam and Matthias materialized by their sides soon after. Peyton hid her grin. It didn't matter that they had just gotten married. Liam still wasn't keen on her spending time with Ethan. And after meeting him, Matthias had seemed to catch his overdeveloped sense of caution around the handsome FBI agent.

"Congratulations," Ethan said, putting his hand out to shake.

Liam hesitated, but he took his hand. "Thank you for coming. I know it was a trek."

"Like I was telling Peyton, I wouldn't have missed it." Ethan turned to Matthias. "Nice country, Mr. President. Or are you prime minister?"

"Neither," Matthias said, putting his hands in his pockets. "We decided on a feudal matrilineal system."

Ethan frowned. "Wait, doesn't matrilineal mean..."

Peyton held up her glass of champagne. "That's right. I'm the queen."

The FBI agent nearly doubled over laughing. When he recovered, he held his glass high. "Well then, long live the queen!"

"I'll drink to that," Liam said, joining in with his own glass.

For the first time in her memory, Liam and Ethan talked like two normal human beings. Peyton wasn't sure they would ever be friends, but it was nice to see them being cordial to each other.

Eventually, the conversation turned to Interpol and the mole. "I heard you offered Mason a position," Ethan said, turning to Matthias.

He nodded. "Ward's done an excellent job of bringing the perpetrators of the Belarus incident to justice. That, and he brought down most of the ring that took Peyton."

"Well, he had some help," Ethan observed. "FitzGeorge kept meticulous records on the people who paid his bribes. We didn't even need him to testify. He'd recorded so many details in his books that the agency had plenty to work with without his direct input."

Both David Travis and Clyde FitzGeorge had both tried to make deals, but Matthias and Liam used their clout to make sure neither man got what they asked for. Both were facing long prison sentences.

"I heard you were at that raid," Peyton said after a moment. "Mason told us. Thank you for that."

He waved her thanks away. "They made the mistake of doing their business on American soil. I'm just sorry the one you call mega-bitch got away."

"For now," Peyton said. "She'll make a mistake sooner or later. I have faith she'll be brought to justice."

Ethan nodded. "Yeah. Mason's on it."

"Unless he accepts my offer," Matthias observed.

"Well, you've got competition now. Interpol offered him FitzGeorge's old job."

"I see." Matthias raised a brow. "Perhaps I need to make a counteroffer."

Rolling her eyes, Peyton nudged Matthias hard in the hip. "Enough business talk. It's Carsonia's first national holiday."

Matthias took her hand. "Yes, My Queen."

Liam echoed his words a beat later.

She giggled. "That's never going to get old."

The strains of a waltz began. Waving goodbye to Ethan, she grabbed her men, pulling them on the dance floor set over the flag-stone tiles.

"I don't know how to waltz as a threesome," Liam admitted as they came to a stop in the middle of the courtyard.

She raised her arms, spinning to make her skirt flare out. "Who cares? We'll figure it out."

Matthias laughed and Liam shrugged, taking her hand to spin her until she whirled into Matthias' arms.

Whoops and cheers followed. The dance was silly, completely unplanned, and occasionally awkward—and it was almost too much fun.

Soon, their friends and family joined in. At one point, Peyton jumped, leaping into Liam's arms.

In one smooth move, he tossed her up, setting her on his shoulder. Matthias joined him so she was balanced between them. It was a dance similar to the hora, but without the chair. A few euphoric spins later, she jumped down into Matthias' arms.

Maggie, who was dancing next to them with Jason, laughed as the crowd cheered. "When did you rehearse that?"

"We didn't," Peyton said, shouting to be heard over the music.

"Then how did you know they would catch you?"

She shrugged, continuing to dance. "I just did."

Liam tugged Matthias by the hand, pulling him around her back so she was pressed between them.

"And we always will," he vowed.

THE END

Need another obsession? It's finally Ethan's turn!

One FBI agent. One single-mother. And a toddler who steals his heart.

All FBI agent Ethan Thomas wants is to come home to his new apartment venture and enjoy the luxury of his new flat screen TV and some frozen pizza. Encountering a tiny toddler alone in the hall changes everything for the rough and rugged agent. Relief sets in when the child's mother appears. But when she collapses at his feet just before a blizzard hits Boston, Ethan's in over his head.
Now, Ethan's changing diapers and playing doctor...and loving every minute of it. The mother and child need a place to stay, and Ethan can't possibly turn them away. But this investigator knows people—and the woman he's falling for is keeping secrets. Can he uncover the truth while protecting them from the dangers of his job?

Read his irresistible romance on Kindle Unlimited today!

AFTERWORD

Need another obsession? Look for FBI agent Ethan White's story in the new 'Of Valor and Villains' series. Coming Soon...

Thank you for reading this novel! Reviews are an author's bread and butter. If you liked the story please consider leaving one.

Subscribe to the Lucy Leroux Newsletter for a *free* full-length novel!
www.authorlucyleroux.com/newsletter
or keep up with her L.B. Gilbert releases
www.elementalauthor.com/newsletter

ABOUT THE AUTHOR

Lucy Leroux is another name for USA Today Bestselling Author L.B. Gilbert.

Seven years ago Lucy moved to France for a one-year research contract. Six months later she was living with a handsome Frenchman and is now married with an adorable half-french toddler.

When her last contract ended Lucy turned to writing. Frustrated by the lack of quality romance erotica she created her own.

Cursed is the first of many regency novels. Additionally, she writes a bestselling contemporary series. The 'Singular Obsession' books are a combination of steamy romance and suspense that feature inter-twining characters in their own stand-alone stories. Follow her on twitter or facebook, or check our her website for more news!

www.authorlucyleroux.com

facebook.com/lucythenovelist

twitter.com/lucythenovelist

instagram.com/lucythenovelist

Printed in Great Britain
by Amazon

87694088R00165